Praise for
Melody Carlson and *Limelight*

"A compelling tale of one woman's journey from the excitement of the limelight to contentment in the twilight. When eighty-two-year-old Claudette is forced to leave her pampered Hollywood life and return to the backward town she escaped decades ago, she isn't sure she wants to continue living—especially if it means facing her estranged sister and the secret she has avoided for years. *Limelight* is a beautiful coming-of-age story at the other end of the spectrum."

> —VIRGINIA SMITH, author of *Third Time's a Charm* and
> the Sister-to-Sister series

"Only a gifted writer like Melody Carlson could present a self-centered character in such a way that the reader can't wait to turn the page and learn more about her. Claudette's poignant yet amusing journey from worldly has-been diva to ~~⸻~~ ⸻est woman grabs the reader by the ⸻ ⸻ ⸻),
even after the end. Highly re⸻

> —JILL ELIZABETH NEL⸻
> Thief Series

"…any st⸻ C⸻ ⸻ ⸻"
> —⸻

FICT CAR
Carlson, Melody.
Limelight : a novel

CANCELLED

NOV 2 4 2009

"Melody Carlson's style is mature and bitingly funny, and her gift for connecting our heart to the character's plight also connects us to the complicated human condition and our need for one another."

—PATRICIA HICKMAN, author of *Painted Dresses*

"Melody Carlson never fails to drag us out of our Christian easy chairs and right into the coals of the confusing culture in which we all find ourselves. She never fails to reveal that place of compassion within each of us. Excellent."

—LISA SAMSON, author of *The Church Ladies* and *Tiger Lillie*

"With great confidence, I can say that Melody Carlson's story will enlighten, encourage, and empower you."

—GREGORY L. JANTZ, PHD, Founder and Executive Director of the Center for Counseling & Health Resources Inc.

DURANGO PUBLIC LIBRARY
DURANGO, COLORADO 81301

Limelight

BOOKS BY MELODY CARLSON

ADULT FICTION
The Other Side of Darkness
On This Day
Finding Alice
Crystal Lies
A Mile in My Flip-Flops
These Boots Weren't Made for Walking
The Four Lindas
The Christmas Dog

TEEN FICTION
Diary of a Teenage Girl Series
The Secret Life of Samantha McGregor Series
Notes from a Spinning Planet Series
86 Bloomberg Place Series
True Color Series
The Carter House Girls Series
Just Another Girl

NONFICTION
Dear Mom
True: A Teen Devotional
By Design series
Piercing Proverbs

Melody Carlson

Limelight

A Novel

MULTNOMAH
BOOKS

LIMELIGHT
PUBLISHED BY MULTNOMAH BOOKS
12265 Oracle Boulevard, Suite 200
Colorado Springs, Colorado 80921

The characters and events in this book are fictional, and any resemblance to
actual persons or events is coincidental.

ISBN 978-1-4000-7082-4
ISBN 978-1-60142-256-9 (electronic)

Copyright © 2009 by Carlson Management Co. Inc.

All rights reserved. No part of this book may be reproduced or transmitted in
any form or by any means, electronic or mechanical, including photocopying
and recording, or by any information storage and retrieval system, without
permission in writing from the publisher.

Published in the United States by WaterBrook Multnomah, an imprint of the
Crown Publishing Group, a division of Random House Inc., New York.

MULTNOMAH and its mountain colophon are registered trademarks of Random
House Inc.

Library of Congress Cataloging-in-Publication Data
Carlson, Melody.
  Limelight : a novel / Melody Carlson. — 1st ed.
    p. cm.
  ISBN 978-1-4000-7082-4 — ISBN 978-1-60142-256-9 (electronic)
  I. Title.
  PS3553.A73257L56 2009
  813'.54—dc22

                          2009014683

Printed in the United States of America
2009—First Edition

10 9 8 7 6 5 4 3 2 1

I used to be a beauty.

You know the sort of woman—she walks into a room and heads turn. Oh, I don't mean just male heads because, believe me, women look too. Maybe they do it a little more inconspicuously, as if they're just checking out the latest shoe styles. But usually, they're comparing, inventorying, mentally tallying up who's the thinnest, fairest, trendiest. Who can turn *more* heads. It's the game we all play but no one ever admits to—a game that ends too quickly. Because, despite our efforts, age creeps in, beauty fades…and along with it, the limelight.

I am a testament to the temporary rewards of beauty. I sit alone in this sorry institution where no one comes to visit and no one gives a whit that I, Claudette Fioré, a woman who once made heads turn and broke hearts, have lost everything. No one knows who I am or who I used to be. No one even cares. It is no wonder that I tried to end my life. And yet I couldn't even succeed at that. Just one more notch of uselessness on the weighty belt of old age.

Of course, there are those fools who think that simply because I am old, I also must be wise. They assume that all these many years of life and experience have somehow broadened something besides my flabby backside. But I fear they are mistaken. I am nothing more than a silly woman who has grown unbearably old. A misshapen and withered shell that holds little more than wounded pride and faded memories. And yet I still manage to deceive a few—but only those willing to be tricked. Like that silly volunteer girl who comes in here twice a week. I suspect she is performing community service, although she will not admit to as much. Her name is Lucy, I believe. Or is it Lindy? Or Lulu? Oh, how am I supposed to remember such trivia?

"You're looking fine today, Mrs. Fioré," she told me this afternoon. It's the same thing she says every time I see her. Why don't they train these girls to use a variety of greetings? But then, what can you expect from a place that uses a rotating weekly menu with entrées like Salisbury steak and liver and onions?

"Fine?" I rolled my eyes and ran my hand through my thinning hair, sadly in need of professional attention and white as cotton since they don't allow me to tint it here in the "home." I've considered asking this girl to help me escape to see André, my hairdresser, to get it properly done, but why bother? Who cares?

She smiled as she straightened the pictures on my bureau. Sylvia, my faithful cook, brought them to me, along with some other things from my home. I suspect she was trying to cheer me up. Most of the photos are of me. Naturally, they were taken when I was younger, prettier, alive. However, one photo is with

Gavin, and another is with my younger sister, back when we were speaking to each other.

She's an intelligent woman but plain faced and frumpy. We make an odd pair, since she wasn't born with the looks that came anywhere close to matching my own, and she never learned how to make the most of what little she had. But all the photos were purposely selected to show me at my best, my prime. Why would I not be?

"So, how are you feeling?" She came over to peer into my pale blue eyes. They were once bright and clear...bluer than the Pacific on a cloudless day. Fiery blue, I was once told by a man who thought he loved me. Now they are faded and weak, and despite laser surgery, I must squint to read her name tag. Lindy, yes, just as I thought.

"As well as can be expected for someone locked up in a place like this." My usual retort to her usual question. But still she smiled, undeterred by my nastiness. It was part of the game we played.

"Oh, Mrs. Fioré, there are worse places to be, you know."

"I can't imagine where."

"Then don't waste your imagination going there. Instead, why don't you tell me about other places you've been?"

Ah, now this was more like it. The only thing good about this silly Lindy character was that she liked to hear about what my life *used* to be like. Or at least she acted that way. I could never be completely sure. I suppose that was the long-term result of having spent most of my days among people who often said one thing and meant another. Still, I was bored silly by myself and my dismal surroundings today, so I played along.

"You were telling me about your mother the other day…" She tossed me the bait as she straightened the sheets on my narrow bed. "I believe she had just sewn you and your sister new dresses."

I nodded as the memory drifted down on me like a downy blanket. I had given myself liberty with this young woman. She was so far removed from my social sphere, so foreign to the world I had inhabited for so many years, that I had come to think of her as a "safe" person—and, trust me, there have been few. I believed she was someone I could tell secrets to, memories that had lain hidden for all of my adulthood.

"Yes, that's right," I began. "Violet, my sister, and I were around four and six at the time. Violet is younger than I, although for decades she's been mistaken for my much older sister. Poor Violet, she's aged so much faster than I."

"What time of year was it?" Lindy fluffed my down pillow, one of my few luxuries in this stark environment.

I actually bribed one of the interns to purchase it for me. Most of my valuables were locked up for "safekeeping," but I tempted the young man with my Cartier Tank watch. Quite a deal for him, considering the watch must have been worth the price of dozens of fine down pillows.

"Spring," I told her. "But these weren't Easter dresses, as I recall. Or if they were, I must've been allowed to wear mine to school." I sighed as I remembered the reception I got at Silverton

Elementary that day. "Of course, all the other little girls were dressed like ragamuffins, and when they saw me, why, their eyes nearly popped out of their straggly heads. I was the envy of the entire first grade. Maybe the whole school, for that matter."

"How did that make you feel?"

I scowled at Lindy. She had this obnoxious way of asking intrusive questions that I'd rather not think about, let alone answer. But I knew the game well enough to know that to keep her attention, I must at least attempt an answer.

"I probably felt a bit bad. And yet...I enjoyed having the prettiest dress. I can still remember the fabric too. It was a pale yellow dotted swiss that my grandmother had sent up from the Bay area. And my daddy said I looked just like a sunbeam in it. And he told me how my blond pigtails shimmered like spun gold in the sunshine.

"Oh, I knew I was pretty, all right. Probably the prettiest little girl in town. And why shouldn't I be? Some people are simply chosen to live above the rest—the crème de la crème, we rise to the top. I think it was around then that I began to suspect I would one day be the golden girl of Silverton. I knew my value would lie in my looks."

"And why's that?"

"Because my folks were poor." I sighed. Surely, I'd told Lindy this already. "Oh, everyone hit hard times during the Depression." I tried to be patient with this poor numbskull of a girl. "But even in the best of times, my folks were fairly strapped, back when I was little anyway. My daddy didn't much care for working; he felt it was hard on his back and callused his hands. And although my mother took in laundry, cleaned houses, did odd jobs when she got the chance…it wasn't enough to keep a family of four fed."

"So it must've been special for you to have a new dress."

"I'll say. I thought I was Queen for a Day. Of course, that was back before I'd ever heard of such a thing. But I'm sure I imagined myself to be a princess in a fairy tale. And in some ways, my fate was set on that spring day. I knew I was too good for our dusty little town. I knew I was destined for greatness."

"You knew that when you were only six?"

"Oh, I probably couldn't have expressed it in so many words, but I had this feeling deep inside me, this undeniable sense that someday I would really be, oh, *something*."

She nodded with a hard-to-read expression, but one that aggravated me to the core. Just who was this upstart of a girl, and why did she come to visit me? Perhaps I should be more careful with my words.

"Is something wrong, Mrs. Fioré?"

"Why are you here?" I peered closely at her pasty complexion. Had this poor girl never heard of rouge or what they called blush nowadays?

She smiled, exposing slightly crooked teeth. "I've told you before that I'm from the university…that I volunteer here to get credit for one of my classes."

I scowled at her, knowing full well that frowning only deepened the creases between my brows, but it no longer mattered how many wrinkles I incurred. Then I smiled at her. It was an insincere smile, but I doubted that she would know the difference. "What is your major, dear?"

She glanced away as if uncomfortable.

"You come here and pester me with your silly questions. Personal queries that I answer honestly. But I ask you a simple question and you close up on me like an angry clam." I leaned forward and peered even more closely at her. She really was a homely little thing with her mousy hair and oversized nose. "Why is that?"

"I'm sorry, Mrs. Fioré. My major is clinical psychology."

My jaw tightened. "So I am your guinea pig? You ask your prying questions without disclosing your purposes. Perhaps you plan to practice your junior clinical psychology on me?"

"No, that's not it…"

I sat up straighter, easing to the edge of my seat. Then placing one hand on each arm of the chair, I hoisted myself to a standing position. "That will be enough." She stood too, but I was still tall enough to look down on her.

"But we've barely started to visit."

"We are finished, Lucy. And do not come back to see me again."

"But, Mrs. Fioré—"

"You are dismissed," I said in my haughtiest voice, the same tone I once used for servants who didn't understand their place in my household. "Good-bye." I turned and slowly walked away.

One of the few things I can be thankful for in my advanced years is my ability to walk. I pretended not to notice others in the room. The pathetic old lump of a woman with greasy gray hair, slumped like a bag of potatoes in her wheelchair…the thin, balding, middle-aged man who chewed his fingernails down to nubs…the doped-up young woman with a tattoo of a serpent crawling down her arm who stared blankly out the window. These people did not interest me. It was obvious they belonged here. I did not.

It was also obvious that I needed to find a way out of this nut house.

2

Even if you were well enough to leave Laurel Hills and return to the outside world…" As usual, Dr. Hampton speaks in his slow, methodic, sedate voice—one I'm sure he's developed to soothe his patients, but the effect on me is that of fingernails scratching on a blackboard. "Where would you live, Claudette? Your house in Beverly Hills has been sold for back taxes. You have no family to speak of."

"Rather, I have no family who speak to me."

He looks down at my chart. "I'm aware that you're estranged from your sister and her family."

"There's Michael."

He glances at his paperwork. "Your deceased husband's son?"

"Actually, Michael is Gavin's *deceased wife's* son. But we've always regarded him as our own." I sort of laugh. "Although Michael and I are close to the same age." Actually, Michael is six years younger, but at this stage of the game, who's counting?

"And where does Michael live?"

"In Hawaii." I think back to the last time I visited Michael there, shortly after Gavin died in early 2000. Michael had invited me over to the big island to help comfort me at my time of loss. I stayed for nearly a month, but Michael's jealous lover, Richard, resented the time Michael and I spent together. Richard is only in his forties and doesn't share the same background that Michael and I have. He would become irate if Michael and I laughed and reminisced about the "good old days" in Hollywood. Finally I decided it was time for me to return to Beverly Hills.

"And do you think Michael would like for you to live with him in Hawaii?"

"Michael and I have always gotten along quite well." I neglect to mention Richard.

"Perhaps you'd like me to give Michael a call."

I sit up straighter. "Perhaps I'd prefer to call Michael myself, Dr. Hampton."

He clears his throat. "You're welcome to call him, Claudette. You know you're not a prisoner here."

I would like to ask for his definition of the word *prisoner,* but I don't want to appear overly hostile. These past several weeks I have strived to convince him that I am perfectly sane, that I have no intention of harming myself or anyone else. "May I use your phone?"

"Of course."

"In private?"

"If you wish." He hands me the phone. "First dial nine." Then he stands, picks up my folder, and exits, leaving the door slightly ajar.

I suspect he is either listening on the other side, or perhaps he has this line tapped. No matter, I intend to plead with Michael to help me out of this place.

"Aloha!" says a voice I instantly recognize as Michael's.

"Oh, sweet Michael, I have missed you desperately."

"Claudette?"

"Yes, dear. It is I."

"How are you, darling? I heard you were hospitalized, but not a word more. I've been worried sick about you. So much so that I've almost returned to the mainland just to check on you."

"Thank you, dear. But I am ever so much better," I say, and then for Dr. Hampton's eavesdropping ears, "I've had the best of care in this wonderful place."

"I'm so relieved to hear that. But is it true? Has the house in Beverly Hills really been sold? I just can't bear to think of that place no longer being in the family. Please, tell me it isn't so."

"I wish I could tell you that, Michael. But unfortunately, your father—rather his accountant—remember Harvey? Well, he neglected to pay our taxes for a few years...*quite* a few years. Apparently the IRS kept track. The estate had to be sold."

"Oh, dear." He sighs loudly. "Whatever will you do now, darling?"

"That's why I'm calling you. I need some help—a place to stay."

"Oh my..." He pauses, and I suspect Richard is nearby. "You know how it is here on the island."

"You mean with Richard?"

"Yes, exactly."

"But I have no one, Michael…no place to go…" My voice breaks, an old trick I learned back in the days when I thought I'd make my living on the silver screen. It has worked well for me over the years, and I'm desperate to have it work now.

"Oh, darling, I do want to help you. But I don't know what to do. I feel caught between a rock and a hard place."

"You mentioned possibly coming to the mainland to see me."

"Well, yes, I'd love to see you, but I don't know…to drop everything… I'm not sure I can get away…just like that."

I can see that I need some sort of tempting bait. Something to encourage Michael to leave his precious island, to make the trip, and to help me. "I've set some special things aside for you. Some of Gavin's film memorabilia and collectibles. Some of those items you've had your eye on for years. They're supposed to be in storage, but I haven't been able to check on anything since I've been, uh, hospitalized. Who knows what may have happened since then?"

"Well, it has been ages since I've been to the mainland. I suppose a little trip might do me some good."

"It would be so wonderful to see you, Michael. And you can help me get out of here, and we'll remove those things out of storage, and perhaps, together, we can think of something… someplace where I could go. I do have some money set aside…" I don't admit that it's hardly anything. "And I've had some furnishings and things spared as well, but I need some help, dear. You know we're not getting any younger."

He laughs. "You're telling me. Do you know I just turned seventy-six?"

"Goodness, you're nearly as old as I am now."

"But knowing you, Claudette, you probably look at least ten years younger. Tell me the truth, darling, were you really in the hospital getting a little work done?"

"If only that were the case." I pat my wrinkly neck and try not to imagine the condition of my frowzy hair. If only I could have something done to it before Michael arrives. Although the blurry stainless-steel mirror in my room hides a multitude of things, I know I must look a fright.

"I will be on the next plane out, darling. Sir Michael to the rescue."

"Oh, thank you, thank you!" I tell him the name of the institution and my doctor, admitting that I have no phone in my room. But I don't mention that my room has a lock that locks from the exterior. Some things are better left unsaid. I've barely returned the receiver to the cradle when Dr. Hampton reenters the room.

"So…has Michael invited you to live with him in Hawaii?"

I slowly stand. "Michael is on his way to get me, Dr. Hampton. We will figure out these details upon his arrival."

He leans forward and looks directly into my eyes. "Are you certain you're ready to leave us? You were in such poor condition when you arrived here. I would hate to see you deteriorate to that level again."

I hold my head higher. "As you know, I have been through a lot in the past year. I lived alone with servants who ruthlessly stole from me, my home was literally sold right out from under me, I had no one to turn to, no place to go. Is it any surprise that I experienced a bit of stress?"

"You tried to kill yourself, Claudette."

I wave my hand, as if to brush away a pesky mosquito. "Yes, I'm aware of that. I was depressed…despondent… I wasn't thinking right."

"But you really believe you're better now?"

"Of course, only this morning you mentioned how remarkable my progress has been."

"I also know that you were once an actress. It's possible you have tricked me."

I hold up both hands, palms dramatically upward. "And suppose that was the case? Would it truly matter? Look at me. I am going on…" I pause now, unsure that I really want to say how old I am or that I care to hear that number spoken aloud. Then again, this man has my medical records and is fully aware of my age. "I am in my eighties." I inwardly cringe at this difficult confession. "Even if I were to expire, I have lived a long and fulfilling life, have I not?"

"Have you?"

I let out a sigh. "I had it all, Dr. Hampton. Beauty, fame,

wealth, envy, adoration, adventure… Really, what more could I possibly want?"

"I think you're the only one who can answer that question, Claudette." He smiles. "Perhaps you will."

I nod. "Yes. Perhaps I will." I return his smile, although mine is most decidedly false. Still, I don't think he's aware of this. He doesn't know how experienced I am at these little charades. He assumes that acting is something I left far behind me, something I set aside eons ago. But if lifetime achievement awards were given to the actor who had fooled the most people for the longest period of time, I might be a serious contender for one of those gold-plated statuettes.

3

I have always been fussy about packing.

For a while after marrying Gavin, I tried to entrust this task to my maid, only to be disappointed once I discovered my precious items wrinkled, snagged, tangled, or crushed. Finally I decided that, like with parachutes, one must pack one's own bags. Because I believe that clothing, when it's well designed and expensive, deserves respect. Respect your clothing and it will respect you. So I start my packing the morning before Michael is to arrive. I expect it will take most of the day to pack these four bags.

My packing reminds me of my old friend Billie. Oh, some people knew her as Joan Crawford, but her close friends called her Billie. Like so many of the old Hollywood greats I met, it was Gavin who first introduced us. Billie was much older than I, even a bit older than Gavin, as I recall. She was nearly old enough to be my mother, although we never spoke of age. That was unthinkable. Besides, she kept herself up, and looking back at some of her photos during that era, I must admit she was still stunningly beautiful. Even so, she was on her way out.

At her age, most actresses were only offered nonstarring roles as mothers or spinsterish old aunts. But Billie wasn't ready to give up her glamorous stardom or the silver screen. And despite the fact that MGM gave her not-so-subtle hints by handing her horrible scripts, she tried hard not to break her contract. But they were, in effect, showing her the door. It was quite sad really.

I sigh as I gently fold a Christian Dior cardigan, smoothing the pale pink cashmere as I lay it flat.

Growing old in Hollywood is not for the faint of heart.

Billie was such a meticulous person, the sort of woman who always packed her own bags. She didn't want anyone to handle her clothing or personal items. In fact, she didn't like anyone to handle much of anything that belonged to her. I even recall seeing her discreetly wiping off doorknobs, lamps, and various items her guests touched while visiting her home. It seemed a bit eccentric, but then that was Hollywood. Everyone had their little quirks.

A story actually circulated that Billie had a brand-new toilet torn out and replaced after the plumber allegedly used it. I do think it's terribly distasteful for a plumber to use one's toilet, but it is a bit extreme, not to mention expensive, to have a perfectly good toilet torn out. A good dousing of Lysol should do the trick. Naturally, I never mentioned this to Billie. I wouldn't dare.

I hold up my favorite silk pajamas with dismay. They have gotten rather ratty looking during my short stint here at Laurel Hills. The laundry service leaves a lot to be desired. So much so that I have avoided sending them more than absolutely necessary. Not only do those careless people destroy perfectly good items of clothing, but they steal things as well. Since I've come here, several of my favorite pieces have gone missing. It's really quite appalling. I've mentioned my concern numerous times, but no one seems to particularly care. I asked the nurse's aide about sending my clothing out for dry cleaning, and she simply laughed.

As I toss the shabby pajamas into the waste basket—no sense taking what needs to be replaced—I remember something else about Billie. She was so particular that she would only wear white pajamas to bed. And she always had a drawer full of them. I thought that was rather glamorous back then, and I even tried it myself for a while, but I soon grew bored with the repetition and returned to wearing a variety of sleepwear—much of it purchased from Frederick's of Hollywood. I was quite popular there...back in the day.

Gavin used to compliment me on my fine sense of style, particularly when it came to things like lingerie and sleepwear. He said that his first wife, Gala Morrow, had no natural fashion instincts whatsoever. And Billie told me that when left to her own devices, Gala might actually leave the house carrying a brown purse while wearing black pumps! But in all fairness, and often to my great displeasure, that was about the only flaw Gavin ever faulted his deceased wife with. In his mind, she was perfection.

Admittedly, Gala Morrow had been a beauty. A striking actress, with dark hair and dark eyes, Gala began her career toward the end of the silent film era. But she had difficulty making the transition to talkies, and before long she was simply part of film history—archived along with the old silent movies. Not long after her career ended, she suffered a severe stroke and died at the age of thirty-seven.

Sometimes I think those are the fortunate actresses, the ones who died early. They remain indelibly youthful and beautiful in our minds. You never witness their old, haggard faces or misshapen bodies plastered across the fronts of tabloids in the supermarket checkout line. No, it's women like Gala Morrow, Jean Harlow, and Marilyn Monroe who will remain forever young. I envy them more than ever now.

For decades after her death, black-and-white photos of the glamorous Gala remained prominently displayed throughout our home. Many a time I would catch Gavin gazing at her sparkling image with longing in his eyes. But would he have yearned for her if she'd still been alive? Goodness, Gala was five years older than Gavin. She would've been old and wrinkled and probably fat as a pig by then. I'm certain she'd have been the type who would've packed on the pounds with age. Even at thirty-seven, she had rounded out some. But those dazzling publicity photos kept her fresh and vital, haunting me endlessly with her bright-eyed youth. Meanwhile, I continued to grow older.

I longed to remove Gala's photos from our home, but I wouldn't dare. So they remained, mocking me from the mantle, from the grand piano, even in our master bedroom suite, right up until Gavin passed on several years ago. That's when I finally took them all down and boxed them up. Naturally, I shipped these off to her son, Michael, in Hawaii. I knew Michael would appreciate them.

Not that he and his mother had ever been close, since a nanny saw to his care until he was old enough to be sent to boarding school. I sometimes felt sorry for Michael, although he wasn't the only Hollywood "orphan" in those days. And later in life Gavin did treat him like a son, but there were times when Michael seemed a bit of a lost soul.

I look at the clock above the door. It's almost five and nearly dinnertime. They serve the evening meal so early here it feels more like a late lunch to me. But then Gavin and I, like so many Hollywood people, never ate dinner before nine thirty. And then we always slept in late.

"You keep Dracula hours," my younger sister, Violet, used to tease me, back when she and I were on speaking terms and she would call before noon, awakening me from my precious beauty sleep—something she couldn't possibly understand.

I close my suitcase, part of a Louis Vuitton set I've used since the seventies. I actually have ten pieces, but only these four managed to make it to Laurel Hills. And I have these pieces thanks to my cook, the only one who hadn't been stealing from me—or so she claimed. Sylvia packed these bags herself. Not as well as I would've packed them. But I appreciated her delivering them to me and bringing me a batch of homemade lemon bars as well.

Sylvia really is a kindhearted woman, and her lemon bars are delectable, but as I keep reminding her, she should cut back on the sweets, since her thick waistline seems to grow larger every year.

I close the leather latch on the case and hope that the other six pieces of luggage made it safely into storage and not into the backseat of a run-down vehicle of one of my servants. I've heard that these vintage pieces are even more expensive than the new ones. Funny how some things grow more valuable with age. Hopefully, my pilfering servants weren't aware of this. Most of their thievery involved newer items, mundane things really. Still, it peeved me. And who knows what they might've stolen after my sudden departure in the back of the ambulance that day. I may have been picked clean by now.

It had been a trying day and a difficult week. I'd been in the midst of sorting out the contents of my home. Naturally, this was necessitated by the unfortunate announcement made by the IRS people two weeks prior. Being old, I wasn't moving terribly fast, and I'd hired some packers and an estate sale lady to help me out. But I'd been doing my part too, steadily plodding along, picking out which items would go to storage, marking some things to be saved for Michael, setting others aside for the estate sale that supposedly took place several weeks ago. My accountant, Jackie Berkshire, assured me that the check had been deposited into my account.

But life those few days had grown very, very stressful. Seeing so many fragments of the past, handling bits and pieces of my life, and preparing to leave the only home I'd known for nearly sixty years was tearing me apart. The thought of losing that lovely house just broke my heart. How could I simply walk away and leave it all behind? It was just too much to bear.

I'm sure that's why I dropped the table lamp. Not just any lamp, mind you. It was a signed Louis Comfort Tiffany lamp, one with the much-coveted golden dragonfly design. It had been an anniversary present from Gavin. It slipped from my hands onto the marble foyer floor, and all that was left of my marvelous lamp lay littered about my feet in a thousand glittering pieces. I stood there frozen, unable to think or move or even speak.

Several of the servants and packers rushed out to see what had happened, and they looked nearly as horrified as I felt. Although I suspect they were greatly relieved that it was I who had done the damage instead of them.

"I help." Marbella ran back to the kitchen to fetch a broom.

After she cleared a path, I walked away from my disaster area and, without speaking to anyone, slowly made my way up the curving staircase, balancing myself with the cool surface of the carved marble handrail until I reached the master suite. I went into the bathroom, opened the gilt-trimmed medicine cabinet, removed an old prescription bottle of Valium, filled a Waterford tumbler with water, and proceeded to ingest all those pretty blue pills, two at a time.

I had barely swallowed the last ones and was just getting ready to take a nice long nap when Sylvia came looking for me and discovered the empty bottle. I was already quite groggy and don't really remember what happened next, but when I woke up I was in the emergency room…and two days later I came here.

The staff physician at Cedars-Sinai assured me that my stay at Laurel Hills would be short and restorative. "Just long enough for an evaluation and treatment," he promised. He also informed me that it was the only way I could be released from the hospital, so I fell for it.

Now, nearly six weeks later, I am more than ready to leave this horrid place. I cannot wait to see Michael again. He's always been such a dear. Nothing like his fashion-challenged mother, Michael always had an expert eye for style. I'm sure that's why he was such a successful set designer. His taste in décor and art is impeccable. I used to adore shopping with him.

If Michael weren't gay, I might've gone after that man for myself. Well, not until Gavin passed on, of course. And not because I never had an affair while my husband was alive, because it's no secret that I've had more than my fair share of men—although rumors as to who I've actually slept with are greatly exaggerated. Even so, I would never have stepped over that line with Michael, simply because if I'd had an affair with Gavin's stepson, life as I knew it would've been over. I'm certain it would've ended our marriage or, rather, what was left of our marriage—a lovely facade of a devoted couple who had been together for many, many years.

This was one of the few things that set us apart in Hollywood. We were considered "the lucky ones," one of those rare couples like Bob and Dolores Hope, Paul Newman and Joanne Woodward, even Aaron and Candy Spelling, who had managed to stay together to the end. Or so it seemed.

But everyone in Hollywood knows that nothing is ever as it seems.

4

D arling." Michael bursts into my room. "You didn't tell me they locked you up in the nut house."

"Oh, Michael." I rush dramatically to him and embrace him. "My knight in shining armor... You've come to my rescue."

"Poor Claudette." He steps back and looks me up and down, finally blinking as he stares at my frowzy hair. At least I have on my pale blue Armani pantsuit and my perfectly matched antique pearls. "You poor thing; it looks as if you haven't been to the salon in—"

"I know, I know. I look simply dreadful. The first thing I want to do, once I'm out of this hellhole, is to make an appointment with André." I remove the Hermès silk scarf from my purse and tie it around my head, as if I'm about to go for a ride in a convertible. To complete the drama, I put on my oversized pair of Chanel sunglasses.

"I still remember his number, darling. I only wish I had him on speed dial."

The orderly helps us get my bags out to the parking lot, and Michael actually tips him.

"Thanks," says the surprised young man. "Want me to put them in the trunk for you too?"

"That would be divine." Michael gallantly opens the passenger door for me. "Terribly sorry about the rental car, Claudette. It was the best they had."

"I am so thankful to be out of that place. I wouldn't complain if you'd driven here in a hay truck."

"Is Dad's Bentley still around?" he asks hopefully.

I shake my head and frown. "The IRS took it along with the house."

He swears at the IRS.

"I'm sorry, Michael."

"Did they take your old Jag too?"

"No, for some reason they didn't want that. It's in storage now."

"Do you still drive, Claudette?"

"When the need arises. I'm not completely helpless."

"But you were able to save *some* things?" His brow creases. Has he given up on Botox treatments altogether?

"Oh yes."

Now I'm fully aware that seeing what I've saved for him is the primary reason Michael made this trip. Oh, certainly he loves me in his way. But more than that, I think he loves the idea of getting his hands on some of Gavin's treasures. And truly, parting with a few original pieces of art and Gavin's Hollywood memorabilia collection seems a small price to pay for Michael's help.

"Where to, darling?"

"I know it's early yet, but I'd love to have some real food today. I believe the cuisine at Laurel Hills was packaged by Purina."

He laughs. "So, where shall we go?"

"How I wish Chasen's were still in business…"

"Don't we all." Michael sighs. "How about Spago, Claudette?"

"Don't you know it's gone too?"

"I'm not speaking of the one on Sunset Boulevard. I mean Spago, Beverly Hills." He actually smacks his lips.

"But wouldn't we need a reservation?"

"Not if we drop our lovely names. Fioré still means something to a few people, and I'm sure Wolfgang might appreciate a little blast from the past to give the place some class."

I can't help but laugh at Michael's silly rhyme. "I'll only agree to go if you call ahead and make sure we can get in. There's nothing more humiliating that showing up at a place and being told we need a reservation. I just couldn't bear to be turned away. Not today."

Michael flips open his cell phone as he stops for a red light, which reminds me that mine, after being locked in the safe with my other valuables, is in need of a charge. Now if only I can find the cord to charge it with. He calls information and waits to be connected. Just like an old pro, he turns on the charm and wit, and I'm not terribly surprised that he actually manages to secure us a table for two thirty.

"You're amazing," I tell him.

"And shameless."

I laugh. "Yes, that bit about possibly meeting up with Tippi Hedren was a bit over the top, don't you think?"

"I just might give Tippi a call. I wouldn't be surprised if she did drop in. She dined with us in Hawaii last year, and she was looking marvelously divine."

"I don't know how she does it. She must be close to eighty now."

"No, she's the same age as I am, Claudette. But I think she could pass for fifty." He laughs. "Do you suppose today's seventies are yesterday's fifties?"

"Thanks to the modern-day marvels of plastic surgery and Botox." I shake my head, wishing that Tippi would pop into Spago. Perhaps I could ask her for beauty tips. I'd like to know who she goes to when she needs work done.

"Speaking of beauty treatments, let's see if we can squeeze you in for an emergency haircut." He flips open his cell phone again.

"Do you really think it's safe to drive on the freeway and talk on the phone?" I suddenly feel nervous. But I'm too late; he's already speaking to someone about a hair appointment. I can tell that André isn't available, but it sounds like Michael is attempting to set me up with someone else.

I'm about to interrupt him, demanding André or no one, when I pull down the visor and examine my image in the mirror. And this is a real mirror, not a blurry piece of stainless steel that makes your reflection so fuzzy you begin to feel as if you've had one martini too many. Good grief, how can I possibly show my face in public looking like this?

I flip the visor back up and just shake my head. Honestly, I don't think I can afford to be too picky in my choice of hair-dressers today. I fumble in my purse for lipstick and my compact. No wonder Michael looked so horrified when he picked me up. I am a fright. But my hands aren't as steady as they used to be, and the jiggling movement of the car on a road that's in need of repairs is not helping as I attempt to apply an even coat of Majestic Magenta. I finally give up, twisting the sleek silver tube closed and blotting my sloppy looking lips with a tissue.

"That's perfect," Michael says to someone on the phone. "Yes, we can make it by eleven thirty. We're on the road right now, only fifteen minutes away. Thank you, darling. You're a lifesaver." He closes his cell phone, then turns to smile at me. "You're on. Angel had a cancellation."

"Do you know Angel personally? Is she any good?"

"For starters, Angel is a *he*. And, yes, he is very good. I've been to him myself on occasion."

"I know I shouldn't complain. Goodness knows when I've let my appearance get this bad."

"You and me both, Claudette. I've put on at least thirty pounds, and everything is starting to sag." Michael taps the loose skin beneath his chin with the backs of his fingertips. "In fact, I think I'll see if I might possibly get a facial while you're with Angel. Flying across the ocean with all that recycled airplane air is murder on the complexion." He glances at me. "Maybe you'll have time for one too."

"Let's do keep our lunch reservation in mind."

Soon we're both comfortably seated and being cared for at the salon. I don't know how Michael finagled his facial appointment, but I'm impressed with his choice of Angel for me.

"Oh my." The large African American man gently runs his fingers through my hair. "We have work to do, Mrs. Fioré. How long has it been since you've been in?"

I do the mental calculation back to my last appointment, before the IRS turned my life upside down. "Nearly three months. I've been, uh, in the hospital."

He makes a sympathetic *tsk-tsk*. "Well, when I'm done, you'll be as good as new again."

A cackling sound that's meant to be laughter comes out. "Well, if you can make me as good as new, you must be a magician."

Then Shampoo Girl (I can never remember her name, but I recognize her by her purple hair) puts a black cape on me and escorts me to the shampoo station. There are many things I do not understand about this new generation, but primarily three trouble me. One, why do they dye their hair such unnatural and unbecoming colors? Two, why do they torture themselves by piercing tender places like tongues, navels, and nipples? And three, why do they use their bodies to display graffiti in the form of horrid-looking tattoos?

As Shampoo Girl towels my hair, she notices that my nails are in need of some attention. "I think there's a manicurist who's free," she says. "If you're interested."

So it is that, as Angel works his magic on my hair, I get a manicure. And when they are both finished, I must admit that I can see an improvement. My hair, now a pleasant platinum blond, is perfectly styled and looks thicker and healthier than before. My nails are neatly trimmed and painted a nice shell pink. The manicurist, Jewel, I think her name was, also talked me into purchasing a tube of matching shell pink lipstick, which she swears makes me look ten years younger. Naturally, I believe her. Why shouldn't I?

Angel turns out to be wrong, because I don't look as good as new. I don't even look as good as Tippi Hedren, although I might be able to pass as her older sister. But at least no one will have an excuse to refuse to let me into Spago now.

"You look marvelous, darling," Michael gushes when we meet up again. I'm primping in front of the big mirror by the door, touching up my lipstick, applying a little powder, patting my already perfect hair.

"Thank you, dear." I smile at him. "So do you."

He pats a smooth cheek. "I feel much better." Then, as we go outside into the bright afternoon sunlight, Michael breaks into a chorus of "I Feel Pretty."

I can't help myself—I have to laugh. But I'm not laughing as we enter Spago. I feel people glancing up at us, curious as to whether we're "anyone" or not. And then, satisfied that they don't recognize either of us, they look away with bored expressions, turning their attention back to their companions, people who are far more interesting than Michael and I.

Everyone here is so much younger, prettier, brighter, livelier. I suddenly feel very ancient, unattractive, sadly faded, and pathetically worn-out. And, despite my minimakeover, I'm painfully aware that I'm just an old woman. A *has-been* who hasn't been for decades now.

Oh, some people might still recall my husband's name, the ones who pay attention to a director's career. And a few savvy fans might even remember some of Michael's work in film. He actually won a few minor awards for set design, although nothing that ever equaled his stepfather's achievements.

But I, Claudette Fioré, am a *nobody*. My life might as well be over. I don't even own a home in Beverly Hills anymore. And as we're seated at a small, insignificant table near the rest rooms, I don't feel much different than I did when I broke the Tiffany lamp several weeks ago. If anything, I feel older...more tired...more depressed. And I wonder, *What is the point?*

"Is something wrong, Claudette?" Michael frowns again.

"You really shouldn't frown like that. Those worry creases aren't getting any smaller."

He touches his forehead. "You're right. I'm overdue for Botox as it is." Now he smiles slightly, relaxing his expression. "But tell me, is something wrong?"

I sigh and fold my hands on the table. "Everything is wrong,

Michael. I am old. I no longer have a home. I'm not wealthy. What do I have left?"

He reaches over and places a hand on mine. "You've been through a lot, darling. You need to put together a plan now. That's why I'm here. We'll get your life back on track."

"Why? What difference does it make? My life is over."

"Your life is not over, dear. You've just hit a hard place. You know what they say: Getting old is not for the faint of heart."

"It's not for me either, Michael."

He holds up his hands. "Consider the alternative."

"I already have. That's what landed me in Laurel Hills." Then, without elaborating, I tell him about my blue pills...the broken lamp.

"The Tiffany?" he exclaims in horror. "The golden dragon-fly design?"

I just nod.

"You *were* having a bad day."

The waiter comes, and Michael orders a glass of Pinot Noir for each of us. As the waiter leaves, Michael just shakes his head. "The golden dragonfly lamp..."

"Yes..."

"So sad."

"I know."

After lunch, I am bone tired. I almost ask Michael to take me home, and then I remember that I don't have a home.

"Where shall we go?" he asks as we walk to the car.

"I don't know..."

"Want to drive by the house? Just for old time's sake?"

I agree, leaning back into the car seat and closing my eyes as he heads up the hill. I'm not sure that I can even look. I feel a nudge on my elbow. Opening my eyes, I realize that I must've dozed off.

"There she blows," Michael says sadly.

A Realtor's sign with Sale Pending is planted by the front gates. By Appointment Only is in bold letters. As if anyone would try to see a house in this neighborhood without an appointment. I turn and look away. This hurts too much.

"Sorry, I thought you might want to see it…for closure."

I nod without speaking.

"I've got a room at the Hilton," he says as he drives away. "Should we see about getting you one there too?"

"Yes," I say soberly.

By five o'clock, I'm settled into a fairly decent room. Oh, it's not the Four Seasons, and it's not the Beverly Wilshire, but considering where I've been these past six weeks, I should be grateful to be here. With its king-size bed, smooth percale sheets, private bath, fluffy white linens, flat-screen television, comfortable chair, and a window with a somewhat pleasant view, it's far better than that horrid place I've just escaped from.

Even so, I feel more lost than ever. All I want to do is sleep. I just want to escape, to forget, to get lost in a delicious dream where I am young, beautiful, and wealthy again. Is that so much to ask?

I t seems I've barely fallen asleep before I'm rudely awakened by the sound of bells. It takes me a while to realize it's the phone. I haven't had a phone in my room for weeks. Something I found greatly irksome but now may have to rethink.

"Who is it?" I growl into the receiver.

"So lovely to hear your voice too, darling," Michael gushes with a sweetly sarcastic edge.

"Sorry," I grumble as I slowly plant my feet on the rug, getting my bearings. "I was asleep."

"Asleep? Why, it's not even seven thirty, Claudette. That seems a bit early to turn in."

"I was tired." I carefully stand.

"Well, far be it from me to disturb you. I only wondered if you'd like to join me and some friends downstairs for drinks. I've assembled a happy little crowd. Some of my old pals from the studio and anyone else who wants to be merry."

There was a time I'd leap at an opportunity to meet for drinks. We'd chat late into the night about the good old days, gossiping about the latest scandal and bragging about whatever personal triumphs we could conjure up to impress the group. And after a few drinks, we were all quite impressed—with each other and with ourselves.

I'm actually considering Michael's invitation as I stretch the phone cord to see in the mirror, curious as to whether I'm fit for a social occasion or not. But my reflection leaves me flat. Just an old lady. A very old lady. And despite my stint in the salon today, my hair is now fanned out on the sides in unbecoming clumps. Bed head. My skin is wrinkled and pale. Even my new lipstick color is disappointing.

"I think I'll stay in tonight."

"Are you sure, darling? I know the gang would be delighted to see you."

I lean forward and peer again. Even my age spots are showing. "No, thank you, Michael. Give them my best."

"Will you order room service then? You need to have something."

"Yes," I promise. "I'll do that."

But after I hang up, I simply turn out the light and go back to bed. I don't unpack my bag, change into pajamas, or even brush my teeth. Why bother?

I wake up early the next morning. It's still dark out. But I can't sleep another minute. My bones ache, and my bladder is bursting. Thankfully I've never had the incontinence problems so many of my generation suffer. My doctor said this is one of the benefits of never having children.

I turn on the light and inch my way toward the bathroom, holding on to the bureau and then the wall as I go. I don't know when I have felt so achy before. It's as if I've been run over by a truck. As I sit on the toilet, I contemplate the cause of my pain. I've not been troubled with arthritis, but my doctor assured me that was due to my fairly active lifestyle. I played golf weekly, attended t'ai chi and yoga classes somewhat faithfully. I even walked on my treadmill while watching Jay Leno sometimes. But all that came to a screeching halt when the IRS intruded on my life. I suppose that's when old age truly began to set in. Perhaps there is no stopping it now.

As I flush the toilet and then wash my hands, I wonder how difficult it would be to get a hold of a prescription for Valium again. Or perhaps there's another way out.

I pace back and forth in my room for about fifteen minutes. And to my surprise and relief, the movement helps some. My joints loosen up a little, and the pain seems to lessen. Maybe I'm stiff and sore from sleeping so long. Twelve hours is a bit extreme.

I open the drapes to let in the first rays of morning sun and then even do some yoga stretches. Not only do I feel better, but I'm hungry. I call room service, ordering up a pot of strong coffee with cream. And then, feeling a bit optimistic and even adventuresome, I proceed to order bacon and eggs, something

I've avoided for decades. "And throw in some pancakes," I add, feeling slightly reckless. "And orange juice."

I return to the bathroom, remove my wrinkled Armani suit, place it in a "to be cleaned" bag, and after protecting my hair with a shower cap, I take a long, hot shower.

I'm thankful for the steamed-up mirror as I emerge from the shower. There is an image I do not care to see. I've barely dried off and slipped into the hotel bathrobe when I hear someone knocking on the door.

"Your breakfast, ma'am," says a nice-looking Hispanic man.

I go to my purse, fumble to find a rather generous tip, then thank him.

"Enjoy."

"Oh, wait." I head for the dry cleaning bag. "Can you see that this gets cleaned and returned to me today?"

"Certainly."

Then I sit down and enjoy my cholesterol-ridden breakfast. Why should I care if I choke my arteries at this stage of the game? I attempt to read the newspaper, but the headlines bore me. Even the entertainment section bores me. All true creativity exited Hollywood in the late sixties...about the same time Gavin and so many of the other greats retired. It's a shame. And now it seems that so many films are simply remakes of the oldies. What is wrong with young people these days? Haven't they fresh or new thoughts in their heads?

I set the paper aside and pour another cup of coffee, which I top off with cream. Then I resettle myself into the club chair by the window. It's not an unpleasant view—well-maintained pool, greens, palm trees. I suppose I could make myself comfortable living in a place like this. Although I would soon be broke at the price of these rooms. Still, I'm sure some decent retirement homes are in the area.

It's not even eight yet, but I call my accountant anyway. I can leave Jackie a message insisting that I must see him today. I need to know the state of my financial affairs. I need to make a plan of some sort for my future, no matter how brief. And I don't know how long Michael will be around to help me sort all this out.

I unpack my bags, hanging things up and setting others aside for dry cleaning, in hopes of undoing some of the damage done by the Laurel Hills "laundry." Then I lay out a Ralph Lauren suit that makes me look rather authoritative. It's a summerweight wool, gray herringbone, dignified with classic lines. I choose a cream-colored silk blouse to go beneath it, along with a paisley silk scarf in shades of blue and gray.

I carefully apply makeup, taking my time to get it just right. Then I fuss with my hair until it finally resembles the style from yesterday. Finally I dress. It's barely nine thirty. Far too early for Michael to be up after a late night last night. Especially if he's still on Hawaii time, which I suspect is the case.

So I turn on the television and sit down to watch Regis and Kelly. Regis Philbin is a bit younger than me but still going strong. Although he does get cranky at times, and I must hand it to that pretty Kelly girl. She has the patience of Job and the wit of Johnny Carson—a real class act for someone her age. I can remember when Regis was Joey Bishop's sidekick back in the sixties. Joey used to pick on poor Regis something terrible. And then one day, Regis walked off the set, right in the midst of a broadcast. He was the talk of the town that week. And here he is still plugging away. I wonder what his secret is.

The television show is just ending when the phone rings. To my relief, it's Jackie.

"I'm so glad to hear that you're out," he says. "How are you feeling?"

"Old." I force a laugh. "But that's not news, is it."

"Where are you staying?"

"Beverly Hilton."

"Nice..."

"The reason I called is because I'd like to go over my financial affairs with you today."

"Oh, today is pretty busy, Claudette."

"Please. I need to know where I stand. I need to plan for my future."

"I really am booked, pretty much for the whole week. But I can let Cindy talk to you. I'm sure she can schedule you in for something next week."

"Next week is not going to work, Jackie." I use my no-nonsense business voice now. "I must get an accounting of my finances as soon as possible. Do you understand me?"

"How about if I have my secretary print something out for

you? I worked out some things on paper while you were in the hospital. A budget of sorts. I can have Cindy fax it to your hotel, if you like. Did you say the Beverly Hilton?"

Good grief, it's not as if I haven't been a good client for Jackie. I most certainly have. He's handled my finances ever since Gavin died, shortly after I discovered Gavin's other accountant wasn't trustworthy, and I've paid Jackie well and regularly. He can't shove me aside simply because of this recent fiasco with the IRS, can he? "Is that the *best* you can do?"

"It is for today."

"Fine," I snap at him. "When do you think it'll be here?"

"Depends on Cindy. But I'll have her get on it ASAP."

"Thank you."

"Uh, Claudette?"

"Yes?" I drum my fingertips on the desktop. I have absolutely no tolerance for this type of shabby behavior. Jackie is a somewhat tacky individual, and to think that I overlooked the fact that he wears unfashionable polyester suits and smells of cheap cologne.

"Well, I don't know how to put this gently…but you might want to brace yourself. I mean, the IRS was pretty brutal. And that estate sale didn't bring in nearly what you had hoped…"

"What exactly are you saying, Jackie?"

"I'm saying it's time to tighten up that old belt." He chuckles.

I sink back into the chair as the light of realization begins to glimmer. *"What do you mean?"*

"Your finances are pretty much tapped."

I'm finding it difficult to breathe. *"I am broke?"* I manage to gasp.

"Not broke exactly...but you're down to the bare bones. And you sure can't keep spending like you were accustomed to. You'll need to live on a budget from now on. I've tried to make some suggestions. But no more buying fancy clothes or expensive meals, if you get my drift."

"Yes...," I say slowly, trying to catch my breath. "I think I understand."

"For starters," he continues, although I'm finished with this conversation, "you probably won't want to stay too long at that hotel."

"I see..." My head is throbbing now. Am I having a stroke? A heart attack perhaps? The doctor assured me that my heart is in good shape, but he couldn't know everything.

"Sorry to be the bearer of bad news, Claudette. But you know me; I always give it to you straight."

"Right." I take in a quick breath. "I appreciate that."

"Take care now."

"Thank you."

A chilling numbness permeates my being as I hang up the phone. Does this mean I'm out of money? What does "tightening up the old belt" really mean? Or that my finances are "pretty much tapped"—isn't that how he put it? That does not sound good to me. But what about our IRAs, Social Security, stocks and bonds? Just how much did the IRS really tap us for?

I lean my head back and close my eyes. Gavin made a fortune in his time. And other than hiring that shiftless accountant who cheated the IRS, Gavin was careful with our finances. He invested and reinvested. Our home was paid for. Our bank account was well padded. How could it come to this?

Perhaps it doesn't matter. Perhaps I won't stick around to see the fallout. It is one thing to be old and to lose your looks. But to be poor as well? That is more than I can bear. I've been poor before, certainly...but it was long ago. I am determined never to go back there again.

If, as Michael says, growing old is not for the faint of heart, then growing old and impoverished must be far, far worse.

G ood morning, sunshine," Michael says when I open the door to my room to see him standing in the hallway. His hair is wet; he has on white linen pants, sandals, and a Hawaiian shirt. Just right for lounging around the pool.

"It isn't morning. And I am *not* sunshine."

"But you look lovely, darling." He nods to my suit. "Are we going somewhere special?"

I shake my head, walk across the room, and sit back down in the chair by the window, the same place I've been sitting for the past couple of hours. I feel as if I am stuck. I have no idea where to turn, which way to go.

"Something is wrong." Michael pulls the straight-back chair out from the desk, arranges it directly in front of me, then sits down, leaning forward with an expression of compassion in his eyes. "Tell Mikie everything."

"I am broke!" I burst out, clutching the linen handkerchief I've twisted into a tight wad. "My accountant just called, and he said I—I am broke." Now I actually do begin to sob, with real tears.

"Oh my…"

We both just sit there, the only sound is of me sobbing, sniffling, and finally blowing my nose. "I don't know what to do, Michael. I feel utterly lost."

"You're completely broke?" He frowns.

"Well, Jackie didn't use those terms."

"Your accountant has a lot of nerve, breaking that kind of news to you on the phone."

"I urged him on. He was too busy to see me, and I was, well, rather unhappy about that." I remember something. "And, oh yes, his secretary was going to fax me a statement…so I'll know exactly where I stand."

"Fax it?" His brows shoot up with horror. "You mean to this hotel?"

"Yes."

"For heaven's sake, Claudette, do you want the whole world to know about your financial crisis? Don't you understand that a fax is an open document that *anyone* can read—?" But Michael is already on his feet and nearly to the door. "I'll run down to the office to see if it's arrived yet. If it hasn't, I'll make sure it's handled with utmost discretion." Then he swears as he closes the door. And I feel like I'm not only old and poor, but stupid as well. What was I thinking?

Michael returns after about twenty minutes, and he has the dreaded papers in his hand. He is just shaking his head as he hands them to me. "Sorry. I couldn't help but take a peek on the way back up. I'm sure others have seen it too. The stupid clerk didn't even bother to put it in an envelope. I've a mind to complain to the management."

I attempt to study the columns of numbers, to force them to add up and make sense, but it's as if my eyes won't focus. Finally I hand the pages back to Michael. "Please, just give me the lowdown. Make it as quick and painless as possible."

So he tells me some figures, but they seem to just float somewhere over my head. I've never been terribly adept with numbers. "Exactly how much do I have to live on? Jackie mentioned I would have a budget. He said he'd made some suggestions."

Michael tosses out another number.

"Is that what I'm supposed to live on for a month?" I feel a tiny bit hopeful since it doesn't seem totally impossible.

"That's for a whole year, Claudette."

I blink and take in a sharp breath. "Is that even possible?"

He frowns and sets the papers aside. "I don't know…"

My vision grows blurry. Perhaps I really am having a stroke. One can only hope.

"I'm calling that no-account accountant of yours," Michael says suddenly. "This just doesn't sound right to me."

I simply nod, eyes closed, body limp, unable to speak. Perhaps paralysis is setting in. I can barely hear Michael as he demands to speak to Jackie. The words seem to tumble about and mix together until I feel certain he's speaking in a foreign language. No matter. I do not even care to listen. It's hopeless. Utterly hopeless.

Michael swears loudly, calling Jackie a bad name, which brings me back to my senses. I sit up and blink at the light. Michael slams down the phone and swears again.

"What?"

He holds up his hands in a helpless gesture. "The man is a moron, but it sounds like he stands by those figures. That business with the IRS was nasty, Claudette. I had no idea."

"Nor did I." I lean back, closing my eyes again.

"I wish I were in a better position to help you. But I'm stretched fairly tight myself. If Richard wasn't still working, we wouldn't be able to afford the place we have."

I just sigh.

"I don't know where you can possibly live on that amount of money per month. Do you have any family who could possibly—?"

I sit up straight, like a woman waking from the dead, eyes wide open. "No! I most certainly do not."

"Excuse me," he says in a wounded tone. "I'm only trying to help."

"I'm sorry…" I press my cool hands against my hot cheeks, willing for this all to be over, once and for all. I wonder if Michael would have any qualms about helping me get some Valium or something that could assist me in bringing my troubles to a grand finale.

"Even if we sell everything that's in storage," he says sadly, "I don't imagine it would last you for terribly long… It wouldn't get you into a nice retirement home."

"I'm not going to a retirement home," I say with a new resolve.

"No?"

"No."

"What then?"

"I need your help, Michael."

"That's why I came, darling." He comes over and takes both my hands. "Tell me, what shall we do?"

So I quickly spill out my plan to end my life—this time successfully. "Do you have anything I can use? Valium perhaps? Any tranquilizers or sedatives?"

"No…" He moans softly. "You don't want to do that."

"Oh, but I do. I am ready to check out, and I want you to help me."

"I can't do that."

"Why not?" I frown at him. "I thought you believed in assisted suicide."

"Perhaps in some cases I do. For instance if someone is suffering with an incurable illness—"

"I do have an incurable illness."

"What?"

"Old age and poverty."

"Oh, Claudette, please don't involve me in this. I want to help you, darling, but not like this. I can't."

"Fine! I'll do it myself." I walk over and look out the window. "I've never been a brave woman, but if I can't get drugs, perhaps I can find something to jump from, or I'll get my car out of storage and find a garage somewhere that I can park it in and asphyxiate myself. Would that be better?"

"Oh, Claudette." He comes from behind me and places his hands on my shoulders. "I hate seeing you like this."

I turn and face him. *"Then help me."*

"I know you're going to find this hard to believe, especially coming from someone like me, but I've begun to reconsider the possibility of an afterlife."

"An afterlife?"

"Yes..."

"What are you talking about?"

"Richard and I have started going to a little church that meets on the beach."

I blink in astonishment. "What? You and Richard in a church? You must be kidding. Are you making this up?"

"I know it must sound strange. But just because we're gay doesn't mean we have been excommunicated from God. According to the Bible, God sent Jesus to the cross for all sinners. This little church loves us for who we are. They know we're gay, but they still welcome us."

I am stunned. "And you go to this church, Michael? *Willingly?"*

He nods. "I'm not claiming to have any answers, Claudette. But I'm not getting any younger either. I remember having a long talk with Gavin, just a month or so before he died. He was thinking a lot about things like God and heaven... I remember him asking me if I was willing to ask the hard questions."

"The hard questions?"

"You know…about what comes next…does God really exist…is there such a thing as heaven. I'm willing to ask those questions now. This church is helping me find some answers."

I don't know what to say. I feel as if I've just been blindsided. Michael, of all people, is actually thinking about religion. Has the whole world gone completely mad?

"So, you see, I can't help you to do this. It would be wrong to help you end your own life when I'm still trying to figure out whether or not there's an afterlife. I couldn't live with myself if I did that."

I sit back down in the chair, lean over, and hold my head in my hands. Everything has been turned upside down, inside out, and I can't begin to make sense of any of it. I do not know what to do.

"There has to be a way out," Michael says calmly. "I mean, besides suicide."

I look up at him, staring blankly.

"Come on, darling. Think this through with me. There must be someone in your family… How about your sister? I remember she used to come down to visit sometimes and—"

"That is impossible."

"Why? She seemed like a nice woman to me. A little frumpy perhaps, but you two seemed to get along. What came between you two?"

"My mother."

He frowns. "Your mother?"

"Yes…my mother died, not long after Gavin died."

"I'm sorry, darling, I didn't know. But, goodness, she must've been very old."

"She was ninety-four."

"Good genetics. You probably have at least twenty good years left for you too, Claudette."

I roll my eyes. "And that's supposed to be *good* news?"

"Still, how did your mother come between you and your sister? Explain."

"When my mother died…she left her house to me. Violet was very hurt. She held it against me."

"And you let that, a mere house, separate you from your own flesh and blood?"

"*I* didn't let it. Violet is the one who held my mother's choice against me. And I was still getting over Gavin at the time… I just didn't need that kind of stress back then. For that matter, I don't need it now."

Michael's eyes light up. "So what became of the house?"

I shrug. "It's still there."

"Do you still own it?"

"I've been paying the taxes."

He's on his feet. "Presto! There's your answer, Claudette. You have a house!"

I frown. "It's not much of a house. It's about a hundred years old and probably run-down. Gavin wanted to help my mother with the cost of repairs. I was worried the old house might collapse around her ears and she'd be forced to come down here and live with us permanently. As I recall, she had to get the wiring fixed and the roof replaced. But Gavin was the one who handled these things; he sent her checks sometimes. And she sent him sweet little thank-you notes."

"So at least the house has electricity and a decent roof." He chuckles. "That's a start."

I shake my head. "This is crazy."

"Come on, darling. This is your opportunity. Your answer. Can't you see that?"

"I can't see much of anything at the moment, Michael."

"Where is this house?"

"Silverton," I mumble.

"Where's that?"

"Northern California…an old lumber town…where I grew up."

"It sounds delightful."

"Delightful?" This man clearly has no idea what he's talking about.

"You mentioned the Jaguar is in storage?"

"That's what I've been told."

"How about a road trip?"

"A road trip?"

"To Silverton."

"You can't possibly be serious." I frown up at him. "That's about an eight-hour drive. At my age and my present state of mind, I doubt I would even survive it."

"Look, Claudette. You wanted to commit suicide just

minutes ago. Why should you fret over an all-day drive? Would you really care if it killed you?"

I consider this, then just shrug.

He glances at his watch. "Let's go check on the things in storage now."

"Why?"

"If you're moving to Silverton, you might want some of your furnishings and personal belongings moved up there."

"You really are serious about this?"

He reaches for both my hands and gently helps me to stand. "First we'll get your car out and make sure it's ready for the road. Is it in good repair?"

"Of course, it's in good repair. I have that car checked regularly, the oil changed like clockwork, and I just had the tires replaced last winter."

"Good girl." He pats me on the back, then reaches for my purse. "And here's your exquisite bag, my dear." He holds it before him, examining it closely. "Versace, I presume?"

I nod, suppressing a groan as I recall how much I paid for that pocketbook a few months ago. I discovered it at an exclusive shop on Rodeo Drive; it was a splurge even for me and far more than what I'm allotted on my new monthly budget. How on earth is that meager sum supposed to cover all my living expenses? It hardly seems possible.

He hands the bag to me and smiles. "Very chic, darling, just like you. You really do look lovely today, Claudette."

I narrow my eyes as the corners of my lips curve into a miniscule smile. "You're attempting to butter me up, aren't you?"

"Moi?" He links his arm in mine as he leads me out the door. "And now the adventure begins." As we wait for the elevator, he merrily hums the tune to "We're Off to See the Wizard."

But I feel fairly certain that at the end of the journey, our wizard, not unlike the one in the movie, will be nothing more than an insecure little man with a receding hairline, hiding behind a heavy velvet curtain and pretending to be something he is not.

I sn't it unseasonably warm for November?" Michael asks.
After a light lunch, we are now at the storage unit place, somewhere outside of Beverly Hills, and Michael is trying to unlock the door to the unit where my belongings are supposedly safely stashed away.

"I suppose." I'm impatient for him to get the stubborn lock open, worried that this large unit will be empty.

"There," he says as the key finally turns. He opens the door, turns on the light, and to my relief, my things are there.

I rush over to a marble-top table that once occupied a prominent place in my foyer. It looks sadly out of place next to the cardboard box marked Small Kitchen Appliances. I run my hand over the cool surface and sigh.

"Wow," says Michael. "There's a lot here."

I nod, looking around helplessly. "Whatever will I do with all of it?"

"How big is your family home?"

"Family home?" I wonder at his choice of words. He obviously doesn't understand this situation at all. But then, how could he? I always kept my roots, both in my hair and in my past, carefully concealed. "It's not exactly what I'd call the *family home*, Michael. It's a small wooden house with a screen door."

"Sounds charming."

I look at the lovely furnishings I saved, items that would enhance the appearance of most homes…but not for the life of me can I imagine them situated in my mother's house. It would be a pathetic joke.

"How large is the house, darling?"

"The square footage?" I shrug. "I have absolutely no idea."

"How many bedrooms, baths, that sort of thing?"

I force myself to remember the house. "Two bedrooms. One bath. A living room and kitchen. That's it."

His brows fly up. "Really?"

"Yes. I told you it was small."

"So…we'll just have to scale down a bit. You'll pick out a few things you know will fit, items that you'll need—beds, tables, chairs, perhaps a sofa. Not the Casino sectional, of course, since I suspect that won't fit in a home that size. How big would you say the living room is?"

"Not big." I remove my jacket, carefully fold it, and set it on the marble-top table. "It's awfully warm in here, isn't it?"

"No air conditioning."

I look around the unit again. "I have no idea where to begin, Michael."

His forehead creases as he gives this some thought. "For

starters, I think we need to get some movers over here to help. We'll point out which boxes and pieces you want to take to Silverton, get them loaded on the truck, and—"

"Do you really think I'll stay in Silverton?"

"What other options do you have, darling?"

I can't think of an intelligent answer. I can barely think at all. So I pull out an armchair from the formal dining room set and sit my weary bones down on it. I vaguely listen as Michael calls Information on his cell phone and inquires about a specific moving company, which is apparently still in business since he's soon talking to someone. It seems he has some sort of personal connection with this place, because he mentions a man's name and then chats for a few minutes.

I close my eyes and lean back into the Mackintosh chair. What possessed Gavin to pick out this design, since it's never been comfortable? Although it is striking to behold with its modern lines and hard shellac finish. Even so, I'm certain this set is not something I'll take to Silverton. If I really am going to Silverton, which seems rather implausible, despite the phone conversation I overhear from Michael's end.

"I know this is terribly short notice, darling, but we'd love to have them come out here today, if possible." He pauses. "You can do that? That's wonderful. Please tell Peter I am eternally grateful and give him my best, will you?" He tells them the address of the storage place and then turns to me. "What is the address of your Silverton house, dear?"

"It's 258 Sequoia Street."

He repeats this into the phone, says "Thank you!" again, then closes his phone with an ear-to-ear grin. "They'll be here in about an hour."

"However did you manage that?"

"Friends helping friends…" He glances around the unit. "You start looking around, and I'll go see if I can get some tools."

"Tools?" I say absently, but he is already gone. I wander around the crowded unit, trying to make heads or tails of all of this—of my life. Finally I sit back down in the uncomfortable Mackintosh chair and convince myself that this is all just a dream. A very bad dream.

Michael returns with some masking tape, a pad of paper, and some felt pens. And for the next hour, he coaches me through the storage unit, saying yea to some pieces and nay to others. I get a glimpse of what he must've been like while working on a film. He seems to have some sort of scheme, perhaps like scene settings, all worked out in his head. And although it's a mystery to me, I am trying to trust him with these decisions.

I watch as he writes down various instructions, taping notes onto boxes and pieces of furniture in a way that reassures me that he really does know what he's doing. I feel as if I am a robot and he is controlling all the buttons. But by the time the movers arrive, there seems to have been a method to his madness. He gives them some directions, then turns to me.

"Our work here is done. Let's go get the Jaguar."

"Am I to drive it?" I ask in a weary voice.

"I can't very well drive two cars," he points out. "All you need to do is follow me to the closest rental car place. I'm sure it's not more than ten minutes from here. Then I'll return this dog of a car, and I'll drive your lovely Jag back to the hotel."

"Where I can take a nap?"

"Of course, darling. And then we'll have a nice late dinner and pack our bags and be ready to leave first thing in the morning."

I take my time to orient myself to my car. It has been a bit more than six weeks since I've driven, but it feels more like six years. I used to pride myself on my ability to drive—so many friends my age had given it up completely. But I still drove out to the country club or to lunch or to shopping. And so far I've never even had a fender bender. But suddenly I feel uncertain...about everything.

"You'll be fine." Michael opens the door and hands me my car keys. "Just relax and focus."

"Relax and focus," I tell myself as I start the engine, which purrs happily, as if she is glad to see me again.

The Jaguar is an XJ6, which means little to me since I know absolutely nothing about engines. I chose this vehicle strictly for looks—lean, elegant, and sexy. I run my fingers over the polished burled wood on the dash. It still gleams like it did the day Gavin brought it home to me more than twenty years ago.

I put the car into gear, checking the rearview and side mirrors before carefully backing out of the storage garage. As I follow Michael's car, trying not to get too close but not far enough to be cut off and lose him, I remember back to when Gavin asked me to pick out a new car. It was a couple of weeks before my sixtieth birthday. My Porsche convertible was starting to ping, and he was worried that it was becoming unreliable.

I'd seen an advertisement, in *Vogue* as I recall, for a car exactly like this. Even the color was perfect: a scrumptious shade of taupe that still leaves me longing for a latte. I think it was called doeskin. Pleased with myself, I'd torn out the glossy page and left it in the center of Gavin's desk.

But straightaway, he tried to talk me out of a Jaguar, and we ended up in a huge argument. I accused him of not loving me, which I think was partially true, and he accused me of being "completely superficial," which was also partially true, although we never could admit to our shortcomings.

"If I were Gala, you'd get me that car!" I'd yelled at him. This was my usual trump card in any argument. "It wouldn't be too expensive if you really loved me the way you loved Gala."

He got very quiet and attempted to calm me down, explaining that his reservations had nothing to do with the price tag. He said he was concerned that a Jaguar could have a lot of mechanical problems. "You'll have to make sure that it's carefully maintained, Claudette. It'll be up to you." Naturally, I promised him I would do that, that I *could* do that. So he conceded to the car.

I made him swear to no big fanfare about my sixtieth birthday. "And do not tell a soul why you got me this car," I warned him. I was still passing for late forties at the time and had no intention of being classified as a senior citizen. It was fine for Gavin, since he was in his midseventies by then and didn't care who knew.

As I follow Michael onto the freeway, I remember how proud Gavin looked when he pulled the gorgeous Jag into our circular driveway. I remember how he smiled when he saw me sliding into the brand-new car, running my hand over the buttery smooth leather upholstery, lovingly stroking the steering wheel...and I remember the sex we had that night to celebrate.

Despite my blues about getting older, it had been a fairly good day, as I recall. But it all seems so long ago now. Like someone else's life, or perhaps just a scene from a movie Gavin directed. And I could laugh, or perhaps I should cry, when I think of how I lamented over turning sixty. Compared to now, that was a walk in the park.

I am amazed at how well my car has held up. I've put less than thirty thousand miles on it, and it's always been stored in a garage. If I do say so myself, it still looks quite spectacular— almost as good as new. And I'm sure if it were to continue receiving the care and attention I've given it, it would remain ageless and lovely forever.

Truly, it's a pity that people weren't designed to last so well.

It's fortunate for everyone else on the road that I am not the driver today. I do not remember when I've been so utterly exhausted, so completely spent and worn out and discouraged. If I thought I felt elderly yesterday, I feel absolutely ancient now.

Overly anxious about today's journey, I'm sure I slept about three hours total last night. I tossed and turned and imagined the worst. Then, when I finally did manage to slumber, I was tormented by horrible dreams, only to be rudely awakened by the jangling of the telephone. To say that my five thirty wake-up call was excruciating is an understatement. Perhaps Michael is right. Perhaps this trip *will* kill me.

Michael's goal was to "be on the road by six o'clock sharp to avoid commuter traffic," and somehow we made it out of the hotel at that ungodly hour. We've been driving for nearly two hours, and I am still a bundle of raw nerves. I'm certain to have a complete breakdown before this day ends.

I peer hopelessly out the window, gazing blankly at the bleak landscape that surrounds us like a dusty brown carpet badly in need of cleaning. This does not help lift my spirits. The scenery northbound from Los Angeles on I-5 must be among the ugliest in the world.

Michael's plan is to drive straight up the freeway, stopping somewhere near San Jose, where we'll have a late breakfast. I lean my seat back and attempt to sleep, but it feels as if someone has hot-wired my brain—and now there is no controlling it. Most of my thoughts revolve around my hometown, replaying memories I'd thought I left behind when I left that lackluster little town back in 1942. I swore to everyone that I'd never go back. And for the most part, I've kept that promise. It's unbelievable that I'm actually going there now.

Oh, there's the possibility that I will die first...not a bad prospect, really.

I didn't return to Silverton until 1981, nearly forty years after my exodus. And I only went back because I was pressured into it by my sister. It was my mother's seventy-fifth birthday, and Violet had planned a "big" party, insisting that, as mother's only other child, I must attend.

"You know Mom never had a fancy wedding," Violet reminded me, "and Dad didn't live long enough for any special anniversaries. This is our big chance to show our mother that she's special, that we love her. And if you don't come, it'll break her heart."

Naturally, it was difficult to argue with this, so Gavin and I both made the trip, arriving in style and bearing beautiful gifts. Also, we footed the bill for this "big" party, which in actuality was only a small gathering of our mother's small-town friends at the shabby old Elks Lodge, where she and my dad used to go dancing on Saturday nights.

Embarrassed by the stodgy steam-table food and dime-store decorations, I attempted to keep my chin up throughout the dismal affair. But once I had Violet alone, I had to inquire if that was the best she could do with my money. Naturally, this resulted in another silent spell between my sister and me—one that lasted for several years.

We didn't patch that up until Violet's youngest daughter, my favorite niece, graduated from high school in 1984. And that was only because Abby sent me an invitation herself. She wrote a personal note on it, and her graduation photo was so gorgeous that I just couldn't help myself. This time I traveled to Silverton alone, driving my brand-new Jag and making a surprise appearance at Abby's graduation. My plan had been to show up, dressed to the nines of course, and without speaking to my sister, I would present Abby with my gift, which happened to be a pair of absolutely perfect one-carat diamond stud earrings.

Abby was nearly speechless over my generous gift, but she pointed out that her ears were not pierced. "Oh, that's easily taken care of." I opened my purse and slipped her a fifty. She squealed, hugged me, and proclaimed me her favorite aunt.

"And you must come down to visit me this summer," I told her, knowing full well Violet was only a few feet away, wearing a drab little floral dress and bad shoes, and eavesdropping.

"You haven't been down since you were sixteen," I continued, "and I had the whole place redecorated last year." Of course, Abby was thrilled with this idea and insisted I come out to her house and join the family for her celebration. "Grandma is already there," she said. "She didn't feel up to coming to the ceremony, but she would flip out if you didn't come out and see her, Aunt Claudette."

"Yes," Violet said, joining us. "Please, do come, Claudette. Mother would be so hurt if you didn't."

"You're sure you have room for one more?" I imagined Violet and Clarence's small ranch-style house overflowing with guests.

"Of course, we do." Clarence came over and put an arm around me. "And we won't take no for an answer."

We were out in front of the school, and my car, which I'd parked in the loading zone because I was late, was being ticketed.

"What idiot parked his car there?" Violet asked.

I laughed. "That would be me." I waved my hand. "No matter, the price of the ticket was worth being here on time to see Abby graduating."

"That's your car?" exclaimed Abby with wide eyes. "The Jaguar?"

I nodded and grinned, I'm sure, like the Cheshire cat.

"I'm riding with Aunt Claudette," Abby informed her parents.

Clarence just rolled his eyes and laughed. But I could see the irritation in Violet's eyes. Or maybe it was hurt. It's odd the way memory works. I suppose I'm not really sure how Violet was feeling in that moment. Probably jealous. Clarence and Violet had both been teachers—he at the high school, she at the grade school.

Oh, they pretended to be happy enough in their boring little lives, doing boring little things in a boring little town. Their old house was as frumpy as they were, and they drove even frumpier American cars. Clarence died a few years ago, and Violet went to the only retirement home in the town. I was stunned when I heard that—I couldn't imagine anyone going to a depressing place like that intentionally. I assumed that meant she had given up completely.

Why am I troubling my mind with all of this now? Really, what is the point? I close my eyes, lean back, and attempt to drift to sleep.

"How are you doing?" Michael asks.

We're in the car again, after filling up on gas and eating a rather horrible breakfast at a chain restaurant, where the food was so greasy I have already consumed two Tums tablets and am ready for my third. It's a bit past eleven, and we're back on the freeway, about fifty miles north of San Jose. Neither of us has spoken a word in the past thirty minutes. And to add to the gloom, it's beginning to rain.

"Do you mean am I still alive?"

He chuckles. "Yes, something like that."

"Barely." I consider complaining once more about our ghastly breakfast, but I think that's a dead horse we're both ready to bury.

"Tell me about this place we're going to, Claudette. Is Silverton a quaint little town with a brick fire station and a charming drugstore that still serves chocolate malts? Perhaps similar to the old *Mayberry R.F.D.* show?"

I can't help but make a *harrumph* sound, which I know is unbecoming. I sit up straighter, clearing my throat. "The last time I was in Silverton, it seemed more like a ghost town, what with the decline of the timber industry and the more intelligent people moving away. It's really rather dismal...the sort of place one might use as a setting for a Stephen King film."

"Really?" He nods. "Well, that could be fascinating too. Any interesting murders take place there?"

"Not that I recall. The truth is that nothing very interesting ever happened there. Truly, they could change the name of the town from Silverton to Boredom, and I doubt anyone would notice or even protest."

"What made your parents live there?"

Usually I find a way to change the subject when someone inquires about my family history and heritage. And that's not so unusual with the Hollywood crowd. So many of us have family ties we're not proud of. For the most part, I find that people— I mean contemporaries, not the intrusive media—do not pry.

"Did you have other family living there?" Michael persists. "Grandparents, perhaps?"

I sigh. Maybe it's time to tell my story with a bit more honesty. When I told that Lindy character about my childhood back at Laurel Hills, it felt almost therapeutic. Oh, I was probably painting it a little brighter and merrier than it actually was, but it felt good to be open and candid for a change. "No, I didn't have grandparents in Silverton. No other relatives either. Just my parents, Violet, and me."

"So what made your parents move there? Was your father involved in the timber industry?"

I laugh, although it sounds rather pathetic. "Hardly. My father felt that logging and millwork were beneath him. He did not like to get his hands dirty."

"What did he do?"

I pause, trying to think of a nice way to say this. There is none. "He didn't do much of anything, Michael. Well, besides drink."

"So your parents were independently wealthy?" Michael glances at me curiously, and I suspect he knows this is not the case.

"No. If the truth must be known, they were independently poor."

"Tell me, Claudette," he pleads like a child asking for candy. "Tell me everything. You know how I do love a good story."

"Perhaps you can develop this one into a screenplay, dear. But I must get a percentage."

"Of course. Now begin at the beginning, darling. What brought your parents to Silverton?"

"My mother's family actually lived in the Bay Area." I glance out toward the west where San Francisco looms, although with these thick clouds, you would never know. "Perhaps not far from here. But my mother never liked to talk about them, and we didn't go to visit them, and they never came to see us. But I do know, from having peeked at old photos and letters and mementos—I was a bit of a snoop as a teenager—that Mother's family had been fairly well off."

"Aha! That explains your fine taste."

"I asked my mother about them, and she tried to brush me off, but I persisted until I wore her down."

"I can imagine you as a teenager, Claudette, becoming a beauty and probably dreaming of being an actress."

I nod. "Yes, that's about right. And I could be very persuasive when needed. So I begged my mother to tell me the truth—who were her parents and why did we not have anything to do with them."

"And?"

"She told me the truth."

"And?"

Now I can tell that I have a captive audience in Michael, so I go with it, play up the drama. Who knows? Perhaps this story would make a good screenplay…although I have no idea how it would end. "It seemed that my mother's family owned a rather large business in San Francisco, and they were quite wealthy."

"What's their name? Do you know?"

"I think it was Lawson, but I'm not positive. Mother was secretive about such things. I think she worried that I would try to look them up."

"Hit them up for money?"

I sort of laugh. "I'm sure she thought something like that. I always wanted more…even as a small child. I had caviar taste on a tuna fish budget."

Michael chuckles. "Continue your tale, darling. This will make the trip go by so much faster."

"Oddly enough, Mother was only two years older than Gavin," I say as I run their birth dates through my head.

"Interesting…that would make her even younger than my mother."

"Younger than Gala?" I try to process this impossible fact. Could it be? "Yes, of course, you're right. Although my mother seemed much, much older. But then poverty does that to a person, makes one old before one's time. Anyway, when mother was a young woman, it seemed her parents had high hopes for her. I think she was their oldest daughter, a debutante, and an heiress. And, yes, she was quite attractive too. I remember being so surprised when I found a photo of her one day.

"It was summertime, and I was sixteen and bored. I'd been poking around the house when I made my discovery. Perhaps she'd been looking at it herself, since it was lying on her dresser with an old handkerchief over it. The photo was good quality, obviously from a studio, and my mother had been about my age when it was shot. I don't recall a date, but I could tell by her dress, which was an exquisite number in some sort of gauzy fabric trimmed in lace, and by her hairstyle, a sweet little bob, that it was taken in the twenties. I remember just staring at that image in wonder. She was so pretty and young, and her eyes sparkled."

"I'll bet she looked like you, Claudette. I mean, when you were young."

"I thought that too when I saw the photo. That's probably the only reason I realized it was her. When I flipped the photo over, it said, 'Emma's Sixteenth Birthday' in delicate penmanship, and then I was certain. Even so, it seemed inconceivable that the girl in the photo was actually *my mother*. The same woman who wore her prematurely gray hair pinned up in a tight little bun and old-fashioned shoes that I wouldn't be caught dead in. And the same woman who camouflaged her bony frame and sagging breasts beneath the horrible 'day' dresses she wore every day. She had two or three pitiful rags that she rotated, not that anyone would notice. How could that fresh-looking girl in the photo be the same worn-out woman whose hands were cracked and dry from taking in laundry? I knew it was true, but it just seemed unbelievable."

"Unbelievably sad for her..."

"Yes..." I don't admit to Michael that it was also personally disappointing to me as well. Or that, not for the first time, I secretly blamed my mother for the state of her marriage and for the way my father treated her. I'd been nagging her to take better care of herself, to use some cream on her hands, to fix her hair and get a new dress, try a bit of lipstick on those pale, tired lips. But she never listened to me. I felt that she was the reason my father strayed. He was an attractive man who kept up his appearance. Who could blame him for looking elsewhere? Why couldn't she understand that?

By the time I became a teenager, I would go far out of my way not to be seen or associated with her. I even denied that she was my mother on occasion. Not that it did much good since Silverton was such a small town. But I did my best to distance myself from her.

"You're not talking, darling." Michael glances at me. "Please, dear, continue the story."

"Where was I?"

"The photo of your mother when she was sixteen."

"Yes, of course. Well, I took that photo to my mother. As usual for that time of day, she was outside hanging up another family's linens on our clothesline. I stood there and demanded that she tell me the truth. At first she seemed peeved at me for snooping, but then I shook the photo in front of her face and told her that I wanted to know what happened to that girl. And if she didn't tell me, I'd do everything I could to find out on my own."

"And she believed you?"

"She did. Fortunately, Violet wasn't around that day. She was probably off with Father on one of his silly nature walks. He thought he was an expert on botany. So Mom gave in to my demands, making a deal with me. If I would continue hanging up the wash, and if I could be trusted to utmost secrecy, she would tell me her story."

"And you agreed?"

"Of course. As I stood in the sun, hanging up lace-trimmed sheets and pillowcases that were far grander than anything I'd ever slept upon, Mother sat in the shade in an old metal chair and told me what had happened."

"Yes?"

"Her father had hired a handsome young man to work in his business, a man named Claude Porter. My mother had gone to the city for something, stopped in to say hello to her father, and met this young man. Claude was handsome and charming and complimentary, and my mother was instantly smitten."

"I think I see where this is going."

"Naturally, her parents were completely opposed to their relationship. Claude was a nice enough fellow, but certainly not in their class, and not the sort of man they had imagined for their daughter."

"A bit of a cad, perhaps?"

"Exactly. But Claude and my mother began to secretly meet. It was summertime, and Mother was seventeen, and she thought she was in love. By the end of summer, she was pregnant."

"And her parents hit the roof?"

"Can you blame them? I know such things aren't nearly as scandalous in this day and age. But back in the twenties, it was a serious situation. Her father was enraged at Claude."

"So, there was a shotgun wedding?"

"No, that was just the problem. Both Claude and my mother desperately wanted to marry, but her father was completely opposed. Apparently he had his own suspicions about his wayward employee. He believed that Claude Porter was a drinker and a womanizer, and he didn't want him for a son-in-law."

"Oh no…"

"Oh yes. In fact, he fired Claude straightaway. And then he informed my mother that she was never to see him again, and if she did, he would disown her. The plan was to send my mother away so she could have her baby and give it up for adoption. They would say she'd "gone abroad to finish her schooling." Then after a year or so, she would return to her family home and hopefully make amends with everyone."

"But she didn't do this…"

"No. She was stubborn. She and Claude got married anyway. My mother actually thought this would force her family to accept him…and her…and their child."

"But that's not how it worked out?"

"No, of course not. My grandfather must've been more stubborn than she. He stuck to his guns, banishing them both from the family home, the business. My mother said her father told her that as far as he was concerned, she was dead."

"So very sad."

I nod.

"But what brought them to Silverton?"

"My grandmother. She was brokenhearted over the whole thing and felt sorry for my mother. So behind her husband's back, she purchased a house in Silverton and gave it to my mother as a wedding gift. But she swore my mother to secrecy. And, other than me and my father, my mother never told a soul."

"And you were the love child, darling."

"The reason they married."

"Thus the name." He sighs, as if this is romantic somehow. "And I always assumed you'd adopted Claudette as your stage name simply because of the lovely Claudette Colbert."

"Gavin thought the same thing when we first met. I still remember that day... I was an extra in *Meet Me in St. Louis,* you know with Judy Garland and little Margaret O'Brien. I think it was Hugh Marlowe who introduced me to Gavin. I was still in that star-struck era, when everyone I met was wonderful and amazing."

"And Gavin Fioré was still a very big name in the business."

"Yes. I was so impressed. And I did all I could to impress him. And when I told him my name and he mentioned his fondness of Claudette Colbert and how I resembled her and how he'd just come from the set of *Since You Went Away,* well, I'm sure I thought I'd died and gone to heaven. But, of course, I didn't show it."

"Of course not."

"But I was terribly flattered."

"Dad was such a fan of Claudette Colbert, and Mother had been gone a few years by then. I know he was lonely. It's no doubt that you caught his eye. And you did look a bit like Claudette back then. That high brow line, those expressive eyes. Although I think of her coloring as a bit darker than yours."

"The first time I actually remember seeing Claudette on the screen was in *It Happened One Night.* I was about ten at the time and highly impressionable, and I liked that we shared the same name, but that movie just completely stole my heart. I couldn't bear to leave the theater. After the lights came on, I slumped down in my chair and then sat through the movie twice."

"That was a sweet little Capra film and I think she won an Oscar for that performance," says Michael. "Clark Gable was so delightful, and Claudette was gorgeously funny."

"Yes. To be pretty and funny and talented..."

"Well, at least you were pretty, darling. One out of three's not bad." Michael tosses me a sly grin.

I bristle slightly, but I don't mention that most people thought I was much more beautiful than Claudette Colbert. Including Gavin. But I suppose that's where the comparison ended. No one ever suggested I could hold a candle to her acting abilities.

"Don't feel bad. Very few had that kind of talent. To think she starred in dozens of films and even did television for a while. I believe I heard that her career spanned at least six decades. Incredible."

"At least I figured out my shortcomings early in the game," I admit. "I knew when it was time to make other plans."

"When life throws you lemons..."

I give him the pretense of a laugh. "Yes, dear, I suppose my acting skills were a bit like lemons." But I don't add that those same skills certainly served me well *off* the screen.

9

I'm surprised to see familiar terrain now. The towering ever-
greens loom menacingly over the road. It's a scene some
might call beautiful, and yet it fills me with anxiety and fear.
What am I doing? Why did I allow Michael to talk me into this
crazy trip?

Perhaps I should demand that we stop this nonsense, turn
my car around, and go back to Los Angeles, where I'll bet it's not
raining. Both Michael and I have been quiet for a bit, and with
each passing mile, I feel more and more nervous.

I estimate that we're about forty miles away from Silverton.
But thanks to the twisting road, which seems to have gotten
even curvier than I recall, as well as the rain coming down in
sheets, I'm sure it will take a good hour to get there.

"So, were they ever happy?" Michael breaks the silence,
interrupting my thoughts. "I mean your parents. After they got
married and moved to the house in Silverton, were they happy?"

I consider this, then slowly shake my head. "Not that I ever
saw."

"And was your grandfather right about Claude?"

"My grandfather had him pegged. My father was both an alcoholic and a philanderer...and a few other things as well."

"Your poor little mother. Pity she didn't listen to her parents."

"And a pity she was too stubborn to ask them for help."

"But it seems her father had made it clear where he stood." He shudders. "Goodness, I couldn't imagine how it would feel to have a parent tell you that you were dead to them. Horrifying."

"Yes, I suppose..." Still, the little girl in me was shaking her fist, wishing my mother had set aside her pride and told her parents that she was struggling. What might it have been like if a set of wealthy grandparents had stepped into our lives and helped us a bit, perhaps even rescued us altogether? How different things might've been. "But we were so pitifully poor, Michael."

"And your father never worked?"

"As little as possible. My mother worked her fingers to the bone. And I have to give her some credit. She did all she could to make things better for her girls."

I try to shove away the image of my mother hunched over her ironing board on a hot afternoon, the sweat literally pouring down her face. She eventually developed a hump in her back. I'm sure it was from all the laundering she did...for the few rich folks in town. Not that they paid her much. "Slave wages," my dad used to say to her in disgust. And yet he treated her like a slave too.

"Even after doing laundry all day long, my mother would still sit down at night and mend our clothes or darn our socks.

She'd cut cardboard into insoles to make our shoes last longer and then she'd polish the shoes so they looked almost new. Or, if she had a bit of fabric, she would sew us something special. She was a whiz at creating clothes or even redesigning old things. A lot of our dresses were fashioned out of old items of her own clothing, remnants of her former life when she'd been well off. So despite being poor and that it was the Depression, Violet and I went out the door looking perfectly respectable. In fact, we were some of the best-dressed girls at school."

"Your mother sounds like a saint."

A tear slips down my cheek. I open my handbag and remove a handkerchief, using it to dab the wetness. "Maybe she was…more than I knew."

"I know your mother passed away around the same time as Gavin, but how about your father?"

"Fortunately for my mother, he died fairly young. I don't think he was even forty. I'd been away from home a couple of years by then, and my acting career, brief though it was, seemed to be taking off. I didn't even go back for the funeral."

"Any regrets about that?"

"I don't see why. My father meant nothing to me. If I'd gone to his funeral, it would have only been to say 'good riddance.'"

"You sound a little bitter, Claudette."

I adjust my posture, holding my chin up higher. "I don't think I'm bitter, Michael. It's just that I simply don't care. All that was so very long ago. I moved on. I left it all behind me. I wouldn't even be going there now…if I weren't, well, *going there now*."

Michael chuckles. "I have a theory."

"And this theory somehow relates to me?"

"Mind you, I'm still working this theory out." He sighs. "But I've come to believe that perhaps life is not meant to go perfectly smoothly."

"Is that so?" I feel skeptical and suspicious. What is he getting at?

"Some people's lives do seem to go fairly smoothly. For instance you and Gavin... Did you know that I used to envy you?"

I smile. "You envied us?"

"Of course. Lots of people did."

"Really?" I turn and look at him with genuine interest now. These are the stories I truly enjoy hearing—people who envied me. Delightfully delicious.

"For starters you and Gavin *appeared* to be happily married, and we all know what a rare accomplishment that is in Hollywood." He chuckles, and I know that he knows more than he's saying, but I must give him credit for his self-control. "You were beautiful, Claudette. You maintained yourself and aged gracefully. Gavin was talented and brilliant and admired. You had a lovely home and an interesting circle of friends. You traveled the world. Really, who wouldn't envy you?"

"I suppose I can see your point," I say modestly.

"For an outsider looking in, or even for an insider such as myself, you and Gavin seemed to have it all. And your lives, like well-oiled machinery, moved along smoothly and elegantly, hardly a bump along the way."

I don't add that this image was more perception than reality. Because, of course, that is the nature of Hollywood. "Yes, I suppose I took it for granted, but Gavin and I did have a rather nice life together."

"And I went through a time of real jealousy."

"But your life has gone well." I hope to sound gracious. "You're a brilliant designer, you've had a good career in film, and—"

"Lots of bumps and bruises along the way." He shakes his head. "Do you remember when my romance with Jerome went sideways, darling?"

"I remember Gavin and I visited you in the hospital after that fight... Your face was a mess. I still cannot believe you didn't press charges."

"Jerome paid all my medical bills. And the dental work too." He points to his front teeth. "Thank God for implants." He chuckles. "I've said that to people before, and they assume I mean another part of my anatomy. But my point is—rather my theory is—I've had some rough times along the way, Claudette. Meanwhile, your life seemed to be going rather well."

"So, are you suggesting it's *my turn* to have some bumps in the road? You think I deserve to lose my home, to become old and poor, and to be forced to live in a place like Silverton?"

"I'm not saying you *deserve* it, darling. If I had my way, your life would continue to be smooth and lovely. You'd still be living in Beverly Hills, and your next plastic surgery would make you look like Madonna."

"Perhaps I don't understand your theory."

"As I mentioned, it's not fully worked out, but I think that life's bumps and bruises are meant to make us into bigger people. If life goes too smoothly, we never get to realize all that we might possibly be. It's like something I heard in church a while back."

"I still find it hard to believe that you go to church, Michael."

"Well, it's not your typical church. Imagine a bunch of people in shorts and Hawaiian shirts, standing on the beach, singing along with a couple of guitars and bongo drums, and then listening to a rather brief talk from a man who seems to be the real deal."

"I'm sure it's perfectly charming."

He ignores my jab. "Anyway, a few weeks ago the lesson was about how God can take the negative circumstances in our lives and transform them into something positive. But we have to let him do this. I don't have it all figured out just yet, but I do like the sound of it. It gives me hope."

"I'm happy for you."

"But you're not buying it."

The rain has let up some. Enough that I can see the sign up ahead. "Welcome to Silverton," I read aloud. "Population 5,648."

"About to become population 5,649?"

I let out a groan and lean back into the seat, closing my eyes to the painfully familiar scene opening up in front of me. Why on earth did I let Michael talk me into this?

"You're not dead yet, darling. So far so good, right?"

I don't say a word. I simply sit there and wish that I were dead. It would be so much simpler.

"Here we are on Main Street of Silverton, California," Michael says in a tour guide voice, obviously for my benefit since my eyes are still closed. I think I am playing dead. "To the right is Frank's Auto Repair; across the street is Harper's Hardware... There is Berryhill Shoes, nice little window display. Silverton Market looks like a good place to pick up some groceries. This is quite charming, Claudette. You can actually walk from one shop to the next. One-stop shopping. And there is the drugstore, Pauline's, complete with Thanksgiving decorations in the windows. I wonder if they still have a soda fountain."

Despite my resolve to play possum, I sit up and open my eyes. "And up ahead, at the next intersection is Sequoia Street. Take a right and go two blocks."

"She speaks." Michael puts on his turn signal.

The town is still dripping wet from this afternoon's rain. The sky is gray, and puddles are everywhere. Only a couple of people appear to be out. A middle-aged woman ducking into the bank and a teenager smoking a cigarette under an awning. I don't know if this is because of the rain or just typical of this sad little town.

Michael makes the turn, and I'm tempted to hold my breath, the way I used to as a child, to see if I could make it the two and a half blocks to our house. My only purpose in holding my breath today would be to see if I could expire—permanently.

"Two fifty-eight Sequoia Street." Michael turns into the short graveled driveway in front of the house. "A bungalow, Claudette! You didn't tell me it was a bungalow. I absolutely adore bungalow style. Pity you don't have some Stickley furnishings to go in it. Oh, hurry, hurry, darling. I can't wait to see everything. How exciting."

To my surprise, his enthusiasm is almost contagious. I fumble to get my purse and my weary self out of the car. My joints feel stiff and sore, but I manage to stand to my feet and slowly follow Michael up the narrow paved path that leads to the front porch. And that's when it hits me. "Oh dear, I have no key."

He turns and frowns at me. "No key?"

I shake my head. "I'm sure I was given one, after my mother died and her lawyer sent the deed to the house and all. But I have no idea where it is right now."

"No key." Michael continues on up to the porch, where he pauses to scratch his head. "Did she ever keep one hidden, Claudette?"

I consider this. "When we were kids, Mother did hide an emergency key, just in case Violet or I ever got locked out. But we seldom locked our doors back in those days… No one did. I don't think anyone ever actually used it. Do you think it could possibly still be here?"

"It's worth a try."

I go back down the steps and over to the rosebush, which is sadly in need of pruning, and there beside it is the same old stone, about the size of a skull. I use the toe of my shoe to push it over, and beneath it is the bottom of a rusty old tin.

Michael stoops down and, using a stick to pry it from the ground, removes the can, which actually crumbles in his hands. But there in the midst of the rusted tin is a brass key, which he presents to me. "The key to your castle, your highness."

"Thank you." Then I proceed back to the porch. "Goodness, I hope the locks haven't been changed." I open the old screen door. But I can tell that the dark bronze doorknob and lockset are the originals, and the key fits. I open the door but am not sure I want to take the next step. I feel as if I'm paralyzed; my feet are stuck to the porch floor.

"Claudette?" Michael says from behind me. "It's a bit cold out here."

I nod. "Yes…I'm going in." I force one foot in front of the other and walk back into time, back into the house of my childhood. Because of the gray day and the large oak tree that monopolizes the front yard, it's too dim to see much. I fumble to find the light switch, which as I recall was to the left of the front door.

"Is the electricity turned ón?" Michael closes the door behind us, eliminating what little light there was.

"I've been paying the bills." I flip the switch that should turn on the entryway light. To my relief it works. I blink in the brightness, looking around the living room, which doesn't even seem familiar. And yet it does. I try to distinguish what has changed and what is the same. "She's put in carpeting," I say with dismay.

"Did it have wood floors before?"

"Yes. Lovely dark wood."

"Then they must still be underneath. We'll have the carpeting removed."

"We will?"

"Of course."

"Look at these windows," Michael gushes as he pushes back the dust-covered polyester drapes. "Craftsman design, leaded glass, all original."

I turn on a slightly tacky ceramic table lamp that's new to me. In fact, most of the furnishings here are not the things I grew up with. I don't know why this surprises me, but it does. I suppose I always imagined my mother stuck in some sort of time warp, still wearing the same sad dresses, using the same sparse furniture pieces. But in a common and unimpressive way, these furnishings have a homier appearance, more comfortable looking than the stiff horsehair couch and wooden chairs I grew up with. And for some reason, I feel a bit better knowing that Mother had this awful plum velvet recliner to sit in. As homely as it is, I can almost imagine her relaxing in it with her feet up. Of course, everything in here is coated with dust, and spider webs give the place the appearance of a slightly haunted house.

"She didn't exactly have your sense of style when it came to decorating, did she, darling?"

"No. I think one might describe this as early tacky or late Sears and Roebuck."

He laughs as he holds up a floral pillow in shades of blues and pinks. "But at least everything matches."

I frown. "I never realized my mother was such a fan of pastels."

"A common and unfortunate decorating mistake of the eighties."

"What will I do with all these things?" I pick a dusty cobweb off the lampshade.

"First we'll call Goodwill. I noticed a store on the way into town. We'll see if they pick up. I instructed the movers not to deliver your things until tomorrow."

"My things will be here tomorrow?"

He nods. "I made them promise not to show up until later in the day. I wanted some time to get a plan in order." He clears his throat. "And I can see that won't be easy."

Despite the dust, I sit on the couch and let out a sigh of deep despair. "I cannot do this, Michael. I just cannot do this. I am too old. I would rather be dead."

"Nonsense, Claudette. You're just a bit worn out. I am too. And I'm hungry. Do you suppose there's anyplace in town that delivers?"

"Delivers?"

"You know, darling, a restaurant that delivers food. Is there such a thing in Silverton?"

"I seriously doubt it."

"Well, I will find out." And he takes out his magical little cell phone, which reminds me that I need to find the charging device for mine, and begins to dial.

While he is preoccupied with this, I use the bathroom, which is almost exactly as I remember it from childhood, and turn on the heat. Everything in here feels damp and cold. Will it ever feel the slightest bit habitable? Or perhaps I will simply develop a serious case of pneumonia, which will bring on my hasty demise. One can only hope.

I go to what used to be my old bedroom. Mine and Violet's, that is. It's interesting how so many of my childhood memories don't even include my younger sister. Why is that? Where was she hiding herself all those years? Probably tucked into a corner behind a book somewhere. She was always very bookish and quiet and self-conscious and insecure.

Surely our home life must've troubled her as much as it did me, but somehow it seemed as if she escaped it better. Or it just didn't affect her to the degree it impacted me. I felt that I would literally suffocate if I didn't leave this place when I did, and I truly believed that she would follow my example and do the same. But then our father died, and I suppose that changed things some. Who can say?

Violet did leave for a while, to get her teaching degree. But like spawning salmon, she and Clarence came straight back to Silverton. I thought perhaps it was only a temporary form of insanity, but then they got married, settled in, bought their home, had their three daughters, and stuck around.

Violet always acted as if she was happy to live here, as if she liked her job, liked being close to our mother and the small-town setting. But I felt that she, like me, was simply acting. Over time, I began to accept that we were just different. I always wanted more and more and more... Violet always settled for less.

I look at our old bedroom, which is exactly the same, with its pale peach walls and the original dark wood floor. The same two narrow twin beds on either side of a window with a painted dresser beneath it. I always used the top two drawers; Violet's were on the bottom. Violet's bed was near the door, which made her space a bit more cramped. Mine was near the closet, which I dominated, and I had a whole wall to myself and enough space to squeeze in a straight-back chair and bedside table, both of which are still there. Why didn't Violet rearrange things after I left? Perhaps she liked it the way it was.

I suppose I might be partially responsible for my sister's shortcomings. I may have trained her early on—I took more, so she had less. She got hand-me-downs and leftovers and settled for it. Really, I can't recall her complaining. She never seemed to expect anything more. So maybe I shouldn't blame myself after all; maybe Violet was just born that way.

It's strange to think that my sister still lives here in town. Even stranger that she resides in McLachlan Manor. I shudder at the very thought. I know for a fact that I would much rather be dead. I'm sure I would leap headfirst from the tallest building in town, even if it is only three stories, before I would let anyone put me in that place. Or if they did put me there, I would escape first thing and throw myself under a train.

I vaguely wonder if I should let bygones be bygones and go visit my poor sister at McLachlan Manor. Perhaps seeing her in such a depressing place would make me feel better about my own sorry state of affairs.

10

When Michael finds me, I am standing in my mother's bedroom. And while it's certainly not my style, I am relieved to see that everything in this room has changed. It feels as if my mother erased all traces of my father, and for her sake, I'm glad. The walls are an improvement. Instead of that dreadful peach color that seems to be everywhere, these have been transformed to a soothing shade of pale blue.

"More pink and blue?" Michael asks from behind me.

I nod. "And more ugly pink carpeting."

"Well, I have good news."

I turn and look at him hopefully. Perhaps he's received a call from the IRS, telling him that they've made a grievous mistake and they are returning my home in Beverly Hills to me. "Yes?"

"First of all, Goodwill is happy to send a truck by in the morning. They will take whatever you'd like to donate and even give you a receipt for a tax deduction."

I roll my eyes. "Excuse me for not cheering."

"But that's not all. I asked the woman at Goodwill if she happened to know of anyone who could remove your pink carpeting and—bingo—her brother-in-law is in the flooring business, and she was going to give him a call for me."

"I don't know how you do it," I say in what I hope is a slightly droll voice.

"I thought you'd be happy."

"Deliriously."

"Unfortunately I struck out on takeout. The only place that delivers is pizza."

I make a face.

"But the Goodwill lady did recommend an Italian restaurant."

"Coming from the Goodwill lady, I'm sure it must be simply divine."

Michael frowns. "You can be such a spoilsport, Claudette."

"I'm sorry." I shake my head. "I know you're being a dear, Michael. And I know I should appreciate your help. And I do. It's just that this is all so disheartening. I feel as if I'm stuck in a very bad dream, and I'd just like to wake up."

He nods and puts a comforting hand on my shoulder. "I know, darling. And I am so sorry for all you're going through. But try to think of this as an adventure." He walks over to the bed and shakes some dust off the pillow. "Goodness, we'll have to do some cleaning before bedtime, won't we?"

"Are we really going to sleep here?" I ask helplessly.

"Would you prefer that Motel 6 on the edge of town?"

I cringe at the thought. "No, I see your point."

"Tell you what," he says suddenly. "Let's pop some linens

into the washing machine. She does have a washing machine, doesn't she?"

"Goodness. The last machine I saw Mother using was her old wringer washer. You don't suppose…"

But when we go out to the back porch, which is now completely enclosed, we find not only a proper washing machine but a dryer as well. There's even a partially full jug of laundry soap. Before long, Michael and I have stripped the beds, he's figured out the settings on the washing machine, and a load of sheets is churning away in sudsy hot water.

"I'm surprised you know how to do such domesticated things," I tell him as he proudly closes the lid.

"Because Richard still works, I try to keep things running nicely in the home."

"Such a good little housewife."

"I do my best."

"Well, you're ahead of me in that game," I admit. "I don't know how I can possibly learn to do those things."

"You'll learn. If I can do it, so can you."

We freshen up a bit and then drive the short distance to town, where Michael parks in front of what used to be Chuck's Diner but is now called Marco's. The décor is a bit campy, with its red gingham tablecloths and wine bottles with drippy candles. But at least it smells good, and I realize that I'm really quite hungry.

"We're new in town," Michael tells the maître d'. "And we're a bit worn out from the road. Are you serving dinner yet?"

The man smiles. "Certainly. Right this way."

The service is unexpectedly good, but then we're the only ones here at this hour, since it's not even five yet, and the food is, well, acceptable. Oh, I'm sure if I were in a better mood, or if I were in Beverly Hills with some of my old friends, I might go as far as to admit the food is slightly exceptional. But I am not in that frame of mind. Besides, Michael makes up for my lack of enthusiasm. He gushes about every single thing—the bread, the wine, the salad, the pasta... Goodness, you'd think the man never had a fine Italian dinner before in his life. And I know that's not true.

But once we're finished, I do feel a tiny bit better. Oh, I'm not happy about my life, not by any means, but I'm not quite ready to jump off the top of the Silverton Bank Building just yet. It's dusky as we go to the car, and although it's barely six, I am exhausted.

"Shall we stop by the grocery store?" Michael starts the car.

"What for?"

He laughs. "Oh, you know, the basics. Things like coffee, toilet paper, dryer sheets."

"Dryer sheets?" I imagine something draped over a clothes dryer.

"You know, like Cling Free, those little sheets you toss into the dryer to make your clothes and linens smell nice. They come in all sorts of different scents. I recently found lavender, and it's really delightful."

"Oh…you really are a domestic goddess, aren't you?"

"Are you saying you don't want a nice cup of coffee in the morning?"

"I'm saying I don't know if my mother even has a coffee machine."

"I noticed an old Mr. Coffee on her countertop."

"You are so observant, Michael." I sigh and lean back. "And energetic. How do you do it?"

"It's all an attitude, darling. You just need to think more positively."

"I'm positively exhausted."

"Well, you stay in the car then. I'll do a little shopping."

I put my seat back and fall asleep even before he gets to the store. In fact, I don't wake up until he's nudging me and telling me that we're home.

"Home…in Beverly Hills?"

"No, darling. In your *new* home. Come now, dear, it's time to play house with Michael."

He helps me out of the car and hands me a bag, which thankfully is not very heavy. Then he gets two other bags, and we go into the house, where he unloads his groceries with plume and pride.

"And see," he produces a box of Kleenex, "something to wipe your nose." Then he removes a package of toilet tissue. "And something to wipe something else." He chuckles as he sets out a bag of what smells like freshly ground coffee. "I would've gotten whole beans, but I wasn't sure if your mother had a coffee grinder."

"I seriously doubt it." I glance around the old tiled countertop, which is a nice shade of green. I'm glad she didn't have that changed to pink or blue.

Michael opens the fridge to set a bag of oranges inside then stops. "Oh my." He quickly closes it and turns to me with a ghastly expression.

"What?"

"Apparently no one cleaned out your mother's fridge when she died." He sets his oranges by the sink.

"Is there a dead body in there or something?"

"No, it just *smells* like it." He frowns. "I wonder if you can afford to replace it on your new budget."

Well, this is just more than I can take. I turn around and go down the narrow hallway to what used to be my old bedroom. I throw myself onto what used to be my old mattress and just cry myself to sleep.

When I wake up, I'm surprised to see Michael standing over me with a laundry basket of what appear to be clean linens. "Feeling better, darling?"

I slowly sit up and blink into the bright overhead light. "What time is it, anyway?"

"It's almost nine. The sheets are clean and dry, and I, for one, am ready to call it a night." He sighs as he sets the basket down. "Is this where you're sleeping tonight?"

I look around and shrug. "It makes no difference to me."

Michael begins to put sheets on what used to be Violet's bed.

"Not *that* bed."

He turns and stares at me. "I thought you said it made no difference."

"Well, it does." I stand up, go over, and snatch the sheets from him. "I can do this myself, thank you very much."

He shakes his head and leaves. "Good night, Claudette," he calls from the hallway.

I am surprised that I still remember how to make a bed, but then I've made this same bed hundreds of times before. It's only natural that it would come back to me. But for some reason, this gives me the slightest sliver of hope. Perhaps I won't be as helpless as I'd imagined.

"Here are the blankets," Michael says as he returns. "I gave them a good shake outside."

"Thank you." I suddenly feel guilty. "For everything, Michael."

He smiles. "So you do appreciate me?"

"I think you are my fairy godmother...or godfather...or my knight in shining armor. Yes, I do appreciate you."

"For that I will bring in your luggage."

By the time he returns with my bags, I've made up both twin beds and am feeling rather pleased with myself.

"Here you go, darling. Your Louis Vuitton has arrived."

"Thanks, Michael. And, by the way, the linens do smell good. Those dryer sheets must be a good thing."

He nods. "See, you can teach an old dog new tricks."

"And I feel like a very old dog tonight."

"Tomorrow is a new day, Claudette."

I try not to think too hard about this, biting my tongue lest I say something offensive.

"And we'll figure out something for that wretched refrigerator. Don't give it another thought."

"You'll be okay in my mother's room?"

"Why wouldn't I be?"

I consider this. For some reason I felt uneasy about spending the night in that room. Oh, it's nice that it no longer looks like it did when I was growing up, but still, just being there... It is unsettling.

"Ghosts?" asks Michael.

"Maybe. Memories can be haunting."

"Well, if I see any ghosts tonight, I'll just send them packing. How's that?"

"Thank you."

"Sleep well, darling," he says as he putters down the hallway toward my mother's room.

"You too, dear," I call back.

I have to smile as I get ready for bed. It is such a pity that Michael is gay. I really think he and I could've been very happy together...in our twilight years.

I am in that delicious state between waking and sleeping, pleasantly dreaming of my luxurious home in Beverly Hills—one of those dreams where I feel as if I have some control over the outcome, but I really don't. Still, it's so enjoyable that I want it to go on and on...

It's early evening, the sky is streaked with amber and amethyst, and the spring air is velvety warm with a faint breeze laced with hyacinth. Gavin and I are outside by the pool, visiting with an interesting mix of Hollywood friends, some still living, many of whom have already passed on. But this is *my* dream and, alas, all things are possible.

I am wearing a strapless platinum gown, and I am still young and beautiful. Robert Mitchum, also young and beautiful, is pouring me a turquoise-colored drink from an oversized martini shaker, looking at me with those sexy, sleepy eyes, when suddenly it all begins to crumble—I hear a banging sound and then a ringing. We must be having an earthquake!

I sit up in bed, grasping the rough woolen blanket to my chin, and as I open my eyes, I realize that not only has Robert

Mitchum disappeared but I am not in Beverly Hills. I look around the small, stark room. I must be back at the horrible Laurel Hills. No, this is my old childhood bedroom in Silverton... Then, like a waking nightmare, it all comes back to me.

Michael peers into my room, pulling on his red and black Japanese kimono. "Someone's at the door, darling!"

"What time is it?" I demand, still grieving over my lost dream.

"Barely morning." He frowns. Just then the knocking and the bell ringing starts up again—this time with a vengeance, as if there is a fire or some other state of emergency.

"Who can that possibly be?" I grumble as I get out of bed and grab my silk dressing gown.

"I'm about to find out," he yells from halfway down the hallway.

"I'm coming too." I shove my feet into slippers and hurry after him.

Michael is fidgeting with the deadbolt. I stand behind him, peering over his shoulder as he opens the door. There, on the other side of the screen door, is the perturbed face of a gray-haired woman, and she's glaring into this house as if she has every right to see what's going on.

"Who are you?" she demands.

"Who are *you*?" Michael shoots back at her.

"I'm Beatrice Jones, and I live next door." She scowls as she shakes her finger at us. "But that's not the point. The point is, who are *you,* and what are you doing in Emma Porter's house? I never heard that it had been sold."

Michael turns to me with a graceful wave of the wrist, as if he thinks he's Vanna White about to reveal a letter. "*This* is Emma's daughter Claudette. And *this* is Claudette's house."

Beatrice's beady eyes open wider. *"Claudette Porter?"*

"Claudette *Fioré,*" I correct her with a tone of irritation, as I step more fully into view, looking down on the squat elderly woman whose lack of manners does not appear to exceed her lack of fashion sense.

She is actually wearing a pair of badly snagged purple polyester pants that are too short, along with grubby white deck shoes and an orange and blue striped polo shirt that's so tight I'm sure she must've used a shoehorn to get it on.

"Oh…" She seems slightly tongue-tied as she stares up at me with a look of shock and disbelief.

"And you have just awakened me out of a perfectly good sleep." I narrow my eyes for emphasis. I have always believed that it's best to put people in their places as quickly as possible— first impressions are lasting impressions.

"Well, I'm sorry to disturb you, but I saw the car outside and thought perhaps it was burglars and—"

"Burglars in a Jaguar?" asks Michael. "And parked in the driveway, in broad daylight?"

"I…I wasn't sure. And no one told me that anyone was moving—"

"Were you given some sort of responsibility for this property?" I ask, ready to lash into her for the state of the refrigerator if by chance she says yes.

"No, well, not officially. But I used to check on Emma from time to time. You know how neighbors are... We look out for each other." She smiles, as if that's going to make everything just peachy. Perhaps she expects me to invite her in for tea and scones.

"Thank you for checking on my mother," I say in a crisp, haughty tone. "Your assistance in that regard is no longer necessary." I start to close the door, eager to be rid of this nosy old lady who has no sense of propriety, not to mention boundaries.

"Wait," she says suddenly. "Don't you remember me?"

"Remember *you*?" I take in an exasperated breath. "Why on earth would I?"

"I'm *little Bea*," she says with a pathetic smile. "You used to baby-sit me."

I open the door wider and take a step forward to see her more clearly. Surely this old woman doesn't expect me to believe she's the cute little redhead I used to watch occasionally for spending money. Good grief, that girl was at least ten years younger than I.

"Really, it's me. I used to live next door with my parents. Remember Audrey and Harry? Well, I grew up, got married, and moved away. But about twenty years ago, my husband left me for a newer model. Then I moved back here to help with Dad after Mother died. Dad had diabetes and terrible eating habits. I tried to get him to eat healthy food, but he died two years ago."

I give her the blankest stare as I attempt to assimilate all this senseless information she seems determined to thrust upon me.

"I used to visit with your mother," she continues, as if she might go on forever. "Emma liked my company. Sometimes we talked about you, Claudette. She was proud of you. She told me all about your acting career and the important people you knew and how you married some hotshot movie producer."

"Director," I say in a flat tone.

"Don't you remember me at all?"

The truth is, I'd like to say, *"No, I do not remember you,"* but for some reason I am unable to do this. So I nod. "I do remember a little Bea...but I'm having a bit of difficulty recognizing her...I mean, *you.*"

She laughs. "Well, we've all gotten older. Although I must say, you look well preserved for your age. Weren't you about twelve years older than me?"

"Eight," I lie.

"Well, you look darn good. I wish I'd held up like that. But then I suppose all you high-rolling Hollywood types can afford to sashay off to fancy spas and spend millions on facelifts and tummy tucks and lipo treatments that take off the years." She chuckles. "Just to make the rest of us look bad."

I clear my throat. "Uh, well, it's been nice to see you again, Bea."

"And this is your husband?" she persists. I almost expect her to open the screen door now, perhaps use her stained deck shoe as a doorstop.

"No," I tell her. "My husband passed on a few years ago."

Her eyebrows lift. "Boyfriend, then?"

I glance at Michael, and he just smiles patiently. I turn back to Bea and, pulling my dressing gown around my neck as if I'm trying to hide something, say, "Yes, you found us out. This is my boyfriend Michael, and you are disturbing our beauty sleep."

She giggles, steps back, and says an embarrassed good-bye.

"Come along, darling," Michael says in a loud voice before he closes the door.

"Good heavens," I say to him as we go to the kitchen. "Can you believe that dreadful woman is twelve years younger than I am?"

"I thought you said eight."

I wave my hand. "Eight, twelve, what's the difference?"

"Worse than that, could you believe what she was wearing?" He begins to make coffee. "And in public?"

"Welcome to Silverton." I sit in a vinyl covered kitchen chair and let out a big sigh. I still cannot believe I'm here. Or that I intend to stay.

"And imagine," continues Michael, "wearing white shoes after Labor Day!"

"Oh," I groan. "However will I manage here?"

"We've got a lot to do today," he tells me as we sit down at the little plastic-top table. Michael has made toast to go with our coffee. "I want you to begin by going through your mother's things and setting aside anything you want to keep before the boys from Goodwill come to cart it all away."

"I'm sure that I don't want to save a single thing."

"What about family photos and memorabilia, Claudette? Surely, you want to set those things aside."

"I don't see why. Besides, I can't imagine there's much left here. Mother never had much when we were growing up. And it's likely that Violet and her girls already took anything worth keeping."

He nods. "I'm sure that's possible. But have a look around… just in case."

So I get dressed and then putter around the house, but for the most part, I seem to be right in my assessment. It appears that Violet and her girls have already removed some things, or there just never was much to begin with.

"I found something of interest," says Michael. He's been working on the kitchen for me, dear man. He holds out a cardboard box full of what appear to be old letters. "The postmark on most of these is Beverly Hills, darling. It looks as if your dear mother saved all your letters."

I look down at the box. "But I didn't write her many. Oh, birthday and Christmas cards. The occasional postcard from a faraway place."

"Well, do you want them or not?"

I take the box from him. "I'll look at them. But they'll probably just end up in the trash."

"You can't look at them today." Michael wags his forefinger at me. "There's too much to be done. Simply set them aside for later."

I nod as if taking orders. "Yes sir, Mr. Director, sir."

He grins. "Good. I'm glad we understand each other."

Naturally, I start in Mother's room. Anything worth saving would probably be in here. And being a fashion-conscious woman, I begin with her closet. I'm shocked at how small her closet is, but even more shocked that she still had plenty of room in there. Although her wardrobe is more extensive than when I was child, it is still extremely sparse. I cannot imagine getting by with so little.

Thankfully the dreadful, old "day" dresses are nowhere to be seen. In their place I find several dark-colored polyester dresses that appear to date back to the eighties. They are what I would call "grandmotherly" dresses, but my mother was elderly back then.

My mother was about the same age then as I am now. How is that even possible?

I take out one of the dreary dresses, holding it up to myself as if I'm wearing it, although I would not be caught dead in something like this. It's a stiff synthetic fabric that I'm certain would never breathe, in a somber shade of yellowy gray that would do nothing for anyone's complexion. Still holding up the pitiful dress, I peer at myself in Mother's foggy dressing table mirror and grimace. So sad, so very, very sad. I toss the pathetic dress down onto the bed, along with the others. Goodwill or no Goodwill, I can't imagine how anyone could possibly want any of these clothes. Still, *this is Silverton.* And if "little" Bea's ensemble is any forecast for what's to come, I wouldn't be surprised to see Mother's old wardrobe parading itself down Main Street by next weekend. Perhaps I should have mercy on this town and simply burn these things.

Finally it's about two o'clock, and I feel weary and dusty and hungry. I've gone through closets and drawers, setting aside very few things to save. I'm not even sure about some of them. So far I've gathered several old photos Violet must've overlooked, a few pieces of Mother's jewelry, mostly gifts from Gavin and me, and the box of letters Michael unearthed.

I actually paused to read a couple of them and am surprised at how Gavin and my mother seemed to have a friendly relationship. In fact, I can tell by what little I've read that Gavin must've been sending her a fair amount of money, because he tells her to "think nothing of it" and "he just wants her to be comfortable." I'm sure she must've written him, thanked him, but told him not to be so generous. It would be like her to respond like that. And it would be like Gavin to continue sending her money. And, of course, that's the only reason she was able to do her little home "improvements" like pink carpeting and flowery furniture. Well, good for Gavin. And now I will have all of it removed.

"I don't think there's anything I want in this house," I tell Michael. "Besides what little I've set aside." He's still in the kitchen. Mismatched glassware and dishes are piled all over the place. He leans down to set a box of pots and pans on the already crowded kitchen floor.

"I'm feeling the same way. I thought perhaps we'd find some collectibles, but mostly it's just odds and ends. Oh, I suppose some desperate dealer might want some of these things." He brushes off his hands. "But that dealer will have to go to Goodwill to find them."

"Right."

"You'll have more than enough to fill this house," he continues. "Besides your lovely furnishings, you've got good linens and nice kitchen things coming. I really see no reason to keep any of this."

"I cannot imagine my things from Beverly Hills in this house. It's just too incongruous. I'm afraid the whole thing will simply turn into a horrible joke." I want to add that the joke will be on me, but Michael is so sincere in his efforts that I hate to insult him too badly.

"I think you'll be surprised, Claudette."

"Perhaps I'll be shocked," I say dramatically. "Perhaps I will keel over with a heart attack. Wouldn't that be lovely."

He shakes his head. "Don't say such things, darling. Have a bit of faith in old Michael." He looks around the compact kitchen, now cluttered with all the old, worn-out kitchen things strewn from one end to the next. "Although I'm feeling a little worried myself."

"Aha!" I point a finger at him. "So you admit it. This is a farce."

"No, no, that's not it. I'm just concerned that I picked out too many things to bring here. I'm afraid it won't all fit in this house."

I sigh. "Well, I'm sure you'll help me to sort it all out, right?"

"You can count on that."

"Is this how it was when you were designing settings for movies?"

He smiles. "Very similar. I would gather a truckload of props and pieces, as well as a crew of able workers, and we'd be off to the races. Oh, it was such fun."

"You honestly find this fun?" I peer closely at him.

"I'm as happy as a clam right now."

"Well, I'm as hungry as a horse."

"We are terribly cliché, darling." Then he looks at his watch. "Goodness, where has the time gone? Those Goodwill boys will be arriving any minute now. Let's go freshen up before they get here. Then you can move the Jag out of the driveway, and I'll give the boys my instructions. After that, you and I will be free to get out of their hair. We'll go have a nice leisurely lunch."

I change into a fresh pantsuit, nothing too spectacular since this is, after all, only Silverton. Seeing Bea's strange outfit was a horrible wake-up call and a nasty reminder of this town's disregard of fashion. I'm sure my tan Michael Kors gabardine trousers and cappuccino jacket are more than adequate. I choose dark brown Ralph Lauren loafers and small matching pocketbook to go with this. And then I put my other clothing and personal things with my luggage as Michael instructed. I would be fit to be tied if the Goodwill boys marched off with those things!

Then, as I'm ready to do a quick inventory on my ensemble, I am surprised to discover there is not one full-length mirror in the entire house. How could Mother have possibly left the house without first inspecting herself in a full-length mirror? What if her slip had been showing?

I fish my car keys from my purse and head outside. I barely move my car out of the driveway and park it in front of the house when I see the big blue and yellow Goodwill van clunking down Sequoia Street. I climb out of the car and watch as they back the clumsy looking truck into the narrow driveway, and to my surprise, I feel an unexpected prick of regret. Really, it's nothing more notable than a mosquito bite—although that's enough. Enough to get my attention.

As I stand there, I must ask myself. Am I a thoughtless daughter? Is it a mistake to discard Mother's things so easily? Is there something I've missed perhaps? Something with meaning, something I should've held on to? Perhaps an item in there could've helped make some sense of a past that seems only worthy of being put behind me?

No, *Mother is not here anymore*—she has no use for these old, worn-out things. Furthermore, nor do I. So I go around and unlock the passenger side of the car. I open the door, sit down, and wait for Michael, trying to shove these foolish sentimentalities away from me. But after I'm comfortably situated, I open my pocketbook, extract a fresh handkerchief, and dab at the stray tears that have somehow found their way down my powdered cheek.

Silly emotions. I don't know why they seem to be getting the best of me now. After I'm done, I pull down the visor and carefully examine myself in the lighted mirror. I take a moment to powder my nose and touch up my lipstick. Then I hold my chin high as I fluff the sides of my platinum-tinted hair. No harm in looking one's best. It's possible I might run into an old friend while we're having lunch. You just never know. It's always best to be prepared.

As I put up the visor, I get the distinct feeling that I'm being watched. First I glance over to my mother's house, which I expect Michael to be emerging from at any moment. But I don't see anyone. The truck is still there, and I'm sure the Goodwill boys are already inside. Then I glance at the house next door, where little Bea and her parents, Audrey and Harry, once lived. And there in the front window, I see a crack in the blinds.

I have no doubt it's Bea and that she's watching me. I casually turn my head away, pretending to look across the street where my old friend Caroline Campbell once lived. I haven't seen Caroline since high school graduation, and I wonder what became of the vivacious brunette.

After several minutes, I turn and look straight ahead down the street. But I still get the sense that Bea is watching. It's unnerving. But then the poor woman has an empty life, and perhaps she's simply curious as to how others live. Or maybe she's envious of me, or even a bit delirious—who can tell? I just hope she's not dangerous.

Then again, who can blame that sorry wretch of a woman for watching someone like me? Truly, if I think my state of affairs is disappointing…then I should simply think of Bea and the sort of life one like her must live. And then, really, I shouldn't gloat.

Unfortunately our choice of lunch places is not as fortuitous as our dinner selection was last night. But we're both hungry, and the food is tolerable and not too terribly greasy, although the service is lacking.

As we're finishing, Michael browses through the local paper. "I have an idea, darling," he says suddenly.

"That it's time to go home to Beverly Hills?" I say hopefully. "Or that you'd like to adopt me like a stray puppy and take me home to live with you and Richard in Hawaii?"

He smiles and pats my hand. "That wasn't my idea." He points to the interior of the newspaper. "How about if I drop you off for this movie. It starts at five."

I frown. "A movie?"

"Yes. It's a perfect way for you to kill some time while I work on the house a bit. Besides, I heard that it's a good movie, and Meryl Streep is in it."

I do admire Meryl's talents, not something I can say about most contemporary actresses. Even Gavin used to sing her praises. "Meryl Streep?" I say aloud, still musing over the idea of going to a movie by myself.

"Yes. It says here that it's a film about women and relationships with both depth and humor. It sounds like just your cup of tea, darling."

"I do so hate attending the theater alone, Michael."

"But I have so much to do at the house. It would be infinitely helpful to have you out of it for a while."

"You don't want me to get in your way?"

"I don't want to wear you out." He winks at me. "And yes, it would be awfully nice not to have you underfoot while I'm putting things together. I was just the same way with my film directors. I would say to them, 'Just leave me be and I will work my magic.'"

"And did you work your magic?"

"Of course."

Now I know I should trust Michael with this little project. Goodness knows he can't make the sad little house look any worse than it does now. And yet a part of me still longs for my old interior decorator. Edouard Beauvais is a living legend in Beverly Hills, and he handled all my design decisions—his signature was all over my home. Whether it was a complete room makeover or simply the choice of an ottoman, I depended on Edouard's guidance for decades. And although he's nearly as old as I am, he still works occasionally, but only for old friends—old friends with deep pockets.

I glance at my Piaget watch. "But it's only three thirty," I tell Michael. "When did you say the movie starts?"

"Five."

"I can't show up at the theater this early." I try not to imagine the dismal image of an old woman sitting by herself in a theater, as if she has no life, just waiting for a matinee to begin. Really, it's pitiful.

"I noticed a coffee shop near the theater," he says hopefully. "Perhaps you could waste an hour in there, darling."

"Sit in a coffee shop for an hour and a half by myself?"

"I think I saw a bookstore on Main Street as well. What if you found a lovely new novel to occupy yourself with while you casually sipped a nice, rich mocha?" He smiles at me. "You look very sophisticated today, Claudette. That scarf is a nice touch. And I'm sure the locals would be eying you, curious as to who the stylish older woman might be." He peers closely at me. "I think they might even confuse you for Joanne Woodward."

"Pity that Paul's not still around."

"Come, darling, I'm offering you a free afternoon to get a steamy romance novel, enjoy a creamy mocha, and take in a movie with Meryl."

"I suppose I could do worse."

"There," he says, standing. "I knew we could work this out."

So it is that I find myself browsing through Page Turner, a small bookstore on Main Street. And, to my surprise, it's not an entirely negative experience. Jazz music is playing, there's an interesting smell that I can't quite describe, and the selection of books, both new and used, is not too bad. I'm looking for the romance section, trying to remember what used to be in this shop, and finally, just as I reach the mystery section, it hits me. When I was growing up, there was a pipe and tobacco shop here. Hence, the aroma.

"May I help you?" asks a woman who appears to be in her fifties. Although it's hard to say since her hair, obviously tinted an interesting shade of red, could be misleading. With her gold hoop earrings and fringed shawl, she doesn't look like the typical Silverton citizen though. I also notice that she's wearing a nice-looking pair of brown suede boots.

"I'm just looking," I tell her automatically, though I really was hoping to find Danielle Steel's latest book.

"Are you a visitor in town?"

I study her more closely, wondering if I might possibly know her, although she's obviously younger than I. "No, I'm not."

"Oh…" She begins to move away, and I feel a stab of guilt.

"I used to live here," I say quickly.

"Oh?" She pauses and looks at me.

"Yes. And it seems that I shall be living here again."

"Really?" She smiles and steps forward, extending her hand. "I'm Page Turner."

"What? I thought the shop was Page Turner."

She nods. "Yes, I know it's confusing. But my name happens to be Page Turner too."

"That's your real name?"

"Yes. And with a name like that, it seemed inevitable that I should either be an author or run a bookstore. Since I can't write…" She waves her hand toward her shelves.

"Did your parents actually name you Page Turner?"

"That was my mistake. They named me Page, and I married a man named Turner and got stuck with it." She chuckles. "Fortunately I didn't get stuck with the man as well. But I did keep his name." Now she looks at me with a curious expression, and I realize that I really am forgetting my manners.

"I'm Claudette Fioré. I grew up in Silverton, but I haven't lived here in more than sixty years. I just came back yesterday."

"Claudette Fioré? Of course I've heard of you. You're the actress who married the wonderful director Gavin Fioré." She smiles broadly. "It's a pleasure to meet you, Ms. Fioré."

"Call me Claudette. Everyone does."

"So you're really going to settle back down here in Silverton?"

"I am."

"That's wonderful. This town can always use a little more color."

"I'm sure that's true."

She laughs. "I know what you mean. We've tried to bring some art and culture to Silverton, but it's not been easy."

"What sort of art and culture have you managed to bring?"

"Have you seen the Phoenix gallery yet?"

"No," I admit. "Where is that?"

"The other end of town. It's next to a restaurant called Maurice's, and their food is actually pretty good. But the Phoenix is in a building that used to house a small car dealership. Maybe you remember it?"

"Parson's Pontiac and Oldsmobile?" I ask, surprised that I do remember the name. I recall going by there sometimes and wishing that we could afford one of those big, beautiful cars. I also remember that my father worked there, briefly.

"That's right. Now it's the Phoenix, and it's owned by Garth Rawlins. He's a nationally known artist who relocated here about five years ago."

"I'll have to go look at it sometime." Not that I can afford to buy things like art anymore, but she doesn't need to know this.

"And there's also Casey's Coffee House. They often have live music on Friday nights."

"Really?" I nod as if this is impressive. "And how's their coffee?"

She smiles. "It's not bad. They roast their own beans. You'll probably catch a whiff of it on Monday, their usual roasting day." Now she looks uncomfortable. "I'm sorry, I didn't mean to interrupt your shopping. But I do try to get to know my customers. Is there anything I can help you find?"

"Well, I was looking for the new Danielle Steel novel."

"It just came in." Page moves down the narrow aisle. "You're almost there. Just another shelf over." She pulls out a hardcover book and hands it to me.

"Thank you."

"And you might be interested in my Hollywood section. I just started it a year ago."

I almost tell her that I doubt I would be interested, that I've lived the real thing and find no need to read about it in a book, but then I stop myself. "Where would I find that?"

"Right this way." She leads me to a table over by the window. "This is a new one about Grace Kelly, and the photos in here are amazing."

I open the book and flip through the pages. "She was beautiful." Then another book catches my eye. Rather the photo on the cover catches my eye. "Claudette Colbert." I put the Grace Kelly book down and pick up what is obviously a used book.

"That's right, her first name is the same as yours. You didn't know her, did you?"

"Yes, actually I did. We weren't close; she was a lot older, but she came to some of our parties back in the day. She and my husband got along well."

"You must've known so many interesting people. I can't even imagine. Silverton is lucky to have you back, Claudette."

"I'll take these two books."

"Of course."

I follow her up to the register and wonder why I hold myself back from certain people. Oh, I know some would assume that it's because I feel superior. And I suppose on some levels this is true. I certainly feel superior to people like "little" Bea. But this one, Page Turner, actually interests me a bit. She seems to be fairly intelligent and somewhat fashionable. And yet, she runs a bookstore…and that is so mundane. I pay her and thank her.

"Come again, Claudette."

"Certainly."

"And, if you're interested, there are a number of book clubs in town. I could easily connect you with one of them. It's a nice way to meet people and talk about books."

I nod as if this is something that appeals to me. "I'll consider that." But the truth is, I can't think of anything more boring than sitting with a bunch of Silverton strangers, discussing a book. Really.

I go to Casey's Coffee House, which is just two doors down from the theater, purchase a mocha, and find a quiet corner, where I sit down with my books. But I feel distracted. I find myself pretending to read, but I'm actually watching other people.

How do they do it? How do they go about their ordinary lives, doing such ordinary things, and act as if it's all perfectly fine? I simply cannot comprehend it. Perhaps they, like me, are all acting. Maybe Shakespeare was right. Maybe the world really is a stage, and we are all simply acting.

I manage to lose myself in the movie for a couple of hours, although I may have fallen asleep for a bit too, since I feel slightly baffled by the way things are wrapped up in the ending. Or maybe it's just old age. I wonder if old age is a bit like insanity—the person suffering from it is the last one to know.

I feel stiff as I stand to leave the theater. There were only about half a dozen people in here. Thankfully no one I knew. No one who knew me. Anonymity could be a benefit in a town like this.

It's dark when I go outside, and suddenly I feel very alone and slightly frightened. What if Michael forgets about me? What if I am forced to make my way home alone? Oh, I realize the house is only about six blocks from here and I could probably walk. But it's nighttime, and I'm alone. What if muggers are about? I consider a taxi, but I seriously doubt there is such a thing in Silverton. I certainly don't recall taxis around here when I was growing up. What shall I do?

"Claudette," calls a man's voice, and Michael's head pokes out the window of my car. He parks in front of the loading zone at the theater, hops out, and helps me into the car. What a relief.

"Sorry to make you wait," he says as we drive away.

"That's all right." I don't admit that it was a very short wait.

"Things are going well at your house. I've managed to put together quite a good crew."

"A crew?"

"Yes. By the time I got back this afternoon, the old furniture was all gone, and Hank, the rug man, was just starting to rip out the carpets. Fortunately they came out in a snap. Then he cleaned and polished the floors. Hank has this amazing machine that really works miracles. Then, just like clockwork, the moving van arrived."

"My furniture is here?"

"Yes. And I offered to pay the movers extra if they'd stick around long enough to help me get things into place."

"And they agreed?"

"They did." He turns down Sequoia now. "And I've got painters lined up for tomorrow."

"Painters?" For some reason I hadn't considered this.

"You don't really like that horrible peach shade, do you?"

"Well, no."

"Exactly."

"How much is this going to cost me, Michael?"

"Don't worry about that, darling. The things we left in storage will more than cover all these expenses."

"Oh…"

"So, how was the movie?" He parks my car in front of the house. The moving van has replaced the Goodwill truck and, I'm sure, given Busybody Bea something else to think about.

"It was okay. Although I think I dozed off a bit." I point at the moving van. "Does that mean the movers are still here?"

"Yes. They were putting your bedroom into place when I left. I told them that was a priority. I figured you'd be tired."

"And hungry."

Michael smacks his forehead. "Of course. I didn't even think, darling. I ran and got dinner for the boys about an hour ago. One of those chicken-in-a-bucket places. And I actually sampled it myself, but I am hungry too. Shall we go get something?"

I consider this.

"You sit tight," he says, opening the door. "I'll go have a word with the boys, then we'll be on our way."

How much more of this can I take? I feel like a displaced person, like a war refugee, an orphan. Will I ever have a normal life again? Would I want to settle for "normal" anyway? Perhaps I don't even care. Then I have to ask myself, just how much can an eighty-two-year-old woman take? Is it possible that this whole thing really might do me in? Wouldn't it be a relief if it did? Oh, I expect Michael would be disappointed. At least, briefly. But then he could gather up my things, sell them, keep them, whatever. It would make no difference to me.

I glance at my mother's—rather *my*—house again. It appears that all the lights are on inside. I suppose I'm mildly curious as to what's going on in there. But another part of me doesn't really want to know. Another part of me would just as soon crawl under a rock and disappear. Why does life have to become so tedious?

Michael, as usual, is optimistic when he returns. "Everything seems to be falling into place," he tells me as he starts the car. "I think we might not even need to paint your bedroom, darling. That shade of blue is rather nice, don't you think?"

"I don't know what I think," I growl at him.

"Now, now, no need to despair. You really should be happy, Claudette. Your little nest is coming together quite nicely. I think you will be pleased."

"The only thing that could possibly please me would be to return to my home in Beverly Hills, to have a miraculous facelift that makes me look twenty years younger, and…" I pause, not sure what else I would want…or even if those things would make me happy. Sometimes I think I shall never be happy again. And sometimes I think perhaps I was never happy to begin with.

"And?" Michael persists. "What else would you wish for?"

"And…I'd like to have all of my old friends return from the dead for a nice big party."

He chuckles. "Now, that really does sound rather divine. May I come too?"

"Of course. Just don't hold your breath waiting for your invitation."

He stops at Main Street, looks to the left, and then the right. "Now, darling, where shall we dine tonight?"

I'm about to throw my hands in the air and ask, "What does it matter? One thing is the same as the next in this unfortunate one-horse town." But suddenly I remember something the bookstore proprietress, Page Turner, mentioned earlier.

"Someone told me about a restaurant, I believe it's called Maurice's. On the other end of town. Apparently there's an art gallery next to it. The Phoenix."

"Great sleuthing, Claudette. I'm proud of you. You might actually make it in this town after all."

"Don't count on it."

"Anyway, these places sound interesting—art and food in the same vicinity."

"I seriously doubt the gallery is open. It's a weeknight, and in case you haven't noticed, we're not exactly in civilized territory anymore."

"Maybe we can simply press our noses against the gallery's windows."

I fabricate a sound that resembles a laugh. Yes, that will probably sum up the remainder of my days. From now on I will be on the outside looking in, my nose pressed up against the windows of civilized society.

I cannot imagine how Maurice's stays in business.

When we are seated, without even waiting, there is only one other party in the restaurant. And before long, it is simply Michael and me and the waiter. The food isn't equal to the places I would normally dine at in Beverly Hills, but it's much better than lunch. I have veal tenderloin, and it's rather good. Unfortunately the décor, a mishmash of old lamps and mismatched tables and rugs, isn't to my taste. But Michael defends it.

"It's simply shabby chic, darling. Some people love it."

"Edouard calls it *shaggy cheap*. And when Helen Caruthers wanted to decorate her guest cottage in it a few years ago, he refused."

"Edouard is a bit of a style snob." Michael sips his wine. "I think there's room for all kinds in this world."

"You are so open-minded."

He smiles. "Thank you." He holds up his glass as if to toast. "Here's to two fine restaurants in this town."

"I suppose that all depends on how you define the word *fine*."

"Oh, darling, you are such an Eeyore."

"An Eeyore?" I frown. "What is that supposed to mean?"

"You know, the old Winnie the Pooh character who was a pessimist about everything."

"Well, thank you very much."

"You weren't always a glass-half-empty sort of girl, Claudette."

"Being poor changes one's perspective."

"You're not poor. Financially challenged, perhaps."

"Call it what you like, Michael. Life as I knew it ended when the IRS stepped in."

"I did have a bit of good news," he says suddenly. "I think I mentioned that I'd called my old friend Alex Granville."

"The one with the décor shop?"

"Yes. I left the key for him at the storage unit office and invited him to go in and look around."

"That's very trusting of you, with my things."

"Alex is an old friend, darling. Besides, some of the things are mine too, remember?"

"Yes, yes… Tell me the good news."

"Alex called this afternoon. He was in the storage unit at the time. And he wants to take almost everything that I'd tagged for him. He's sending me a check."

"He's sending *you* a check?"

"Well, yes. As you know, I've been stuck with the bill for everything involved in this move so far. I'm not financially destitute, but I'm not exactly rolling in dough either. And keep in mind, it's not an enormous check, but it's enough to cover the cost of our Sequoia Street project."

"And that's it?"

"I thought you'd be happy."

"Delirious."

Now Michael's sunny disposition fades, and as he signs for the check, I can tell I've wounded him.

"I'm sorry. I must seem terribly ungrateful."

He solemnly nods as he puts his pen back in his pocket.

"You've been extremely helpful, Michael. Under normal circumstances, I'm sure I would be a much better sport." I sniff, as if I'm about to cry, although I don't think I am. "It's just that this is so hard." I shake my head. "It's taken such a toll on me."

He pats my hand. "Yes, I know, darling. That's why I'm doing all I can to make things better." He smiles now. "Speaking of which, let's go home and see how the moving boys are doing."

"Aren't they finished yet?"

"Well, there's been a lot of rearranging going on. It's not easy making it all fit and work together. Just before we left for dinner, I arranged for them to do a little painting, and they promised to stay as late as necessary."

"How did you talk them into that?"

"Money talks."

"Oh yes. But where will they sleep?"

"I'm putting them up at the Motel 6."

"How *luxurious*."

"They didn't complain."

When we get home, the moving van is still parked in the driveway, and Michael parks my car in front of the house.

"I don't like leaving my car on the street. It's bad enough this house doesn't have a garage, but—"

"I'll move it to the driveway after the boys leave."

Then, as we're about to go into the house, Michael makes me cover my eyes. "I don't want you to see anything until it's all done."

"How am I supposed to—?"

"I'll guide you to your bedroom. At least it's mostly in place. Then you must promise not to peek."

I'm so tired that I cooperate, allowing Michael to lead me along as if I can't see. "So now I know how it feels to be old and poor *and* blind," I say when we finally stop at what I assume is my mother's old bedroom.

"Open your eyes."

I open my eyes and, for a moment, can't remember where I am. "Is this really my mother's bedroom?"

"It is. See—the pale blue paint is the same."

I walk around the room, taking in the dark cherry furnishings, the pale blue and cream bedding and window coverings, the elegant lamps on the bedside tables, the art on the walls, the gleaming hardwood floor, and the Oriental carpet. "I cannot believe it." I run my hand over the silky duvet cover. "This was

from the guest room in the Beverly Hills house. I'd almost forgotten it."

"It's like new, darling. And the blue and cream damask is so
perfect with the walls. Do you like it?"

"I do, Michael." I turn and look at him, and to my surprise,
tears are in my eyes. "Thank you."

"I know it's a comedown from your master suite, but I hope
you'll be comfortable."

I nod. "Yes, my master suite was bigger than this entire
house."

"But this is cozy. And look." He opens the closet. "I even
unpacked some of your things for you."

I frown. "There's not much room in there."

"No. It's time to pare down."

Michael tells me good night, reminding me again not to
peek at the rest of the house. "Well, other than the bathroom,
of course. I've put some of your nice linens in there, but the rest
will have to wait until it's painted tomorrow. We must get rid of
that ghastly peach color, darling. That color should be called
dead salmon."

"That sounds about right."

As I get ready for bed, I try to imagine what my life in this
house will be like in the days to come, but it's like looking into
a pitch black tunnel...a tunnel with no light at the end. I feel as
if I've been sent to prison, serving a life sentence with no parole.
Or perhaps it's more of a death sentence. But, not unlike so
many murderers living on death row, I don't know when the

execution will actually take place. Perhaps tonight. Oh, to sim- ply die in my sleep. It sounds so easy.

I pick up my novel as a distraction from these depressing thoughts, and I get into my comfortable bed with its down com- forter and pillows, its eight-hundred-count percale sheets—the best bed I've been in for weeks. But I'm so exhausted that I set Danielle Steel aside and turn out the light.

And here I lie in the darkness, haunted, it seems, by the past. It is strange and unsettling to realize that this is the room where my parents once slept and fought and occasionally, when my father forced his drunken way, even had sex. I shudder. Naturally, I don't want to think about such things. What child likes to imagine her parents together like that? Although it was hard not to know what went on in a house so small. And yet I know my anxiety has deep roots, something that lies beneath, buried below layers and years of distraction.

I have been quite adept at pushing unpleasantries away, sup- pressing those parts of childhood that make me uncomfortable. Over the years, I've worked hard to block old things out, putting them behind me.

Haunting memories can slice into one's soul… They can torture the mind.

I've seen it happen to others, seen them broken down, locked up, forlorn and forgotten. It is very sad and terribly unfortunate. But I always made sure it didn't happen to me. And somehow, without the aid of psychological therapy, which so many of my friends have relied upon, I have managed to keep my demons at bay. So far, I've kept them away for my entire adult life. And I have no intention of losing this battle now.

For no particular reason, I wake up at dawn. No one is pounding on the door, demanding to know who I am or why I'm here. And yet I sit up in bed and wonder why I'm awake. I turn on the bedside lamp to see that the room still looks rather nice. Small, yes, but at least it's elegant. That is something.

It's unlike me to be wide awake at this hour, but it's no use. I might as well get up. I go to use the bathroom and almost venture down the hallway and into the kitchen, but I remember my promise to Michael and stop. I suppose it's the least I can do, considering all that he's doing for me. And if his efforts for the rest of the house are even half as nice as my bedroom, I can at least show my appreciation by keeping my word. Besides, I don't relish the thought of being caught by him as I tiptoe past my old bedroom, where I suspect he is sleeping.

So I return to my room, get dressed, carefully put on makeup, and finally sit in the easy chair in the corner and read about Claudette Colbert. I knew that she'd been born in France, just one more thing I've been jealous of. However, I didn't know that she'd gone to art school or that her career began on Broadway, more envy-worthy facts.

"Good morning, darling." Michael taps on my door.

"Come in."

"I thought I heard you up early. Did you sleep well?"

I shrug. "I suppose…"

"I have coffee brewing. Can I bring you a cup?"

"Meaning I still can't see my house?"

"Of course not. I'm not ready for the unveiling yet."

"What am I supposed to do?" I close my book with a snap. "Stay in here all day like a prisoner?"

"Let me think about that as I get your coffee."

Michael returns with a tray that's set with china dishes that look vaguely familiar. "Is that my Limoges?" I pick up a delicate white cup trimmed in a narrow but sophisticated band of dark green, black, and gold.

"I thought it went well with your mother's dark green tile in the kitchen, and it sort of lends itself to the style of your home."

"I haven't seen this in years," I say as I admire the cup.

"It may not be replaceable."

I shrug. "So little in life is…" I take a sip of the coffee. "This tastes better than yesterday's."

"It should. It was made in your very own espresso maker."

"You know how to use that thing?"

He chuckles. "And so shall you before I leave." He nods to my unmade bed. "You know, darling, you don't have a house-keeper anymore."

"Oh…"

"Would you like me to teach you how to properly make a bed?"

"Does one really need lessons for all these mundane chores?"

"It can't hurt." And then, as if he thinks I'm an imbecile, he proceeds to give me a step-by-step lesson on the correct way to properly make a bed. Everything from how you fluff a comforter to arranging the pillows. "I learned this on *Martha Stewart*," he admits.

"Really," I say in exasperation. "Do you think I'm completely helpless?" Or just helplessly lazy, I almost add.

"Not completely. Just mostly."

"And what difference is it if I don't make my bed every day? Will the Silverton housekeeping police arrest me and throw me in jail?"

"No, but you may create a prison of your own, darling. One that you would not be happy in." He artistically folds the pale blue chenille throw just so and sets it at the end of the bed. The bed looks so lovely now that it could be a page in a magazine. Funny how my housekeepers back in Beverly Hills didn't make beds nearly as well as this.

"Did I tell you what I found in here yesterday?"

"What do you mean?"

"When the Goodwill boys were removing your mother's bed...there was something amusing beneath it."

"Beneath her bed?"

He chuckles. "Yes, it gave us all a good laugh."

"What was it? A sex toy?"

He waves his hand. "No, no, nothing like that. It was a cast-iron frying pan."

I frown. "A cast-iron frying pan?"

"Yes."

"A bit odd, don't you think? Do you suppose she kept it there for protection? To arm herself against burglars?"

"I don't think so, darling. It was neatly wrapped in a raggedy yellow towel, and this was placed in an old department store box and tied with string, almost as if it were a keepsake of sorts."

"Really? And what became of said frying pan?"

"The Goodwill boys took it. One of them liked it so well that he asked if he could keep it. Of course, I let him. He planned to use it on hunting trips. Do you know these good ol' boys actually go out in the woods and shoot animals up here?"

I conceal my disgust. "Yes." But I don't admit to him that venison stew, made with meat given to us by neighbors, was often a staple in our diet. "So did you come up with anything to get me out of your hair today?" I ask, eager to change the subject. "A nice visit in a day spa, perhaps?"

He laughs. "If there were such a thing in Silverton, I would sign you up right now."

"Pity."

"Didn't you mention that your sister still lives in town?"

"My sister who is not speaking to me."

"Perhaps you should be speaking to her."

I roll my eyes as I sip my coffee.

"You and your sister aren't getting any younger, Claudette. Maybe it's time to make amends... You know, before it's too late."

"Too late for whom?"

"For both of you. Think about it, darling. How would you feel if your sister died while you two were in the midst of this silly disagreement? You'd never get the chance to make things right with her."

"What about her? She's the one who should be making things right with me."

"Does she even know how to reach you?"

I consider this.

"Why not make the first step, Claudette? Extend the olive branch, so to speak? If she refuses, you'll at least know that you tried."

"I don't know..."

"Well, think about it. And keep in mind that you'll have a very long day cooped up here in your room. The sun is shining out there. You could drive around in your lovely car, which needs to be moved from the driveway before the movers return."

"Oh, fine," I snap at him. "I'll go."

"How about if we go find some breakfast first? I need to bulk up on carbs. I have a marathon day ahead of me."

So I finish my coffee and, once again, close my eyes as Michael guides me to the front door. I am not ready to see my sister today. And no one can make me.

14

I noticed yesterday that Casey's Coffee House serves a limited breakfast," I inform Michael as he drives us to town. "Naturally, I can't vouch for it."

"Naturally." Michael turns down Main Street and parks across from the coffee shop. "You know, Claudette, you could easily walk to town on days when weather permits. It's such a short ways. And it does seem a bit wasteful to take the car all the time, especially when you consider the cost of gas."

"Yes, and I suppose I could grow my own vegetables and sew my own clothes. Perhaps I should be like my mother and take in the neighbors' dirty laundry as well. Would that make you happy?"

Michael laughs. "You are such a delight."

After breakfast, Michael insists on walking back to the house. "Why?" I demand as we stand out by the car. "Are you showing off or simply trying to make a point?"

"I just want to, Claudette." He hands me my keys. "You run along now. Have fun. I'll be fine."

"Fine," I snap at him. But once I'm in the car, it's not fine.

I have no idea of where I should go…what I should do…and I need to use a rest room. I start up the engine and carefully pull out onto the street. I drive clear to the edge of town, where I notice the moving van is just leaving the Motel 6 parking lot, and then I turn right.

I drive very slowly, like the little old lady that I am, but it's only because I'm trying to decide what to do next. I go past the old high school, where little has changed in the past sixty years. Oh, they've got a new sign, one that lights up, as well as an improved football stadium. But the boxlike, two-story brick building still resembles a small prison. As I loop around and go down Main Street again, I realize that I'm driving in circles.

Then, as if my car has taken over, covering for my ineptness, I find myself on the road that crosses the railroad tracks and leads straight to McLachlan Manor. I drive down the long drive-way, assuring myself that I don't have to go in. I can simply drive by and think about it. I'm a grown woman, and no one can make me do what I don't want to do. Well, besides the IRS. I never did get my way with those stubborn people.

Even from the driveway, I can see that this place has changed. For one thing, the grounds appear to be better kept, and the trees, newly planted when Violet and I were kids, are now big and tall. As I get closer, I see that the original structure has been remodeled and enlarged, with two wings now flanking the entrance. I park in a spot marked Visitor and just sit there. But after a couple of minutes, my bladder gets the best of me, and I decide to simply go inside and use the rest room.

"May I help you?" asks the woman at the front desk.

"Yes, I'd like to look at your facility, but I need to use the rest room first."

She smiles. "Oh, I know how that goes." She points to a hallway off to the left. "It's right there."

As I'm using the rest room, I firmly make up my mind. I am not going to see Violet today. My reasoning is twofold. For one thing, I can tell that this is a fairly decent facility, or at least it seems to be, so my pity factor has just been removed. Violet should be just fine. It doesn't even smell too terrible.

The other reason is just plain old stubbornness on my part. As I wash my hands, I ask myself, *Why should I be the one to go to her first?* I don't care what Michael says; if anyone needs to apologize, it's Violet. In a week or so, I'll simply drop her a note, letting her know that I'm in town and I've moved into the house. I'll even give her my cell phone number. Of course, that means I'll either have to find that stupid charger device or get a new one.

Just as I'm exiting the rest room, a young blond woman in a navy business suit approaches me. She smiles and extends her hand.

"I'm Cynthia Winters, and I manage the assisted living facility. I just happened to be going by the reception area, and Barb told me that you wanted a tour."

"Well, I don't want to trouble—"

"It's no trouble at all. I assume it's the assisted living facility that you're interested in since you seem to be in good health and fully ambulatory."

"Well, it's not—"

"Oh, unless you're here for someone else. I'm sorry. I should've asked first. Perhaps a husband?"

"No, no. My husband's deceased."

"So the tour is for you then?"

I'm tempted to tell her the truth, but then I'd have to divulge my sister's name and that might complicate things. Oh, what can it hurt to have a quick tour? This seems to be a fairly large place. What are the chances of running into Violet?

"Yes, why don't you show me the place." I glance at my watch, as if I'm pressed for time. "But, if you don't mind, let's keep it short. I have an appointment at ten."

"No problem, Ms.—uh—did you tell me your name?"

"You can call me Claudette," I say with a smile.

"Great." She smiles back. "By the way, I love your handbag. Is that a Birkin?"

I nod. "It is."

"Very nice."

I feel that I have this under control as she shows me the dining room, where breakfast is just winding down. Then she shows me the large "family room," where a number of residents are scattered about, some reading, some watching a big-screen television, some sitting around a table just visiting. Very congenial. Then we go to a game room with pool tables and game tables. Then a crafts room, where a class is in session, and finally she shows me a kitchen set up for residents to use.

"We want people to feel free to cook if they want. One resident makes the most delectable sugar cookies. You can smell them all over the place. Do you like to cook, Claudette?"

I laugh. "Hardly."

"Well, that's okay. Because you never have to lift a finger here, and the food is really good. Everyone says so."

"That's nice." I'm ready to go now. I think I've been lucky not to have seen or been seen by Violet. But my luck could run out at any moment.

"And we even have housekeeping service for those who want it. It costs a little more, but some of our residents, particularly the men, swear by it. The housekeepers even leave a mint on the pillow." She laughs. "Can you imagine?"

I nod as I consider the prospects of making my own bed for the rest of my life. "Yes, I can." I make a conspicuous effort to look at my watch.

"I know you need to go to your appointment, but I'd like to show you our sample room first. We keep one room open for potential residents." She opens the door to a room that's not much bigger than my current bedroom, although it does have its own bath.

"It's not very large," I say.

"No, but that's only because we encourage our residents to get out and mingle with the others. We don't think it's healthy to spend too much time alone."

"I see."

"The double rooms are bigger…but then you have to share them with a roommate."

I shake my head. "I could never do that."

"Any questions?"

I am curious as to what these rooms go for, so I ask. Using my best actress face, I conceal my shock when she tells me the monthly cost. It's more than twice my new monthly budget. I am stunned to think that I cannot afford to stay in a place like this. Not that I'm interested...just shocked. How can Violet possibly afford it? Plus, she's been here for several years now.

"So, what do you think?" asks Cynthia brightly.

"I think it's a very nice facility," I admit as we leave the room.

"But not what you're looking for?"

"The truth is, I'm just not sure I'm ready for this yet."

"And I totally understand. But we do have a waiting list. It's not terribly long at the moment, but you might want to get on it. You just never know."

"Oh, I don't think that's—" I stop as my sister emerges from the next room. I look the other way, hoping she won't see my face. But it's too late.

"Claudette?"

"Do you know each other?" Cynthia asks happily.

"Yes," I say in a frosty voice.

"What are you doing here?" Violet asks.

"She's just had the tour, Violet," bubbles Cynthia. "I was just suggesting that she put her name on the waiting list."

"You're trying to get in here?" Violet clearly seems confused.

"Well, I…"

"Maybe you can encourage her," says Cynthia. "How do you know each other, anyway?"

"She's my sister," Violet says in a flat tone.

"Really?" Cynthia turns and looks at me with surprise. "You didn't tell me your sister was a resident."

"Well, I wasn't positive she was still here, and I just happened to be in town and I—"

"That's great." But Cynthia is eying me with a slightly suspicious expression. "I'll just leave you two to catch up. That is, unless you really do have another appointment to get to, Claudette."

"Thank you for the tour," I tell her stiffly.

Then Violet and I are left standing in the hallway. I don't know what to do, and she's not saying anything.

"I should go," I finally say.

"Why did you come here?"

"I…I was just curious."

"You wanted to see how the rest of the world lives?"

"Something like that."

"You come here, find out that I'm still living here, and then without even speaking to me, you just leave?"

"I only wanted to use the rest room."

Violet's eyes flash with anger. "You came all the way to Silverton just to use the rest room? You might think you're a good actress, but I'm not buying that nonsense."

"Oh, I didn't come all the way to Silverton to use the bathroom. I was in town...and I just happened to be driving by...and I needed to go. I saw this place, so I stopped in."

"And then while you just happened to be here, you decided to take the tour?"

"That's right," I snap.

"Well, you are a piece of work, Claudette. You always have been."

"Thank you."

"Claudette?" A woman with a cane hobbles over to us. She's peering at me as if she knows me, and I wonder if she might possibly be a crazed fan, someone who followed Gavin's career and somehow knows I'm his widow. "Violet?" she says to my sister. "Is it really?"

"Yes," says Violet dryly. "This is Claudette. She's been touring the facility."

The woman comes closer now, looking into my eyes and smiling. "Claudette Porter. Don't you remember me? I used to be Caroline Campbell. We were good friends, remember?"

"Caroline? From across the street? Of course I remember you. Although I never would've recognized you in a million years. You live here too?"

"I do." She nods over her shoulder. "Let's go sit down and catch up. I have a bad hip and can't stand in one place very long without screaming bloody murder."

"I think Claudette has an appointment to make," Violet says in a snippy tone.

"No." I take Caroline's free arm and walk with her. "As usual, my little sister is wrong again."

Caroline laughs as we make our way into the family room. Soon we're settled into a pair of club chairs, and Violet simply stands there, looking at us with a mixed expression of what must be rage and jealousy.

"Aren't you going to join us?" Caroline asks Violet.

"No, thank you." Violet turns on her heel and stomps off.

"Who put the bee in her bonnet?" asks Caroline.

"I think she was born that way."

"So, tell me, what *are* you doing here? Violet mentioned that you took the tour, but you couldn't possibly be thinking of moving up here, could you? You wouldn't leave sunny Southern California for Silverton, would you?"

"Not intentionally." Then to change the subject, I focus on her. "What brought you back here? I thought you'd moved away."

"I had moved away—eons ago. I went to Eureka and got a job at the newspaper. Then I started dating an editor there, and I married him when the war started. Jack made it back home in one piece. We had two kids and a good life. He eventually owned the newspaper. Our son took it over when Jack retired. Then Jack died in 1993, and I had some health problems that made me give up my home. I tried living with my kids for a while, but that just about drove us all mad. Finally, I started looking around for a good assisted living setup." She waves her hand. "And can you believe I ended up back in our old stomping grounds?"

"I was surprised to find this place is much nicer than I remember."

"So was I. My son discovered it for me on the Internet. It was ranked pretty high. And it's not that far from Eureka. So here I am." She stares at me and then shakes her head. "And here you are, Claudette, looking just as fantastic as ever, which is completely unfair. How do you do it, anyway?'

"Thank you. The truth is, I don't feel terribly fantastic. Whenever I look into the mirror, I just see a faded old lady looking back."

"You should try looking into *my* mirror sometime." She laughs. "But really, what are you doing back in town? Did you come to see your sister?"

"Did it look like that to you?"

"Not unless you wanted your head torn off. Why is Violet acting like that anyway? Usually, she's quite nice. In fact, she and I have become close friends. When I first came here, she kept me up-to-date on your doings down there in Hollywood and wherever you were off traveling to with that talented husband of yours. But, come to think of it, she doesn't do that anymore. And if I bring up your name, she usually just changes the subject."

"She's mad at me."

"Why?"

"Oh, it's silly, really."

Caroline leans over and puts her hand on my arm, smiling with conspiracy. "Come on, you can trust me, Claudette. We go back further than Violet and I."

So I tell her about my mother's home being left to me.

"To you alone?"

"Yes. It seemed a bit odd at the time, but I was distracted with my own problems. Gavin died shortly before Mother, and I had things to deal with. When Violet threw her hissy fit, well, it's possible I said things that hurt her feelings too. It was all rather unfortunate."

"I've heard that wills and property disputes can result in the worst kinds of family feuds. Jack and I made sure that everything was split evenly among the children, grandchildren, and even the great-grandchildren so none of them will have anything to argue about."

"In my mother's defense, I think she may have left the house to me because Gavin and I had helped her out so much financially. Perhaps she felt she owed it to us. I don't know…"

"That's understandable. But it's a shame that it came between you and Violet. I hope you can work it out."

"As you can see, it's probably up to her."

Caroline doesn't say anything now.

"So, are you happy here?" I ask to change the subject.

"Happy as anyone in my condition can be." She grins. "Do you remember that time we played hooky, Claudette? What were those boys' names? The twins?" She squints, as if to remember, then snaps her fingers. "John and Ronald Green."

"Johnny and Ronnie!"

"Yes. Johnny and Ronnie. We went to the lake and drank beer." She sighs. "Oh, those were the days."

"Remember when we got caught smoking in the rest room?"

"Yes. It was such a scandal. My parents were fit to be tied."

I nod and say yes, as if my parents were furious as well, but the truth is, my mother barely reacted. She and my father were in one of their terrible fights, as I recall it, because he'd wasted some money that she'd set aside. Consequently my letter from the principal went mostly unnoticed.

Caroline and I reminisce about some of our other outrageous antics for quite some time. We really were rather wild and fun loving back in our high school days, and as we stroll down memory lane, we try to top each other in remembering crazy stories, sometimes laughing so loudly that others in the room begin to take notice.

Before long, some of Caroline's friends come over to see what's going on. So she tells them about how we were as teens. Then she tells them who I am and who I was married to, and she even mentions some of my famous friends. As a result, our little party gets bigger and better. People are asking me questions about Gavin and Hollywood and filmmaking back in the good old days, back when a motion picture was a big event. I answer their questions with drama and polish. They are a good audience, and I feel like I'm a star.

"You must stay for lunch," says Eddie, who, according to Caroline, is one of the few "available" male residents—and highly sought after.

"Yes," the others agree. "Stay for lunch, Claudette."

So I stay. Of course, the food isn't very good, but I'm not feeling terribly hungry anyway. I'm having too much fun entertaining my new fan club. But I notice that my sister is not among this crowd, and that troubles me a little. As I scan the dining room looking for Violet, I try not to be too obvious. I'm not all that surprised to finally spot her over by the kitchen doors, sitting by herself with her head down. Playing the wounded little sister again, the perennial wallflower, the outsider.

Well, that's her choice. I don't see why it should be of any concern to me.

15

I stick around for a while after lunch, but I can tell Caroline is tired. It seems that her friends are either snoozing in front of the television or have all tottered off to their rooms for their afternoon naps, which actually sounds rather appealing to me too.

"Well, dear," I say to Caroline, "I should be on my way."

"Oh, I hate to see you leave, Claudette. It's been so long... and so fun to see you again. Are you going back to Beverly Hills now?"

I realize that I haven't confessed to her or anyone, including my sister, that I've returned to Silverton for good—rather for bad, which is more how it feels. I try to think of a creative way to tell her this news, a way that's not completely humiliating to me. Especially after being the star with her friends today. I hate to see the limelight growing dim as people, even Silverton people, discover how degrading life has become for Claudette Fioré. It's all so embarrassing. "Actually...I've decided not to go back to Beverly Hills."

"Why not?"

"Oh, you know how it is… Everything is so busy and noisy down there. So many of my friends have passed on. I want to try a simpler life."

"Really?"

"Yes. I came up here to check on my mother's house and decided to do a little renovation, move some of my things up, and try living here. I've heard of other people from my circle of friends who enjoy small-town life, and I thought perhaps it was time for me to give it a try as well. Also, Silverton has gotten a bit of culture since we were kids, what with the new restaurants, coffee house, gallery. I even found the little bookstore to be charming, and I enjoyed meeting the owner, Page Turner."

Caroline smiles happily. "That's wonderful."

"I hope it's not a mistake."

"Well, at least you still have your home in Beverly Hills to return to. You might try living here for part of the time, then going down there." Now she frowns. "Although you seem to be doing it backward."

"Backward?"

"I'd think you'd want to winter down there and come up here during the warmer months. But we're just going into winter."

I wave my hand. "Oh, well, I'll just have to see how it goes."

"Anyway, I'm so happy to know my old friend is back in town. I hope you'll come out and visit here. Perhaps I can come visit you sometime too. I don't drive, of course, but there's a van that takes residents to town."

"Yes. When I get all settled into my house, I'll have to give a little party."

"A party." She sighs. "That would be such fun, Claudette. You have just made my day."

"And now I'll let you get some rest," I say as I stand.

"How I wish I had your stamina. I don't know how you do it."

"I've tried to remain active with yoga, t'ai chi, golf, walking with friends… It's just the way people are down where I lived." Now this used to be true. But it's been nearly two months since I've pursued any real form of physical exercise, and I'm afraid the time off is taking its toll. However, it's never too late. Or is it?

"Does your sister know of your plans?" Caroline grunts as she pushes herself to a standing position, balancing herself with her cane.

"No…" I frown. "I really didn't get much of a chance to talk to her."

"Would you like me to tell her?"

That seems to be an easy way to break the news. "Feel free. It's not a secret."

She grins. "Oh, I can't wait to tell everyone here. They enjoyed your visit so much, and I know they'll be pleased as pie to hear that you'll be around."

"Take care now, Caroline."

"You too."

I'm surprised at how I feel slightly energized as I walk out of the building and to my car. I'm not sure if this is due to the attention I got here today or, perhaps, my observation that, in comparison to Caroline or even my sister, who seemed to be dragging, I am actually doing rather well for my age. I suppose things could be worse. Still, as I check out my image in the visor mirror, I look old and wrinkled and worn out. I poke at the creases in my temples. Is there a reputable doctor who gives reasonably priced Botox injections up here? Perhaps Michael will have ideas.

As I drive back toward town, I wonder how Michael is progressing on my house. I'm sure he doesn't want me to come home yet, but I don't know where else to go. Although I'm feeling a little hungry since I barely touched my lunch at McLachlan Manor. Perhaps I could kill a bit more time by getting something to eat. I wonder if Marco's has a lunch menu. If I were as adept as Michael at driving and using my cell phone, I would try to give them a call. But my cell phone is still dead, and until I find or replace the charging cord, I am completely cut off. As I turn to go down Main Street, I notice a Radio Shack store. Maybe someone in there will be able to help me with my phone. Perhaps I'll drive back after I have some lunch.

Marco's turns out to be open, but I barely make their cutoff, since they stop serving lunch at two thirty. I'm seated at a small table by the fireplace. I order the eggplant ravioli and a salad, which are much better than what they were serving at McLachlan Manor.

As I eat, I feel a flicker of hope. Perhaps I *can* make this work. I think of the lies I told Caroline today. But maybe I can turn those lies into the truth. Maybe, in time, I will be happy that I moved up here. Or maybe I will simply die in my sleep…with the aid of some sleeping pills. Would Caroline and her friends all come to my funeral? Perhaps I should do some planning for it in advance. It would be so pitiful, not to mention humiliating, to have it handled poorly. I suppose I should put that on my to-do list.

After lunch I drive back to Radio Shack, where a young man with shaggy hair and bad skin helps me find a charging cord. Of course, it turns out that it must be ordered, but he promises that it will be here within a week.

"We'll give you a call."

"On what? My cell phone is dead."

"You don't have a landline?"

"No, not yet. I suppose I'll have to look into that." I shake my head as I go out to my car. So many things one has to do just to live in this world. I never really grasped this before—not for years and years anyway. Gavin took care of so much…and then my household staff looked after so many other necessary things. I feel a twinge of guilt when I consider how I treated them sometimes. But I am a woman with high expectations. I do not like to settle for less than excellence.

I think about my cook, Sylvia, and wish that I could've brought her with me. Oh, I know she has family and friends down there, but it would've been so nice to have help. I don't even want to think about all the things I'll have to do for myself now…all the things I must learn. It's overwhelming.

"You're home, darling," Michael says as I stand on my doorstep waiting to be let inside.

"Yes, I'm home, and I'm tired. I stayed away as long as I possibly could. Please, let me in, and I promise to go directly to my room and take a nice long nap."

He grins. "It's a deal." Then he makes me cover my eyes as he walks me through the house. I can smell paint as we go. I'm curious as to what color he chose. I do trust his taste, although he can get carried away at times. For instance, his home in Hawaii is far more colorful than anything I could ever live with. But then, I feel that he knows my likes and dislikes. I just hope he hasn't done anything too outrageous.

"Here you are," he says.

I open my eyes to see that I'm back in my peaceful bedroom, and to my surprise, I feel comforted to be here. "Thank you."

"Rest well, dear. I think I shall have this all wrapped up before dinner."

"I look forward to seeing it."

"Really?" He sounds pleased.

"Yes, of course."

He claps his hands. "That's the most enthusiasm you've shown me since we started our little journey. You give my heart hope."

Hope, I think as I remove my shoes and lie down on the bed. It seems such a fleeting thing, so slippery. Just when you think you have a grasp on it, it evaporates. As I'm dozing off, I vaguely remember a time when I felt hopeful as a child. It's not something I usually allow myself to think of, but I'm so tired and my resistance is low.

And like a ghost floating through this bedroom, whispering its dark memories into my ears, it almost drifts into my mind, like a dream. It's amazing how quickly these things can flash through one's mind, unbidden yet unrestrained, simply because one is too tired to hold them back.

I'd just turned thirteen at the time that life seemed to change for my family. My mother had recently gotten a job in town. Now, besides taking in laundry, she worked in the bakery as well. Not out in the front with the sweet rolls and pies, where the girls wore pink and white checked aprons and crisp white hats. No, my mother, in her ugly, old day dresses, worked in back where no one could see her. She worked the night shift, leaving the house about the same time that Violet and I went to bed.

This was a relief, because I didn't relish the idea of her being spotted on the street in daylight as she walked back and forth to the bakery in her ugly, worn-out shoes. Her job was to operate the big dough machine and bake the loaves of bread that were sold each morning.

Naturally, my father hadn't been happy about this new development. He said she only took the job to embarrass him.

And naturally, he used his anger as an excuse to go off on his binges even more regularly than before. Part of me was relieved at his absence because life grew calmer, but another part of me missed his humor and wit.

Despite my father's shortcomings, the man knew how to liven a party. After the first few weeks of Mother's new job, we fell into something of a routine. Violet and I helped out around the house a little more, and Mother rewarded us with a bit more spending money. Not much, of course, since it was still the Depression, but enough to buy a soda or see a movie. And that in itself was enough to make me feel a bit hopeful. I thought things were truly changing for us.

One night, my father seemed to confirm that good things were ahead. He came home in a jolly mood, whistling. I knew this probably meant he was drunk. But at least he was a happy drunk. It was pretty late, and I'd just gotten up to get a glass of water. I was about to turn off the light and tiptoe back to bed when he came into the kitchen.

At first I expected to be scolded for being up so late, but he simply smiled and told me he'd gotten a job at the car dealership in town. He was so excited that I felt excited too. He said that things were looking up for us and that Mother could quit her job at the bakery soon.

"I'll be changing oil and doing tune-ups to start with," he told me. "But in time I can work up to a sales position and make some good money. Old man Parson promised me a promotion by summer."

I told my father congratulations and that I was happy for him. And I really was happy. This seemed to be the beginning of a new era. Then my father did something that surprised me. Our family had never been demonstrative, and we rarely displayed any form of physical affection. But that night, my father hugged me. And as he hugged me, he sort of swayed and danced with me, humming for quite some time.

We were still in the kitchen, and I remember my bare feet got cold on the wood floors, since it was winter, but I didn't complain. I danced with him anyway. Finally I told him it was a school night and I should go to bed. But once in bed, I replayed the scene I'd just participated in.

On one hand, I felt very special… I'd been the first one to hear my father's good news, and he actually danced with me. But another part of me felt uneasy and confused…and I wasn't even sure why. Of course, by the next day I didn't really think of it at all. By then we'd all heard about my father's new job.

He actually made us breakfast, laughing and joking as he flipped oversized hotcakes on the big cast-iron skillet. Even my mother, who looked weary from a long night's work, appeared slightly hopeful. It seemed we had truly turned a corner, and we were all happy that morning. Although there was no dancing in the kitchen.

My father had been working at Parson's Pontiac and Oldsmobile for about a week, I think. I'm sure we were still on pins and needles, wondering if this job might really last; he rarely stayed employed for more than a week or two. I know I continued to feel hopeful. I imagined how nice it would be to have a father who worked regularly and brought home a paycheck. I envisioned us living like "normal" people and perhaps even getting ahead. I imagined walking around town holding my head high, being proud of my family and what we'd become. I'm sure Violet felt the same, and consequently, we were all doing all we could to keep this thing rolling smoothly.

It was Friday and my father had taken Violet and me to the theater. We'd seen *Mr. Deeds Goes to Town,* and I imagined that Mr. Deeds, played by Gary Cooper, was the sort of person my father was transforming into. A generous and caring man—a man who enjoyed a good time, occasionally drank too much…and a man who also just happened to come into a whole lot of money.

I felt hopeful. I also felt special because I got to sit next to my father and he'd even put his arm around me during the film. I'm sure Violet felt jealous—that would be like her. Then, later that night, after Violet had gone to bed with her silly horse book, I stayed up and talked to my father.

I liked the way he was treating me more and more like a grownup, telling me things about his job and his life…things that he didn't tell my mother. And when he complained about being tired from working underneath the hood of a car all day and asked me to rub his sore back, I didn't hesitate.

"It'll be easier if I lie down," he told me. So I followed him to the bedroom and began to massage his back.

The memory gets blurry at this juncture. I remember my

father saying that he should repay my kindness by rubbing my back too, and I didn't argue since my arms were getting tired. At first it felt good. But then I realized he was rubbing more than my back. His fingers began creeping around to the front, fondling me in places I knew should be private. I felt confused and embarrassed, and I didn't know what to do. Finally I stood up and told him to stop it.

He acted as if he didn't understand. And then he seemed hurt. But I didn't care. I straightened my mussed-up clothes and walked out of there. I stormed into the bedroom, where Violet was still reading her stupid book.

"What's wrong?" she asked me. But I didn't tell her. That would've been too humiliating. Instead, I acted as if nothing whatsoever was wrong. I acted as if I'd just had a very enjoyable time visiting with our father. And I never told anyone, not even my mother, about what happened that night.

I suppose I didn't fully understand it myself. Except that I felt it was wrong. My father stepped over a line, and he knew it. I knew it too. And that's when hope died.

Not surprisingly, my father got fired the following week. And this sent him on another binge. He stayed away from home longer than usual this time. I heard that a slutty woman named Gloria was harboring him. She lived on the bad side of town, and I secretly hoped he would stay with her for good. I think perhaps we all did.

But, like always, he eventually came back. And as usual, he acted very sorry for being gone, for having hurt us. He begged us to forgive him, promised that he was changing his ways. He even tried to explain what had derailed him this time, blaming everything on the fact that he'd been "unfairly fired" from his job. Although I'd already heard that he was drunk at work and had botched Mayor Fenwick's tune-up and oil change so badly that the mayor nearly blew up in his car while driving to Fresno.

After that, I kept a safe distance from my father. And I partially blamed my mother for our convoluted problems. If only she could handle things differently...if she fixed herself up more...made him happier...made him toe the line...then life might've gone better for everyone. But I think I knew it would never happen.

In my teen years, I began to devise a plan of my own. As soon as I was old enough, I would leave this horrible place. I would never come back. Never.

16

"Yoo-hoo?" A male voice pries me back into a partially awakened state. I open my eyes, but other than a crack of light coming from what must be a slightly opened door, the room is dark, and I am disoriented.

"What?" I sit up in bed, trying to get my bearings.

"It's just me, darling. Did you have a good nap?"

"Oh, Michael." I reach for the light switch on the lamp and turn it on, blinking into the brightness. "What time is it anyway?"

"It's almost seven." He steps into the room. "You slept for quite a while. Are you feeling all right?"

"Under the circumstances, you mean?" I put my feet on the floor and slowly stand, stretching a bit to loosen my stiff joints.

Michael peers curiously at me. "Your eyes are red and your makeup is smeared. Have you been crying?"

I touch my hand to my face, then turn to look in the mirror. My face does seem slightly ravaged. I reach for a tissue and face cream, doing some minor repairs as Michael looks on from behind. Finally I turn to face him again. "Better?"

"I know this is hard on you," he says with compassionate eyes.

"I'm perfectly fine."

"Well, good." He presses the palms of his hands together. "And I am ready for the unveiling."

I am not ready for anything...except perhaps crawling back into bed. "Yes. Let me put on my shoes first."

"Oh, I just can't wait to see your reaction, Claudette."

I wish I could muster up more enthusiasm, but it feels as if I am climbing a mountain just now. Oh, I do appreciate Michael's effort, but how can it possibly be worthwhile? Really, what difference will this all make if I am unable to stick around and make this thing work? I shove my feet into my loafers and even attempt to fluff up my hair in the back since I'm sure it must be flat as a pancake after my nap.

"Are you ready?"

I nod. "As ready as I'll ever be."

"Good." He takes my hand and leads me out. "We'll start with the other bedroom."

"Fine." We go down the hallway, which is now painted sort of a golden beige, perhaps the color of sand. Light enough that it feels brighter than the previous "dead salmon" color, but not so light that it's harsh. "I like this color. And I like the selection of art you've put up here."

"I'm so glad. I was really challenged with some of your pieces. Wall space is rather minimal in this house."

"Wall space as well as square footage."

"Well, yes, that's true." He points down. "Do you like the runner?"

I look at the carpet that runs down the wood floor in the hallway. It has an interesting geometric design in desert tones. It's vaguely familiar. "It's nice. Was it from my things?"

"Yes. I almost didn't bring it, but I'm glad I did. It's perfect in here, such a nice contrast to the wood floors, and it lightens it up a bit, don't you think?" He stops by what used to be Violet's and my bedroom, his hand on the doorknob. "I was rather bewildered about this room, how it should be used. At first I thought a small office or library, but then I realized you might need a guest room as well." He opens the door. "So I tried to make both."

I take in the full-size bed, which is flush to the wall with lots of colorful pillows piled along one side so it resembles a comfortable sofa or lounge. And on the other side of the room, nestled into the corner adjacent to the window, sits a leather chair with ottoman. A small antique desk and matching credenza are attractively placed as well. The walls are painted a soft sage color and adorned with several pieces of well-chosen art, including what was once Gavin's favorite, an unusual piece by Julian Schnabel. He always thought it looked like a swan, but I never could see it. Today, as I look at it in this new location, I can almost see the swan.

"I would never have imagined this room could hold so much furniture," I tell him.

"That's because those two twin beds used up a lot of space. This room is only a foot narrower than the other bedroom." He turns to me. "What do you think?"

"I think you're a magician."

"See, it's both a guest room and an office."

"Clever." I'm feeling a twinge of hope.

"On with our tour."

Next we go to the bathroom, which isn't greatly changed but is still refreshingly different. Now painted a celadon green, the feeling is soothing and peaceful, providing a clean contrast against the white-tiled floor, claw-foot tub, and bathroom fixtures. He's put what used to be a lawyer's bookcase in here, only now it's outfitted with linens and bath things and topped with a pleasant little lamp that used to be in my bedroom.

"Very nice," I say.

"I know it's a bit Pottery Barn-ish, but I think it works."

"This carpet is a nice touch," I say when I notice the silk Oriental rug alongside the tub. As I recall, Edouard picked that out to occupy one of the more formal guest rooms. He warned me that it was very expensive and needed to be cleaned carefully. I consider mentioning this, but why bother? It looks right in here.

The kitchen is next on the tour, and it's truly transformed with a warm and welcoming buttery yellow paint. Again the art is arranged attractively on the walls, adding just the right touches of color. But it's the new stainless-steel appliances that take me by surprise. I just stare at the stove, refrigerator, and microwave in amazement. "How did you get these?"

"As you know, that nasty fridge had to go the way of the wicked. And the Goodwill boys told me about an appliance store that's only about an hour away. I got a salesman on the phone and told him what I wanted and the sizes. They were delivered late this afternoon while you were napping."

I open the refrigerator and peer in. Clean and neat at the moment, but will I be able to keep it that way for long? I turn back to Michael. "How did you pay for these? Aren't appliances expensive?"

"Like I told you. Alex Granville is sending me a check for the things in the storage unit. It should cover everything I've put out and then some."

"You really are amazing, Michael." I look at my Limoges china and sparkling crystal glassware, so prettily arranged behind the glass doors of the dark cherry cupboards, giving the cabinets an unexpected touch of elegance. "I had no idea this kitchen was this nice."

"I wish we could've put in a dishwasher. Unfortunately, that would've required some major remodeling."

"Oh…"

"Which means you'll be washing dishes by hand, darling. Can you manage?"

I try to shrug this off. "I don't know why not. I used to wash dishes by hand all the time when I was a kid. Right here in this very same sink."

"It's a good sink," he assures me. "Soapstone."

I run my finger over the smooth surface. "I always did like the feel of this sink. Although I remember how the dark color bothered me. I wanted a shining white enamel sink like my friend Caroline had in her house."

"This sink is actually much more valuable."

I look over to the small dining area, where a square oak table and four matching chairs are arranged. In the center of the table is a gold ceramic vase from Tuscany, complete with fresh flowers in shades of orange, yellow, and red. "Is that table from my old breakfast nook?" I try to remember the padded banquette seating and the bay window that looked out over the beautifully landscaped backyard and pool. Sometimes I had my morning coffee there, usually around noon.

"Yes. I took the leaves out and removed the padded cushions from the chairs. I think it works."

"And that rug is interesting." I point to the antique Kilim that used to be in Gavin's den.

"Don't you just *love* those harvest colors in here?"

"It really is nice," I admit. "But I never would've dreamed of putting that rug in a kitchen."

"Well, Kilims are made to last. And if you ever decide you don't want it, just toss it my way. I'm sure I can find a home for it."

"You really are good at this, Michael." I stare at the kitchen and try to remember what it looked like before. "Everything has come together so well…and I know that couldn't be easy in such a small house. But you've managed to make it look bigger and better. I am impressed."

"Thank you, darling. That means a lot coming from you." He rubs his hands together. "But we're not finished."

Michael leads me out into the living room, and I actually

have to take in a quick breath—the transformation is so incredible I'm stunned. "Is this really the same room?"

He nods and actually giggles.

"Michael…" I just shake my head as I walk around the surprisingly spacious room. The walls are painted a very rich yet mellow color that reminds me of pumpkins or squash, a comforting golden-orange shade. I'm sure I would've instantly balked at this color if he had asked me first or shown me a swatch, but it is perfect in here. It brings the dark wooden window trim, baseboards, and crown molding to life.

He's arranged an interesting mix of furniture too, pieces that were previously in different rooms of my house. I recognize the sofa, a dearly loved piece that had been in my bedroom; its rich, golden chenille with goose-down pillows has always been perfect for napping. There's also a pair of Italian leather chairs that once flanked the desk in Gavin's office, arranged nicely by the small fireplace that I'd nearly forgotten was here. I think my mother must've had a chair or something blocking it. An oversized ottoman with autumn-toned tapestry that came from our formal living room now serves as a coffee table. The art Michael selected for this room is unexpected, but perfect.

"I never would've dreamed of putting these things together," I tell him. "And that Scully abstract over the couch"—I study a painting I've taken for granted for years—"is absolutely lovely in here."

"Isn't it? I think of this room as eclectic. Do you really like it?"

"I do." I nod as I walk around the room, trying to take it in. The familiar lamps, end tables, pillows, furniture… It's as if I'm seeing it all for the first time. Then I notice an arrangement of old photos on the wall by the front door. Candid shots of Gavin and me with various Hollywood friends taken over the years. I just stare at the pictures in wonder and amazement. I almost feel at home now. Finally I turn to Michael, with real tears in my eyes. "I don't even know how to thank you."

"That's all I needed, darling." Then he stretches out his arms and we embrace.

"Thank you so much." I step back and look at the room again.

"I know it's not the same as your Beverly Hills house, but hopefully it will begin to feel like a home to you."

"It already does. Oh, it's a different sort of home, much smaller, but I do feel somewhat at home here." I don't admit that I also feel uneasy about all this. How will I keep these rooms looking this nice? At the moment, the floors and the woodwork are gleaming. All is clean and tidy and attractive. I remember the housekeepers I employed and how hard they seemed to work. What is involved in maintaining a house, even one as small as this?

"And maybe having your things arranged attractively…well, perhaps it helps you through the challenges of your new life."

I extract a slightly used handkerchief from my jacket pocket and dab at my eyes. I want to be as positive as Michael, especially after all the work he's invested in this, but I just cannot begin to imagine how I'll ever manage without him. "I wish you were staying here with me."

"My work here is done, darling." He smiles sadly. "And Richard called twice today. He's already getting jealous." Michael chuckles. "He keeps saying that I've left him for you."

"If only I could talk you into it."

"What you can talk me into is dinner. I'm starving."

"Yes, of course," I say. "What would you like?"

"I've been thinking about that charming little Italian place."

"That sounds fine. I'll get my purse." I don't even complain that I already ate there once today, and I feel proud of myself for that. Tonight I do the driving. It's my way of thanking Michael, showing him that I can be an independent woman. As I drive, he fills me in on some of the house details.

"You should have everything you need in the kitchen," he says. "I tried to keep it simple since I didn't expect you'd be doing a lot of cooking. But just in case you become adventure-some in the kitchen, there are a few extra appliances and odds and ends in the storage area of your laundry room. Also, I used both closets in both bedrooms for your clothes, but as you'll see, everything is not there. I stored the other things in one of those hanging canvas wardrobes as well as some crates, which are also in the laundry room. However, if I were you, I might simply give those things away, darling."

He pauses to catch his breath. "Sometimes less really is more. Speaking of less, I sent the items I was unable to use in the house back with the movers. They'll put them back into storage for Alex to deal with. I've also asked Alex to ship me the things I've marked for Hawaii."

I park my car on Main Street. I am amazed at how Michael is able to keep all of these things organized in his mind and under such control. But, really, I do not understand how he expects me to do the same. I do not see how I can possibly handle this on my own. I'm afraid it is simply too much and that I will be lost without him.

As we enter the restaurant, the hostess at Marco's greets us, nodding to me. "Nice to see you again so soon, Ms. Fioré."

"Good evening," I answer in a stiff voice.

"See how friendly the locals are?" Michael says after we're seated. "Already they know our names. I am starting to simply adore this town."

I ignore his comments as I peruse the familiar menu. I wonder how long it will be before I have it memorized. But then I remember my monthly budget... Even though Marco's isn't as expensive as the places I would normally dine, I won't be able to afford it on a daily basis.

"I've made a list for you," Michael says after we've ordered. He opens his Day-Timer and removes several sheets of paper. "Things you need to do and to buy and people to contact."

"A list?"

He smiles as he hands me the papers. "Actually, it's several lists. I had a feeling you might need a bit of help, sort of a jump-start, just to get you going. I'm sure you'll be fine once you find your groove."

"My groove…" I glance over the first page, which seems to be house maintenance things like, "Call for garbage pickup, order oil for the furnace, rake the leaves, get phone service, cable service," and so on. I point to the line that says, "Call plumber." "What am I to call the plumber?"

He chuckles. "Nothing bad, I hope."

"Then why am I calling him?"

"Haven't you noticed the pipes seem slow?"

I consider this. "The bathtub did seem to take a long time to empty."

"The carpet guy mentioned the toilet was pretty slow. He told me that sometimes when a house is left vacant for a while, roots will grow into the sewer lines. He suggested that you call a plumber and get them cleaned out."

"Cleaned out?" I say, vaguely wondering how people can bear to do that sort of work. Whatever cleaning out a sewer line entails, I do not care to know the details. I turn to the next page. This seems to have more to do with business things. "Open bank account in town, call accountant, change homeowner's insurance," things like that. The final page appears to be a grocery shopping list.

"Really?" I look at Michael. "You think I'm unable to fetch my own groceries without specific instructions?"

He laughs. "Well, you never know. I'm just trying to be helpful."

I narrow my eyes. "Just why have you been so helpful?"

He shrugs. "Because we're friends. Because of Gavin. Because although we're unrelated, Claudette, we are family. I care about you."

I hold up my hand. "Stop, stop… You're going to make me cry again."

"They say that tears are good for the soul."

I look back down at my lists as a distraction. "Oh, you should be proud of me, Michael. I ordered a cord for my cell phone. You know, to recharge it. I walked right into Radio Shack and simply ordered it myself without having it on a list or anything."

"That's marvelous." He holds up his glass of Cabernet in a toast. "Here's to you, darling. May this be the beginning of great things to come."

I hold up my glass too and do my best to feign a smile. But the level of my confidence in my own abilities is not nearly as high as his.

17

I drive Michael to Eureka in the morning. He's booked a flight to San Francisco on one of those horrid little commuter planes that feel as if they might plunge from the sky at any moment. After that he'll fly directly to Hawaii, first class. How I wish I were going with him.

"You'll be fine," he assures me as we say our good-byes in the loading zone in front of the terminal.

"I will not." Of course, I am crying now—no acting skills necessary. I feel as if I'm losing my last and best friend. "I don't see how I can possibly do this on my own."

He shakes his head. "Don't keep telling yourself negative things, Claudette. You can do this. You *must* do this. Be strong, darling."

I suddenly remember a scene from *Casablanca*, at the end of the movie when Rick (Bogie) is telling Ilsa (Ingrid) to get on the plane and leave him behind. And although it's Michael who's leaving right now, I pretend that I'm Bogie, playing Rick. And I try to remember how he had to be strong when he stayed behind.

"I've got to go now, or I'll miss my flight."

181

"I know, Michael." I look him in the eyes and repeat the old line. *"And if that plane leaves the ground and you're not on it, you'll regret it. Maybe not today. Maybe not tomorrow, but soon and for the rest of your life."* He throws back his head and laughs. "See, Claudette, you *are* a trooper. That's Rick's line from *Casablanca*—and you delivered it perfectly, darling. You're going to be just fine. I know it."

I force a smile that I hope is convincing. "Yes. It seemed apropos."

"Here's looking at you, kid!" Then he kisses me on the cheek, loads his bags onto a cart, and heads into the terminal.

I stand there watching him as he goes into the building, waiting until he's out of sight, probably at the ticket counter. I slowly get back into my car, the way a very old woman would do, lifting one foot and then the other. I feel so tired, so alone. So completely cut off from everything. I get back on the highway and drive toward Silverton in silence.

I still have options. There are other ways out. I even consider the possibility of a car accident, except I do not like pain or the possibility of disfigurement, and there are no guarantees that I would not survive a horrible wreck.

I feel exhausted when I get back to town. I park my car in the driveway, go into my house, and lock the door behind me. A part of me is convinced that I will remain in this house indefinitely. I will not go out. I will not speak to anyone. I will find a way to end this thing.

But then I see the living room and how transformed it is from the living room I remember as a child, or even the living room I knew only shortly, the one my mother occupied all those years. And I walk through the house, and I see all the work that dear Michael put into this place. All of his loving attention to detail…and I know I cannot give up this easily. For Michael's sake, I should at least try.

I open my purse and take out the lists he gave me. Some of these things seem impossible to accomplish without the help of a phone. Those things will have to wait. But then I realize I'm hungry. I'm tempted to go to one of the few restaurants in town; then I remember the grocery list Michael made for me, so I decide to go shopping.

First I go to the bathroom and freshen up a bit. I powder my nose, put on some lipstick, and fluff my hair. I'm not sure if it's because of the lighting or perhaps because my laser eye surgery is wearing thin, but I really don't look too terribly bad for a woman my age.

As I go out to my car, I try to remember other actresses in their eighties or thereabouts, women who are still taking care of themselves, still leading active and fulfilling lives. It's a game I used to play when I needed to lift my spirits, although the list grew shorter each year. Mitzi Gaynor, Angie Dickinson, Shirley Jones… They're all a bit younger than me. But then there is Doris Day; she's held up well. And the glamorous Zsa Zsa Gabor, who must be over ninety by now. Finally, as I'm parking at Raleigh's Food Mart, I think of Lauren Bacall. She's still going strong, and we're the same age. Suddenly I feel much better. I can hold my head high.

I go into the store and just stand there. I'm not even sure what to do next. But I think of what I've seen on movies and television and pretend that I'm playing a role. Starring as today's grocery shopper. I can carry this off.

I take a few steps forward to where grocery carts are lined up. But stacked near the carts are the smaller baskets, the type you carry on your arm. Somehow carrying a basket seems a bit more elegant than pushing a clunky wheeled thing about. Besides, I cannot imagine how I would begin to fill an entire cart with food for just me.

"Can I help you?" asks a woman who appears to be a clerk, since she has on a rather unbecoming red smock with a name tag pinned on it.

"No, thank you." I pick up the smaller basket and hook it over my arm, as if this were something I do all the time. Now if I were shopping for shoes, clothes, art, or jewelry, I would be perfectly comfortable, right within my element. But finding myself in a large, cluttered store that smells a bit like overly ripe fruit and damp cardboard, and with elevator music blaring over my head, I feel rather lost.

I fumble to balance the bulky plastic basket as I open my purse so I can remove Michael's grocery list, but I don't see it. I hunt and hunt but finally accept that it's not there. Either I left it at home or lost it. Still, how hard can this be?

The first section seems to be the bakery, and while some of these sugary items are tempting, it's best to avoid sweets. Instead I choose a loaf of whole grain bread that resembles what Sylvia used to serve as toast with my orange juice in the morning. Orange juice—of course! But where would I find it? Certainly not with the doughnuts. I walk for what seems a long way without seeing anything that resembles orange juice, and my arm is already feeling the weight of the basket. But I find the wine section and think a nice bottle of Cabernet Sauvignon might be an asset to my kitchen. I select one with a label from a vineyard I recognize and place it in my basket, next to the bread.

Then I notice a good bottle of Merlot and put that in my basket as well. Unfortunately this makes the basket quite heavy, and my arm becomes sore from carrying it. Perhaps I should've gotten a frumpy cart with wheels on it after all. I look around, hoping to spot an empty cart, but without luck.

I do not relish the idea of walking the distance of the store, back to where the wheeled carts are lined up. But neither do I like the idea of my poor left arm being permanently disabled due to the handle of the basket, which feels as if it's cutting through my skin. I walk as quickly as these old legs will carry me.

And just as the wheeled carts are in sight and I think I can bear the pain no more, the weight in the basket shifts. And the next thing I know, the whole thing goes topsy-turvy and turns upside down, dumping the two bottles of wine and the bread to the floor with a loud crash. The Cabernet Sauvignon survives the fall, but the Merlot shatters, spewing red wine in every direction, including the direction of my nice pale blue pantsuit, my favorite Armani, which I wore to see Michael off at the airport.

The clerk who earlier asked me if I needed help is about fifteen feet away, in a check stand, bagging groceries for a man. They both stare at me with surprised eyes, and the clerk asks if I'm okay.

"No, I am *not* okay."

"Cleanup by check stand one," she says into a loudspeaker. She finishes bagging the groceries, then comes over to survey the damage. "Oh man," she says when she sees my splattered pants. "That's gonna leave a stain."

"Do you really think so?" I say wryly. I read the name on her tag. Trudy. That sounds about right.

Trudy looks down at the floor, taking in the tumbled basket, broken shards of glass, red wine spewed in every direction, the loaf of bread. She bends over and picks up the unbroken bottle, holding it up. "Bread and wine...looks like you were going to have communion or something."

"Or something," I say sadly.

"You want a towel for your pants?"

"Thank you." I am still standing in the exact same position I was in when the accident occurred, as if my feet have adhered to the ground. Just then a young man comes up with a mop and bucket, and I manage to peel myself away from the mess.

"Gross." He begins to mop it up.

"Here." Trudy hands me a fistful of paper towels. "That should help sop it up—off of your pants, I mean."

I set my purse on the checkout counter, then bend over to attempt to clean up the mess, but it's useless. The towels absorb some of the liquid, but the damage is clearly done. Finally I give up.

"Here." I hand the red-soaked paper towels back to Trudy and pick up my purse. "I think I should go."

"You don't want to finish shopping?"

I don't even answer as I exit the store. An older couple going into the store pause to look at me, staring at my suit as if they think I'd been shot. I suppose the red stain on pale blue might look like blood. But without saying a word, I simply hold my head up and walk straight to my car. My plan is to never set foot in Raleigh's Food Mart again.

I take in a few deep breaths before I begin to drive. It's a centering trick I learned in yoga. It helps to calm your nerves. But as I drive straight home, my heart races and I'm sure my blood pressure is rising. Perhaps I will suffer a stroke and that will solve everything. Yet to be found dead in my ruined Armani suit seems such a shame. I make it home, get out of my car, and am halfway up the walk to my house when I see my neighbor coming my way.

"What happened to you?" Bea hurries over to see me better.

"I had an accident."

"Is that blood?"

"No, it is *not* blood."

"What is it?"

"If you must know, it's wine."

"What on earth have you been doing? Stomping grapes?"

I glare at her. "No, I have not been stomping grapes."

"What then?"

"I was grocery shopping. A bottle of wine fell and broke."

She frowns at me. "If you were grocery shopping, where are your groceries?"

I simply throw my hands in the air, make a groaning sound, and stomp off into the house, where I remove my ruined pantsuit and stuff it into the garbage can beneath the kitchen sink. It fills the entire thing. I close the cabinet door, trying to put the loss behind me. I am certain that even the best dry cleaner cannot save that suit. I go to the bathroom, clean myself up, then change into a wine-colored Michael Kors velour warmup suit. Too bad I hadn't worn it to the grocery store.

I go and sit down in the living room. If I were a more resilient woman, I might march myself out to my car, drive back to Raleigh's Food Mart, and start all over—using a cart with wheels this time. But I do not feel any more resilient than my Armani pantsuit at the moment. I feel beaten. I feel tired. I feel old. My little pep talk about aging actresses faring well left out one very important fact—at least I believe it's a fact—those actresses are not impoverished. They still enjoy the pleasures and comforts that money can buy. I, on the other hand, do not. This is unfair.

I also feel hungry. It's half past two now, and I haven't eaten since the quick bite Michael and I had on our way to the airport early this morning. Yet the mere thought of returning to Raleigh's Food Mart is too much. I cannot bear it. I get off the couch and go to gaze out the front window. It's actually a very nice day outside. If I were a stronger, braver woman, I might consider walking to town. Michael encouraged me to do as much. But after my catastrophe at the grocery store, I'm not sure I care to take the risk. What if I tripped and fell? What if that horrible Bea came out and accosted me with more questions? I peer toward her house and don't see anyone. Still, she could be lurking.

Finally, hunger gets the best of me. Perhaps it's the Michael Kors warmup suit, but I'm suddenly aware of the fact that my body is in need of exercise. My yoga instructor warned that women my age cannot let things go and expect to get them back. I also remember what I learned from my walking friend Marsha. You do not walk and carry a purse. For two very simple reasons: One, it's bad for your posture, and two, it's an invitation to a mugger. So I remove some cash, tuck it into my pocket along with a tissue, and feeling somewhat clever, I prepare to make a quick exit and hopefully avoid my nosy neighbor.

To my relief I make it out of my yard and down the street without being spotted by Bea. I slow my pace some, since it's obvious by my short, quick gasps that I'm out of breath and out of shape. Still, I find that walking feels somewhat empowering, and although I would never walk alone in Beverly Hills, I feel relatively safe in this small town. I look at the houses along the way, trying to recall who lived where back when I was growing up.

Once I make it to Main Street, I decide to get something to eat at Casey's Coffee House. Their selection is limited, but I am so hungry I do not care. I go directly to the counter, which is not busy, and order a poppy-seed bagel with salmon cream-cheese spread, the fruit cup, and a latte. I pay the good-looking young man, wait for my latte, then take it and the number he gives me, head over to a small table by the window, and sit down. There's even a fairly fresh-looking newspaper there, so I can pretend to be reading, which is always an easy way of appearing occupied when one is eating or drinking alone in a public place. My order arrives shortly, and I thank the attractive young man. I almost ask him if anyone has ever told him that he looks like a young Jimmy Stewart, but then think better of it. I wouldn't want him to get the wrong idea.

I take my time eating my bagel sandwich, using the plastic knife to cut it into small, delicate pieces. One of the secrets of keeping a trim waistline is to eat slowly, carefully, enjoying each bite. I've heard this is how French women manage their weight. That and walking. They do a lot of walking and a lot of stair climbing. Finally I'm done with my late lunch. I set the newspaper aside, thank the young man behind the counter, and leave.

It's surprising how this small achievement bolsters my spirits and increases my confidence. I almost feel ready to tackle the task of acquiring some groceries, although I do not feel ready for Raleigh's Food Mart. Still, there is the little market down the street. Michael went there and seemed to feel it was adequate. Perhaps if I only got a few things, not so much that I couldn't easily carry them home. I think of those healthy French women again, getting their skinny loaves of bread, tasty wedges of cheese, a bit of fresh fruit, and a good bottle of wine.

Although I think I shall pass on the wine. I've had more than enough already today.

I am feeling rather pleased with myself as I walk toward home. The smart woman at the little market talked me into buying a handy canvas grocery bag with straps that can be looped over one's shoulder. I realize that carrying even this fairly light load isn't good for my posture, but every couple of blocks I switch it to the other side.

Being in a French state of mind as I shopped, I bought a small loaf of whole grain bread, a bit of nice sharp cheddar, two Fuji apples, a half pound of smoked turkey, and some cream for my coffee. And I am feeling quite smart as I carry my bounty home.

I am just turning up my walk when, once again, Bea appears out of nowhere, coming from behind, calling my name, and nearly causing me to jump. Honestly, this woman must be lurking around the corner just waiting to catch me.

"Why do you do that?" I ask her.

"Do what?"

"Sneak up on people."

"I was just putting away my hoses."

"What?"

193

"You know, for winter, so they won't freeze."

I just shrug and continue up my walk.

"You really need to get those leaves raked," she says.

"Yes, I know."

"Where's that boyfriend of yours? Maybe he can do it."

I turn and glare at her. "Michael has left."

She looks curious. "Did you break up?"

"No. He simply returned to Hawaii."

She brightens. "He lives in Hawaii?"

"Yes, with his other lover…Richard."

She frowns. "He's bisexual?"

"No. He's gay."

"So, why was he with you?"

I sigh. "You are the nosiest person I have ever met."

She nods. "Yes. Everyone tells me that. But sometimes you learn things by being nosy."

"I can only imagine." I'm on my porch now, ready to make a fast break and get into the house.

"In fact, I know something about your family, Claudette."

I feign a yawn. "I'm sure you know all kinds of things."

"Something no one else knows."

"Really. I don't think I care to hear about it, thank you anyway."

Bea steps forward, cupping her hand around her mouth as if she thinks someone else might possibly be listening, which is insane since there is no one else within fifty feet of us. *"It involves a frying pan."*

I nod, rolling my eyes. "Yes," I tell her as I unlock my door. "Does it involve bacon and eggs as well?" Then I tell her a crisp "Good day," go into my house, set down my bag, and lock and deadbolt the door.

That woman is really starting to annoy me. Not only that but she's a little frightening too. And I don't simply mean her wardrobe, which would get her mistaken for a bag lady if she were to be seen walking the streets in Beverly Hills. But her whole intrusive demeanor is unnerving. I would be wise to keep my distance.

It's not until I'm unloading my few bits of groceries that her words come back to me. *"It involves a frying pan."* Of course that sounds perfectly crazy. But it also reminds me of what Michael told me about finding a cast-iron skillet beneath my mother's bed. That made no sense either. And suddenly I wonder if there might be a relationship between these two very odd things.

"No," I say aloud as I set my cheese, cream, and turkey in the refrigerator. "It's just like when Bea was a little girl; she always wanted my attention. And in her old age she has gotten a bit unbalanced." It's only as I'm closing the refrigerator that I realize I'm talking to myself.

My meager rations last me into the next day, but by late afternoon, I am growing tired of the repetition. I've searched the house for Michael's missing grocery list, but although I found the other two lists, the grocery one seems to be permanently lost.

My guess is I dropped it at Raleigh's Food Mart. Still, I should be able to prepare my own list. How difficult can it be? I used to make lists before. Of course, those lists included interesting things like "hair salon at ten, golf at two, magenta heels for tomorrow night's premiere, meet Edouard at Design Central..."

Oh, to return to those days. I go into my office/guest room and open up the little secretary desk, relieved to discover that it's still outfitted with the basics like pens and paper and envelopes.

I sit down and begin to make a list. First I write down *orange juice,* and then I stop. What else? I move at a snail's pace, trying to decide what I need. And yet, after half an hour I only have *orange juice, butter, crackers, lemons, eggs, skim milk.* It's hardly worth making the trip to Raleigh's Food Mart for just these six items. And yet with two liquid things, the canvas bag will be heavy by the time I get home from the market on Main Street. Finally I go walking about the house, taking my list with me and hoping that somehow this little tour will enlighten me as to what is needed.

I notice that I have dirty dishes in my sink, and when I look for some sort of soap to wash them with, there is none. I add *soap* to my list. And then also put *washing things,* although I don't know what that might be. I proceed like this for another full hour until my list seems worthy of the dreaded trip to Raleigh's Food Mart. I only hope Trudy's shift is over by this time of day.

For this trip to the store, I wear dark colors and flat shoes, just in case. I would wear dark glasses as well, but it's cloudy today and I don't think I'd be able to see very well inside the store with them on.

To my relief, I make it to the car without experiencing another strange confrontation with Busybody Bea. Perhaps if I take enough time at the grocery store, I won't be home until after dark and I can sneak into the house unnoticed. Oh, for the days of locking gates, security systems, and neighbors who respected privacy and maintained boundaries.

I still find it hard to believe that it's gone...forever gone. I know how Scarlett O'Hara felt after Atlanta burned. But Scarlett was lucky: she still had Tara to return to. Oh, certainly, it was in disrepair, but at least she wasn't locked out and cast into the wind.

It takes me quite some time to find all the things on my list. I walk back and forth, this way and that, through the grocery store every which way...until it feels that I've pushed this cart for miles and miles. Perhaps I have. Do they give out maps to grocery stores? Maybe one could somehow design a list that followed the blueprint of the store to save time and energy.

Still, I suppose the exercise is good for me. And at least I have a grocery cart to push and not one of those horrid little baskets that so easily tip over. I even bravely select a bottle of wine. But not Merlot. I don't think I'll want Merlot anytime soon.

When I finally make my way to the checkout, my cart is surprisingly full. The store seems much busier this time of day, and most of the lines are full. I suspect that's because of people who work during the day and have no choice. I make a mental note to come back at an earlier hour next time.

I notice a line toward the end with only two customers waiting in it, and neither of them has much to purchase. This must be my lucky day. I hurry over and get in line behind them. Feeling pleased with myself, I browse through the magazine rack while I wait and eventually decide upon the December issue of *Architectural Digest,* which is featuring "Hollywood Homes for the Holidays." It will be fun to see if anyone I know is in here.

"Excuse me, lady," says the sales clerk in a loud voice. "If you wanna check out, you'll have to put your stuff on the conveyer."

I look up from my magazine. "Oh…" I nod and place items on the black rubber belt that moves toward the cashier.

"Wait a minute, wait a minute!" He holds up his hands. "Don't you know this is the express line?" He points to the sign above his head.

"Well, yes. That's all right; I *am* in a hurry."

"No, that's not it, ma'am. You can't have more than ten items in this line."

"Ten?" I look into my fully loaded cart. "But I have more than that."

"My point." He shakes his head and nods to the people waiting behind me. "You'll have to go to another checkout."

"But I—"

"Sorry, lady, that's the rule. No exceptions. Especially during rush hour."

Feeling embarrassed and confused, I start to back up my cart.

"Get your stuff first," the man commands.

As I load my groceries back into my cart, I can feel the eyes of the people in line behind me watching. I'm sure they must think I'm a silly old fool. I pull out of the checkout and go to the end of another line. A long line this time.

"Hey, it's you again," says the cashier. I look up from the *People* magazine I'm now reading to see Trudy. "Did you get that stain out?"

"No." I set the magazine back and begin, once again, to set my groceries on the conveyor belt. I feel clumsy and slow, barely able to keep up with her as she rings up my purchases.

"That's too bad. Paper or plastic?"

"I'll pay with cash."

"No, I mean bags. Do you want paper bags or plastic ones?"

"Oh." I frown now. "What's the difference?"

She laughs. "One is paper. One is plastic. We usually have those reusable bags you can buy, but we're out today."

"Plastic, paper, what difference does it make?"

She studies me for a moment. "Is anyone helping you with these?"

"Helping me?"

"You know, once you get home? Anyone to help carry them into the house?"

"Well, no..."

"I think plastic then. And I won't load them too heavy. Plastic is easier to carry."

"Oh, okay." I look at her name tag again. "Thank you, Trudy."

"You new in town?"

"I grew up here. But I haven't lived here in ages. I recently moved back."

She nods as she puts my bananas in a plastic bag. "Where did you move from?"

"Beverly Hills."

"Wow." She stops and looks carefully at me. "Does that mean you're famous or something?"

I shrug. "Not too famous. I was an actress long ago. My husband was a director…"

"Really?" She looks impressed now. "What did he direct?"

"Oh, probably nothing you would've seen. It was a very long time ago."

"I watch Turner Classic Movies," she says. "I love the oldies."

"Have you ever heard of Gavin Fioré?"

"No way! He was your husband?"

I nod, a little self-conscious but also slightly vindicated after my embarrassing moment in the express line, which couldn't have been slower.

"That is so cool." She continues ringing up my items.

She chatters at me as she hits buttons and scans things. I don't know how she can talk and work simultaneously. She mentions some of her favorite old films and really does seem to have a grasp of classic Hollywood.

Finally she tells me the total, and I open my purse. I didn't realize groceries cost so much. As I search for the right amount of bills, I realize that I'm running low on cash. I remember Michael's suggestion that I open a local bank account and contact my accountant to transfer some money, since I asked for him to cancel all my credit cards when I suspected my staff was stealing from me. Fortunately I have enough cash to pay for my groceries. I'm not sure if I could've handled the embarrassment of being short.

Trudy hands me my change. "I'll call someone to help you out with that."

"Thank you."

"And it's very nice to meet you, Mrs. Fioré."

"You too, dear."

A young Hispanic man shows up and takes my cart for me. He's shorter than me and could pass for a twelve-year-old. I lead him out to the car and hand him the keys to open the trunk, waiting as he loads the bags of groceries. As I stand there I wonder, *Do you tip these people?* No one has ever told me about these things. So, not wanting to insult him, I open my purse again, pull out a five, and hand it to him in exchange for my keys.

His dark eyes grow large. "What's this for?"

"It's a tip."

"Wow, thanks, lady. This is my first tip."

That answers my question about tipping. Now I wonder if that young man will be overly eager to help me with my groceries whenever I shop here. And if so, should I continue tipping him, or should I simply explain my ignorance? *Live and learn,* I tell myself as I start my car.

At least it's dark out now, and I don't think Busybody Bea will be running out to chatter nonsense at me. And if she does,

I'll hand her some bags and ask her to help carry groceries for me. That should shut her up. As many bags as are in my trunk, it'll take an hour to get it all into the house.

It turns out that I'm not far off in my estimate. By the time I've made at least a dozen trips from the car to the house and back again, it is well past seven. As I stand in my kitchen amid what looks like a blizzard of white plastic bags, it occurs to me— I still have to put all these things away.

I feel like crying or simply going to bed and forgetting about the whole thing. But then I realize they'll still be here tomorrow. Not only that, but some of the things might spoil. I may not know much about housekeeping or cooking, but I do know that meat and dairy products need to be refrigerated.

I open a bag and focus on things that need to be chilled. But soon I have dozens of items, everything from toilet tissue to Tums to cottage cheese strewn on all the countertops, the dining table, and even the chairs. I don't even know where I'll put all these things.

I finally take a break, clearing a chair so I can sit down. I open a box of rye crackers and eat directly from the box as I survey the dismal mess I've created. Oh, why is this so hard? And why did I buy so many things?

And perhaps the hardest question is, how do ordinary people live like this?

Eventually I manage to put the perishable foods in the fridge. But that's where I give up. Then I pour myself a tall glass of orange juice, wishing I'd bought some vodka to go with it. I break off a banana and take these out to the living room, which feels blessedly uncluttered compared to my kitchen.

I open the cabinet that contains a small television, take the remote back to the couch, then kick off my shoes and settle back. Hearing Trudy at the grocery store talking about Turner Classic Movies has put me in the mood to watch an old film, but when I click on the television, all I see is a blank blue screen. I try changing the channels and pushing all sorts of buttons, but nothing seems to work. Then I vaguely remember something on Michael's list about cable service. I turn off the television, peel my banana, sip my orange juice, and try not to envy the people who understand these simple complexities of daily living.

The next morning, at half past nine, I am rudely awakened by the sound of knocking and doorbell ringing. I remain in bed, trying to ignore the noisy interruption, but it goes on and on.

Finally I put on my robe and go out to see what's the matter. I suspect it's my busybody neighbor, and when I open the door, I'm proven right.

"Good morning," Bea says brightly. She's got something wrapped in foil in her hands. For all I know it might be a bomb or a dead animal.

"What do you want?"

"I want to be neighborly," she says with a smile. "I brought you some pumpkin nut bread. I just made it fresh this morning."

"You made it *yourself*?" I say, imagining the worst.

She pulls open the screen door and thrusts her foil-wrapped offering directly beneath my nose. "Take a whiff. It's still warm."

To my surprise it smells rather good.

"Got any coffee?" Bea asks.

"I do have coffee, though it's not made."

And then to my utter surprise, she pushes her way into my house. "Well, let's make up a pot and have some of this pumpkin bread with it."

"Well, I—"

"No problem. You go get yourself dressed, and I'll make up the coffee." She literally pushes me through the living room as I protest. "Go on with you. I'll slice up the bread and get the coffee going, then we'll sit down and have a nice little chat. Your mother and I used to do this all the time."

Flummoxed and annoyed, I go back to my room. I am half tempted to get back into bed and pretend I haven't just been invaded. However, that will not get this woman out of my house. I find my warmup suit on the chair and grumble as I pull it on.

Just who does this woman think she is? Perhaps my mother didn't mind such intrusions, but I am not my mother. I march out to the kitchen, fully prepared to give this obnoxious woman a large piece of my mind.

"What happened in here?" she demands when I walk in.

"What do you mean?"

"All this stuff all over the place... Looks like we had an earthquake or something."

"I was putting things away."

"I thought you were sleeping."

"Last night," I snap at her. "I got tired and left it until morning."

She puts her hands on her wide hips and just shakes her head. "I think you need lessons in housekeeping, Claudette. When I saw this place the other day, while your gay boyfriend was still here, it was all in apple pie order. Now he's been gone a few days, and you've let the place go to hell in a handbasket."

"Michael let you into this house?"

"Sure, he gave me the complete tour. And I was impressed. That man might be fruity, but he sure knows how to put a place together." She makes a *tsk-tsk* sound. "And you sure know how to mess it up. I can't even find your coffee maker."

I am about to tell her to take her pumpkin bread and stuff it where the sun doesn't shine, but she suddenly starts opening cupboards and poking around.

"What do you think you're doing?"

"Helping." She puts a can of soup away. Then she picks up a box of bran cereal and holds it up. "You really eat this stuff?"

I don't answer her. I just stand there, staring in amazement as, one by one, she puts my groceries away. She talks the whole time, saying why you put cans in one cupboard and boxed things in another, as if that should all make sense. Eventually I go and sit down, continuing to watch this crazy woman putting things away.

Today her outfit is a bit more subdued, although tacky as usual. Her polyester pants are a rust color, and her top, which I suspect is also polyester, is a floral design I think is supposed to resemble autumn leaves but looks more like a bad buffet table. And once again she's wearing those horrible canvas deck shoes that were probably white at one time but look grayer every time I see her.

It takes a while, but finally she is done. And despite my irritation, I must admit, at least to myself, that the kitchen does look better. Will she wash my dirty dishes next? I don't think I'd complain. Even so, I do not let on that I'm pleased. More than anything I'd like this woman to leave.

"Now, where is your coffee maker?"

With a grim expression, I point to the espresso machine situated in the corner. I've only used it a couple of times, and although Michael wrote explicit instructions that I keep in the knife drawer, I still feel challenged.

"That's a coffee maker?" She bends over and peers at the large stainless-steel machine. "How on earth do you use it?"

I slowly get up, go over, extract my cheat sheet from the drawer, and following it step by step without saying a word, I grind the coffee and go through the paces of creating espresso. As I'm doing this, Bea slices her pumpkin bread, still chattering as if she thinks I care to listen.

"I used to make pumpkin bread from real pumpkins, but then I tried using canned pumpkin and I realized the bread was even better. And, good grief, the time it saves you. Instead of cutting, peeling, and cooking a pumpkin, you just take out a can opener. Couldn't be easier."

She's sitting at the table now, the sliced pumpkin bread on a plate beside my vase of flowers. She's even put out a couple of small plates and napkins. I pour two cups of espresso, put them on saucers, then go to the fridge for cream. I set these things down for myself and my uninvited guest, and then I sit down.

"That's awfully strong coffee," she says after a sip. "You sure you made it right?"

"It's espresso." I reach for a slice of pumpkin bread. I smell the slice and pause before I take a bite, waiting to make sure she does the same. Not that I think anything is wrong with it, exactly. I seriously doubt this woman came over here to poison me this morning, although she probably shouldn't trust me not to poison her.

"Mmm-mmm." She actually smacks her lips. "Nothing like nice, warm pumpkin bread, fresh from the oven."

I nod but do not speak. It is actually very good, but I refuse to give her the satisfaction of knowing I like it. I do not want this woman on my doorstep every morning—even if she does come bearing gifts of food.

Bea pours a generous amount of cream into her espresso, and I take another bite of bread, savoring the spices and nuts. Perhaps I could purchase a loaf from her. Or would that only encourage her?

"Your gay boyfriend told me—"

"Please. His name is Michael."

"Fine." She waves her hand in the ridiculous "fairy flip," as Michael sometimes calls it. "*Michael* told me you weren't used to keeping house. He even suggested that I come over and give you some tips."

"He did, did he?" I reach for a second piece of pumpkin bread and imagine the scathing conversation I will be having with Michael when my phone is functioning.

"Yes. And I can see that he's right. You need help, Claudette."

"I've always had housekeepers and servants." Perhaps the pumpkin bread is softening me up a bit. "Taking care of these things myself is new to me."

"Do you know how to wash dishes?"

"Well, of course. I used to wash dishes as a child, and I'm sure it's like riding a bicycle."

"How about laundry? Do you know how to do laundry?"

"I saw Michael do it. It seemed rather elementary." I don't tell her that I even know about dryer sheets.

"There's a lot to housekeeping—dusting, vacuuming, washing windows. Most people don't go about it right, but I believe a well-maintained house is its own reward."

"Right…" I restrain myself from rolling my eyes.

"Your mother was a good housekeeper."

"My mother spent the best part of her life cleaning, cooking, doing laundry…and I do not intend to imitate her in that regard."

"You could do a lot worse. Your mother was a fine woman. I respected her a lot." Bea actually sniffs. "And I still miss her."

"Yes, I'm sure…"

"Well, I know you consider my visit an invasion of your privacy," she says as she finishes off the last of her coffee. "And I get the feeling you're not the friendly, outgoing type. Come to think of it, you never were. So I figured it was up to me to reach out to you. We're not getting any younger, Claudette, and like it or not, neighbors are like birds of a feather—we need to stick together. So you might as well count on me knocking on your door from time to time. And I hope you'll do the same to me someday." She wipes her mouth on the napkin. "I'll leave you be now, but if you need any housekeeping tips, I'm right next door."

"I'll keep that in mind."

Bea slaps her forehead. "Oh, I plumb forgot what I came over here to tell you. I'll be heading out to my daughter Polly's house around noon today."

I nod in a vague sort of way, wondering why she thinks I need this bit of trivial information from her.

"And I'll be gone clear until the weekend. I just thought you should know." Then she peers curiously at me. "What are you doing for Thanksgiving?"

"Thanksgiving?" I frown. "When is it?"

"Thursday, of course."

"*This* Thursday?"

"That's right. Have you got plans? Maybe spend time with your sister and her kids?"

"Yes…something like that. By the way, what day is it today?" I am so embarrassed to have to ask this, but I really have no idea.

"It's Tuesday. Thanksgiving is two days away."

"Oh yes. I suppose I lost track of time…since the move and all…"

She laughs as she stands. "I know just how you feel. I used to have trouble knowing what day it was too. Then I got myself a nice big calendar that's easy to read, along with one of those boxes you keep your prescription pills in. You know the kind with days of the week printed right on each compartment? Real handy. Do you have one of those?"

"No."

"Why, you should get yourself one. How else can you keep track of when you took your last pills?"

"I don't take pills."

She looks shocked. "No pills?"

"Well, I did take vitamins. Just a multiple and one with calcium and those horrid-tasting fish oil pills, but I seem to have misplaced them during the move."

"But no prescriptions?" She shakes her head. "And here you are older than me. I take one for blood pressure, one for high cholesterol, one for my bone density since I started getting osteoporosis. And besides that I take a baby aspirin every day. You don't even take a baby aspirin?"

"I used to give them to my husband. But, no, I haven't taken them myself."

"Well, you should. Everyone our age should do that."

"Thank you for the medical advice," I say in a chilly voice. "I'll consider it."

"Sure. And if you want to read my AARP magazine, it's full of good tips for old girls like you and me."

"Yes, I'm sure it is…" I start to stand now.

"Don't you get up, Claudette, I can see myself out."

"Thank you for the pumpkin bread."

"You're welcome. And you have a nice Thanksgiving, you hear?"

"Yes…the same to you."

I listen as she walks through my living room. She pauses, as if she's looking at something in there, but then a few seconds pass and I hear the front door open and then the screen door slam shut. She's gone. I let out a relieved breath. And then I reach for another slice of pumpkin bread. It's really not bad.

Bea is obnoxious, there is no doubt, but the fact that she put my kitchen back in order is somewhat encouraging. So I clear the table and add the dishes to those that have been collecting in the sink. It's really gotten to be quite a pileup. Feeling slightly inspired by the cleared countertops, I decide that the time has come to wash the dishes.

I stand there for a moment, leaning against the sink and straining my memory back to my childhood, trying to remember how this was done. I used to do the dishes quite a bit…and I usually complained about it too. I didn't like how it made my fingernails soft. We used to have this horrible dishpan we put in one side of the sink. We'd fill it with hot, soapy water and then rinse the dishes alongside it. We also had a wire dish drainer to place the clean dishes in. Neither of which I have now.

Even so, I should be able to do this. Really, how hard can it be? I remove the dirty dishes from the soapstone sink. Then I scrub the sink with the dishwashing soap, but when I search for something to stop the sink and keep the water from going down the drain, I find nothing. I stand there for several minutes, just trying to figure out the answer to what I know must be a very simple question. And yet it evades me.

Why not simply do this the old way—with a dishpan and a dish drainer? Except that I have no idea where one purchases such things, or if people actually use them anymore. My Beverly Hills house had two automatic dishwashers. Not that I ever used them myself, but I do recall seeing them in the large kitchen. Sometimes one of them, or even both if we'd had a party, were running.

I briefly entertain the idea of asking Bea about where I might find these tools, but that could entail another long, drawn-out conversation that would only contribute to her because-we-are-neighbors-we-must-now-become-friends theory. I consider the grocery store, but I'm not ready to return to Raleigh's quite yet. Besides, I don't recall seeing things like that, although I might've missed them.

Then I remember Harper's Hardware. I sometimes went there with my mother when she was looking for a light bulb or an extension cord or some other odd household item. Perhaps Harper's would have what I need. If my phone were charged, I could call them and find out. And that reminds of Radio Shack, and I wonder if the phone charger cord has arrived. So I decide to drive to town.

I go to the hardware store first, because that seems more pressing. And to my delight, a young woman directs me to exactly what I need. Not only that, but I also notice a bucket of rakes for leaf removal, and I put one in my cart as well. By now I know that a shopping cart with wheels, like matching shoes and handbags, is a must. Feeling confident and assured, I get into the line—after making certain it's not the express lane— set my selected purchases on the counter, and wait as the clerk rings them up. But as he's telling me the total, which isn't very much, considering, I realize that I only have six dollars and some change. And that is not enough.

"Is there a problem?" he asks as I stare at my wallet.

I look up at him, I'm sure, with flaming cheeks. "Well, yes... I'm sorry, but I seem to be short of cash." I take in a quick breath.

"We take Visa, MasterCard, American Express, and—"

"I only have one card with me, and I'm afraid it's expired. You see, I just moved to town, and I'm—"

"You can set up an account with us." He pulls out a yellow sheet of paper. "It's pretty easy. You just fill in the form, we put it in the computer, and if you buy enough stuff you even get bonus points."

"Bonus points?" I echo, unsure of what that even means.

"Yeah. Why don't you move down there and fill it out while I wait on the dude behind you?"

So I take the form and carefully fill in the blanks—some of which I leave blank—and then hand it back to the clerk. For whatever reason, he seems content with my effort and punches some things into his computer register, prints out a receipt, which he has me sign, then bags up my items and tells me to "have a good day."

I thank him and feel slightly like a thief as I leave. But as I put my rake and things into the back of the car, I remind myself of how many other things—very expensive things—I once bought on credit. I'm sure it should be just fine. However, now I'm not sure if I can afford the charging device at Radio Shack. And yet without it, how will I call Jackie Berkshire and get my funds transferred? Perhaps they have some sort of a revolving account as well.

To my relief, not only is my phone charger there, but the sales clerk is happy to open a Radio Shack account for me. "Your card will come in the mail in a few weeks, and you can even upgrade it to a Visa account if you want," says the sales clerk. "And the more you use it, the more rewards you get."

"Rewards…" I say, pretending to be interested. Then I thank him, sign the receipt, and leave with my charging cord.

It's noon by the time I get home and take my packages out of my car. I glance nervously toward Bea's house, but all is quiet there. Her old blue Buick is gone, and I think she has already left for her daughter's. It should be a nice reprieve to have her gone a few days; no more unexpected morning visits for a bit. I should be relieved…but instead I feel slightly lonely.

I walk up to the porch and set my rake by the door for when I might possibly feel like raking, although I don't expect it to be today. There's a nip in the air, and the breeze is picking up. I overheard two men talking at the hardware store earlier, saying that the weather pattern was changing and that "the temps were going to get low tonight."

It's been so long since I've lived in a place that gets cold, and after sixty years, one's personal thermostat grows accustomed to the warm Southern California climate. So much so that I have no problem wearing lightweight wool or cashmere during the winter months, although I've noticed that younger people dress as if it's summertime year-round. But how will my old bones adjust to these extreme changes in temperature?

Once I'm in the house, I set my dishwashing tools in the kitchen and even briefly consider tackling this lackluster chore. But I really feel tired, not to mention a bit chilled, and perhaps a short nap is in order.

Before I allow myself to nap, I plug in my new phone charger. I place this on my little secretary desk in the office/guest room, which at the moment is the tidiest place in the house. Then I set my cell phone in the cradle and wait until the little blue light goes on to show that it's working. I expect the phone should be up and running in a few hours. Perhaps I'll even call Michael and tell him how well I'm getting on. Although "well" is probably an exaggeration, but at least I'm still alive and I haven't given up yet.

I go to my room, where my bed is still unmade (ever since Michael left), and a rather unbecoming pile of clothing is accumulating on the easy chair. Oh, how I miss my maids and housekeepers…dry-cleaning services that delivered…fresh, clean sheets and towels.

The bedroom, like the rest of the house, is rather chilly. I must remember to turn up the thermostat when I finish my nap. Michael showed me how to do that before he left. I just hope I can remember. But if it's going to be cold, a bit more heat would be most welcome.

I put the throw blanket around my shoulders like a shawl, then get into bed and reach for my novel. After a few minutes my hands are so cold I set the novel aside and pull the comforter up to my chin. Thank goodness for down feathers, because soon I'm feeling warmer. And then I'm sleepy.

When I wake up it's dusky outside, and my nose is so cold it feels slightly numb. I get out of bed to discover it's even colder now than it was earlier. With the throw blanket still wrapped around my shoulders like a granny's shawl, I dash out to the end of the hallway where the thermostat to the oil furnace is located. This is not the same furnace we had when I was younger. I don't know when Mother replaced it, but this model is much smaller and, according to Michael, much more efficient. Or at least it was when we arrived.

Right now the thermostat is set on seventy-two degrees, which Michael assured me should be comfortable, but then he's not here for this cold front that's swept in. I turn the thermostat up to eighty-five degrees. If that's too hot, I'll simply turn it down before bedtime. But when I reach down to where the hot air is supposed to blow out, it is stone cold. No air seems to be coming out at all. Is this thing even on? But the little light on the thermostat is glowing orange so it must be getting some sort of energy. Perhaps some part of it is broken.

I run back to my bedroom to put something on my bare feet, which are now freezing cold. I dig through my drawers until I find a couple pairs of thick socks, and I layer these on. Then I take out several cashmere cardigans, also layering them on. I must look very unstylish, but it's preferable to freezing. I also layer on pants, pulling my looser velour warmup pants over two pairs of lightweight wool. I look at myself in the full-length mirror and gasp. The fashion factor is bad enough, but with all these layers of clothing, I now look as if I've gained thirty pounds. Well, no matter. No one will be seeing me tonight.

Feeling a bit warmer, I check on my phone. It's high time to start making phone calls. My plan is to begin with my accountant. I'll ask Jackie to transfer some funds to Silverton immediately. It's not quite five yet; he might even be able to do this today. But when I try to use my phone, it doesn't seem to be working. It appears to be charged just fine, but when I dial the number, it simply says "no service." I try several different numbers, including Michael's, thinking he might be able to tell me how to fix this little problem, but nothing seems to be working.

It could be my fault, since I've never been terribly clever with all these modern-day electronic devices. Gavin always seemed to understand these things. He would set up computers or video machines for us. Even my phone was purchased and programmed by him. When he first got it for me, I simply had to punch the speed dial button and the number one and I would reach Gavin within seconds. If only I could do that now.

Finally I give up on the stupid phone, which I'm tempted to toss to the floor and stomp on. I have a more pressing need at the moment. Thanks to having taken an extra large dosage of Citrucel this morning, I am headed for the bathroom. Once there, I quickly discover that it's not easy to use the toilet when one is wearing too many layers. It takes a while to finally get myself situated, and then I'm so cold I'm literally shivering. The bathroom must be the coldest spot in the whole house, and the sooner I'm out of here, the better. Fortunately the Citrucel quickly does its magic.

I hurry to flush the toilet. Then as I'm pulling on my first layer of pants, I notice that instead of going down, the murky looking contents are rising. In desperation, I push the handle again, hoping this second flush will do the trick, but now the water is dangerously high, about to overflow.

With one pair of pants now zipped and two others still around my knees, I hop about, pulling up my pants as the white tile floor begins to resemble a fetid cesspool. I back away from this foul mess, trying to keep my feet on high ground, when I notice my expensive silk carpet from India is about to be ruined.

I lunge for it, hoping to snatch up the rug before it's too late, but the combination of wet floor and slippery socks causes me to lose my footing, and I plunge sideways, falling smack into the nasty, reeking mess.

There I lie for a few stunned seconds, unsure as to whether I have broken any bones or permanently injured myself. But as

I use the edge of the tub to pull myself up to a standing position, I seem to be in one piece.

Seeing that it's too late for the precious carpet, not to mention myself and these layers of soiled and stinking clothes, I allow the silk carpet to play the role of a giant sponge, sopping up the foul sewage water. I stand there next to the shower, peeling off my ruined clothing, including three layers of cashmere, and tossing all these soggy items to the floor.

Standing there buck naked and freezing and feeling as if I've just taken a tumble into an outhouse, I cannot imagine how life could possibly get any worse. I am certain I have reached an all-time low. Either I will die tonight or things will get better. I'm not sure I even care which way it goes.

Shivering uncontrollably, I turn on the shower, wait for the water to get steaming hot, and then get in. I lather Christian Dior shower soap from head to toe and am just beginning to thaw out when I realize that my feet are in standing water. For some reason the shower is not draining properly and the water level, reminiscent of the toilet episode, is about to flow over the edge.

I turn off the water, then grab for several towels. Some of these I throw onto the floor, hoping to create something of a path, an escape route to the door. I wrap the remaining towel around me, making a quick exit and closing the door to the useless and malodorous bathroom.

By the time I reach my bedroom, I am concerned about the possibility of hypothermia. And part of me thinks I should simply give in to it and die. I've heard of old Eskimos being set out on icebergs and left to perish. Perhaps I should surrender to the chilling temperature as well. The problem is that I have always loathed being cold. So I hurry to towel myself dry, rubbing so hard that I'm certain my skin will be raw and bleeding when I'm done. And, once again, I must layer on clothes. Unfortunately I've already used and ruined my warmest items of clothing.

Then I remember the extra clothing Michael stored for me, things that didn't fit in the two closets and that I might want to get rid of. Perhaps some of those clothes are warm. I dash out to the laundry room, which is little more than an enclosed porch and, believe it or not, far colder than the frosty bathroom.

I open some plastic crates and unzip the canvas wardrobe, ransacking through my old clothes until I have a heavy armful of items and run back into the house. I throw these things down into a heap in the middle of the living room and return to search out some more. As odd as it seems, I almost feel as if I'm searching for lost treasure.

I return to the living room and sort through these random pieces of warmer clothing. Most of these things are old, and I don't even know why I held on to them, although I'm glad now I did. I carry a bunch of things to my bedroom and begin to layer on my odd assortment of miscellaneous pants and tops and socks. I even managed to unearth a red woolen ski hat, a souvenir from a long-ago ski trip in Switzerland; a lime green cashmere muffler from a few Christmases back; and a pair of thick suede gloves in an awful shade of purple. And once I'm dressed, I add these colorful accessories to my already strange ensemble.

When I'm done, I stare at the image of myself in the mirror and don't know whether to laugh or cry. Not only do I look forty pounds heavier now, but I'm a complete fashion nightmare in clownish colors. I'm sure I could beat my neighbor Bea out of a "fashion don't" magazine spot.

The truth is, I've thought about Bea a couple of times throughout tonight's crisis. I actually wish she were home. I think I would happily take refuge there, or at least use her phone to call for some emergency assistance. I don't know what to do. I consider going to the hardware store to see if they have some sort of heating unit that can be run on electricity, but it's after six and I feel fairly certain they're closed.

Besides, would I really want to be seen in public tonight? Not only do I look frightening, but I'm sure I don't smell very nice either. Despite my hasty shower and Christian Dior soap, that nasty sewage smell still clings to me, even after I douse myself and my clothes with a generous splash of expensive Bvlgari perfume. Even if I do get free of the smell, I doubt I will ever be able to erase that stench from my memory.

The only good that's come out of the plumbing catastrophe is that, due to all the running about, I feel slightly warmer. I go check on the furnace again, thinking perhaps it's working after all. But it's still cold as ice. I give the machine a kick, in case something is jammed. But still nothing. I go and try my cell phone again, but it's not cooperating either. It's obviously charged, but it refuses to connect.

I pace about the house, feeling like a trapped animal about to be led to the slaughter. Finally I stop in the living room, still clutching my useless phone in an ugly purple glove. The living room, no longer my peaceful pumpkin haven, is now strewn with the clothing I carried in here earlier. It must look like the dressing room of a homeless shelter. But what difference does it make? Why should I even care?

In complete frustration, I use my last bit of strength and fury to hurl my useless cell phone into the fireplace. Then I begin to sob. "*Why me? Why me?* Oh, God, if there is a God, *why me?*" Tears run down my chilled cheeks now. "Please, God," I cry out even louder now. "If you are really there, can't you please, please help me?"

In a state of complete destitution, I sink down into one of the leather chairs that flank the fireplace. I just sit there, staring at the shiny silver pieces of my smashed phone against the soot-darkened bricks. I keep asking myself, *What should I do? What should I do?* And then, like a bolt from the blue, it hits me—my own mother used to make fires right here in this very fireplace.

Occasionally when it was cold out and we actually had firewood, Mother would make a nice, cozy fire. Violet and I loved it when she did this, and sometimes we'd even make popcorn in a clever basket Mother had concocted out of an old piece of window screen and a wire hanger.

A fire could take the chill off this house. Perhaps if I close the doors to the rest of the house, this room would get warm enough that I might bring my down comforter in here. I could sleep on the sofa tonight. It might even be cozy. The question is, do I have firewood? Is there any chance that Mother had stashed some away before she died?

I remember how kind neighbors would sometimes bring us firewood. I know they felt sorry for us; they knew Father was a good-for-nothing…and that Mother struggled hard just to get by. I also remember that what little firewood we managed to accumulate was kept dry in the little woodshed out back.

And despite our love of a nice, warm fire, Violet and I despised going into the woodshed because it was full of spiders. We'd heard that spiders, including brown recluses and black widows, enjoyed inhabiting dark, musty places just like that. Consequently, we would argue about whose turn it was to go out there to get a Mason jar, a garden tool, or some firewood. And for the most part, unless there was an emergency, we only went out to the shed in the daytime.

"But this is an emergency," I remind myself. I can do this task very quickly. I will simply go straight in, grab some wood, and then come straight out and back to the house. However, I do not relish the idea of carrying pieces of spider-infested firewood in my arms. I must find something to put the wood into.

I walk around the house trying to spot something large enough to carry a few sticks of wood. Finally I remember the trash container beneath the kitchen sink. I pull out the white plastic bin to discover that my wine-stained Armani suit is still stuffed into it. I remove it, toss it onto the kitchen floor, then telling myself this is an "adventure" and something I can tell Michael or even Caroline about later, I go out to the back porch, turn on the outside light, and march outside.

It takes a few seconds for my eyes to adjust to the darkness, but the path that leads to the shed, though somewhat over-grown, is still visible. And when I open the door to the shed, the light from the back porch illuminates it just enough for me to see that there is indeed a small stack of firewood there. I am greatly relieved, although still worried about spiders. So I reach in very gingerly, using my purple suede gloves for protection, to pull out one piece at a time and drop it into the garbage can.

Soon I have several pieces and room for no more. But cer-tainly this should be a good starter. I'll get things warmed up a little and come out here for more. Perhaps I'll bring a candle next time. My teeth are chattering as I carry my bucket up the back porch steps, and it occurs to me that I'm wearing my slippers.

I set down my bucket of firewood so I can open the door. That's when I discover it's locked. I give it a pull and push and a tug and finally a kick, which thanks to the lightweight slipper manages only to bruise my toe. It's no use. This solid wooden door is securely locked.

I try to recall if I locked the front door when I came home. So much has happened tonight that my memory feels blurry.

But I sometimes forget to lock the front door until I'm in bed and it's late at night and I'm worried about a break-in. So, carrying my bounty of firewood, I hurry around the side of the house and up onto the front porch. But this door is locked as well. And now my slippers are thoroughly soaked from the wet grass. And despite my layers and this most recent form of exercise, I am growing colder by the minute.

I glance over to Bea's house, but it's dark and quiet, and I know she's not home. She cannot help me. I look across the street to where Caroline once lived. But a new family lives there now, a family I haven't even said "boo" to. Besides, what can they do for me? What can anyone do for me? Do I really want the world to know that I'm in such straits? Do I really want to be seen like this, dressed as I am? Smelling of perfumed sewage?

I sit on the little wooden bench that has been on this porch for as long as I can remember. It's where Violet and I were supposed to sit on a rainy day to remove our rubber boots before going into the house. Too bad I didn't wear rubber boots tonight. My feet would at least be dry.

I look through the screen and through the leaded glass window and into the house. It looks surprisingly warm and cozy in there. Even if it's on the chilly side, it can't be nearly as bad as this. If I stay out here much longer, I probably really will develop hypothermia. And as much as I feel ready to depart this world, I do not relish the idea of being found frozen, in ugly clothes and bad hair, and locked out of my own house.

I don't know if there's such a thing as humiliation after death, but I don't think I care to find out. And I don't like thinking about the news article that might be written. "The late Gavin Fioré's widow found dead on porch, dressed like derelict, and smelling of raw sewage. Authorities question her sanity..." No, if I'm going to leave this world of my own volition, I would like to do so in the way that I have lived, at least until recently—*in style*.

I stand up and kick the trash basket of firewood, spilling the contents out on the porch. A lot of good that does me now. I pick up a piece of wood and shake it in the air. And then, just like a scene out of an Alfred Hitchcock movie where the burglar breaks through a glass door to gain entry, it hits me. Of course! How simple. How stupidly simple! Even if I have to pay to replace the leaded glass, what is that compared to freezing to death out here?

I swing the sturdy piece of firewood, testing it. And then, holding it like a club, I bash it into the window right above the doorknob with a blast. Then, carefully, just like a real second-story man, I reach in through the shattered opening and unlock the deadbolt. And just like that, I am in.

I'm surprised that it actually does feel a tiny bit warmer inside. I go back to the porch and gather up the rest of the wood. Then, pretending I'm a Boy Scout or perhaps a member of one of those survivor shows that are so popular on reality television, I set out to make a fire. Now, I've seen Gavin make a fire before, but that usually amounted to simply striking a match and igniting something one of our housekeepers had already laid out for him. But I do recall that crumpled-up paper and smaller pieces of wood were involved. So I go off in search of something that will possibly suffice. I don't have any smaller pieces of wood. And based on this evening's luck, I don't trust myself with an ax. Not that I would even find one. But I decide to create my own kindling (I believe that's what it's called).

I discover a good-sized cardboard box in the laundry room in which Michael had placed some miscellaneous kitchen things. I dump these items onto the already messy kitchen floor, and then I locate a big knife and begin to shred this box into smaller pieces. After that I search for paper.

Unfortunately I don't find any newspapers, but I do notice the issue of *Architectural Digest* I recently bought. And without sacrificing the feature on Hollywood homes for the holidays, which I've yet to read, I tear out a number of other glossy pages and crumple them up into neat little balls that I stack on top of each other to make a small hill.

Upon this I lay the strips of cardboard, then on that I place the firewood I brought in from outside. I stand back and smile at my efforts. I really do think this will do the trick.

Except that I need a match or a lighter. Michael lit candles the evening before he left. I remember the drawer he set up for me in the kitchen. He called it my "everything" drawer and said it might contain whatever odd thing I'd be looking for. I pull it open and there, along with some small tools, masking tape, nails and screws, and some things I don't even recognize, is a box of old-fashioned wooden matches. I truly feel victorious now. Certainly I may have been bullied tonight and even beat up some, but I refuse to let this house get the best of me. Not yet. And not without a good fight. After that, well, I'll have to wait and see.

As I'm leaving the kitchen, I notice a bottle of Cabernet on the counter. That might be just the thing to celebrate my triumph over the nonworking furnace and the possibility of freezing tonight. I imagine myself by my crackling fire, sipping some fine red wine, reading my novel. It's a happy scene. Perhaps I'll fix myself a nice plate of crackers and cheese, maybe even slice an apple to go with it.

I open the wine bottle and take it, along with a goblet and my precious box of matches, back to the living room. Then I stoop down, strike the match, and ignite my fire. To my pleasure, it immediately takes off. The magazine pages and the cardboard leap into colorful flames. I then fill my wine goblet and actually toast myself and my fire as I sit down. But just as I take my first sip, I notice that the smoke is not going up the chimney like it's supposed to. Instead, it's puffing out sideways, billowing toward me and threatening to fill the living room. I set down my glass and attempt to blow on the fire, thinking perhaps I can force it another direction, but my blowing only increases the flames and the smoke, which is still not going up the chimney. This fire must be extinguished!

I race back to the kitchen. Water…water will put a fire out. I look through the cupboard for a container to carry water in, but all I see is a crystal decanter that holds perhaps a quart or two. No matter! Smoke is now coming into the kitchen! I grab the decanter, rush to the sink, and turn on the water full blast. As I'm filling the decanter, my elbow knocks over one of the stacks of dirty dishes, sending pieces of Limoges crashing to the floor. I cannot deal with that now. I have a fire to put out.

I race back to the living room, now full of smoke, and douse the fire, shaking the heavy decanter so hard it slips from my hands and flies smack into the fireplace to shatter on the bricks. But the water quenches the flames, and soon my fire, along with my hope, sputters and smolders and slowly dies…until all that's left are ashes, damp charred wood, and splinters of broken crystal.

The fire may be out, but the house is still blue with smoke, and I'm beginning to hack and cough. I open the front door to let in some fresh air. I briefly, very briefly, consider the possibility of an intruder walking in, but what kind of desperate burglar would dare enter this house of horrors? And if someone really is that stupid, I simply do not care. He can rob me and slit my throat, and before I die I will sit up, shake his hand, and thank him for putting me out of this misery.

I am done trying. This house, this life, perhaps even God himself, have beaten me. I am finished. I pick up my goblet and the bottle of Cabernet and slowly walk to my bedroom where, thankfully, the closed door has kept some of the smoke at bay. I go in and close the door behind me. Still fully dressed in my ridiculous layers of clothing, with bottle and glass in hand, I get into my bed, where I proceed to drink every last drop. This is far more than I would normally drink, but I do not care. I hope it will either poison me or numb me long enough for hypothermia to set in and kill me.

I turn off the light, pull my comforter up to my nose, and prepare to meet my maker. If I have a maker, which I seriously doubt. And if I do have a maker, I am fully prepared to give him a generous and candid piece of my greatly troubled mind.

When morning comes, I am surprised to still be here, but I think perhaps I'm dying. My head is throbbing, my throat is raw and dry, and my nose feels as if it's frostbitten. I'm still in my bed, still wearing my red ski hat, purple gloves, and all the layers of clothing. But I am not getting up. My plan is to stay here indefinitely, until the end, which I hope isn't too far off now. I close my eyes and try to remember my home in Beverly Hills...try to remember Gavin...try to remember what it felt like to be young and beautiful...and warm.

I've nearly conjured up a pleasant image, something to transport me far away from this hellish place, when I hear the sound of footsteps. It sounds as if someone is on the front porch. Is it possible that Busybody Bea is back? that she will be knocking on my door? No matter, I will not get up. I will not answer. Let her knock all day.

"Claudette?" I hear a woman's voice calling. I'm not sure it's Bea, but it sounds as if she's actually inside my house. I sit up in bed, remembering that I left the front door open last night. Oh, good grief, can't an old woman simply die in peace?

"*Violet!*" yells the same voice. "Get in here now! Something is wrong!"

"Will you look at that!" says a male voice.

"Oh dear!" exclaims a voice that must belong to my sister. "Something is terribly wrong here."

"Someone has broken in," says the male. "Did you see the broken window?"

"And it smells like smoke."

"And look at all this—someone has torn the place apart."

"Where is Claudette?" asks Violet.

"Do you think she's been hurt?"

"Should we call the police?" asks the male voice. "I think Roberto has a phone out in the van."

"Maybe we should see if she's still here first," says Violet.

"Yes, she might need help."

"Oh no!" cries Violet.

"A knife!" screeches the other female. "Is that blood?"

"What is that smell?" says the male.

"It smells like something dead," says the woman.

"Oh, my goodness!" cries Violet. "Do you suppose she's been murdered? Perhaps lying here dead for days?"

"It's coming from the bathroom."

"I can't bear to look!"

"Stand back, ladies."

I hear the squeak of the bathroom door, then a gasp.

"What is it, Eddie?" cries Violet.

"Oh!" exclaims the man. "I thought it was a body...but I think it's just clothing. There seems to be a plumbing problem in here."

"I'm going for Roberto!" cries the woman, and I hear the sound of clumping down the hallway.

"I'm going into the bedroom," says Violet urgently. "My sister may need help."

"This looks bad."

"Roberto!" screams the woman from the porch. "Get in here now! And bring your phone! There's been a crime! Hurry!"

I flop back down in bed, pulling the comforter all the way over my head. Oh, how I wish I were truly dead now. Despite the embarrassment of being found like this, I think this level of humiliation is more easily endured in death. At least no one expects you to explain anything. If I had a knife, I think I could actually slit my own throat just now. Blast that burglar who never showed up last night! My bedroom door slowly opens, and I pray for my heart to give out...or a stroke...anything.

"*Claudette?*" my sister's voice is shaky and barely audible. "Are you in here?"

"It looks like someone is in the bed," says the male voice quietly. "Not moving..."

"Do you think?" Violet's voice cracks, and she begins to sob. "Oh, Eddie, do you think she's—she's dead?"

"Roberto is here to help!" cries the other woman. "I have his phone. I am dialing 911 right now."

"Roberto," says my sister. "We think there's been a break-in...possibly a murder."

"Ees there a body?" asks a voice that obviously belongs to Roberto.

"We don't know," says Violet. "I can't bear to look."

"No, no...," says the other male voice, which must belong to Eddie from McLachlan Manor. "Let someone else do it for you. Why don't you step outside, Violet."

"No...I need to be here."

"Yes, we have an emergency situation. There's been a burglary and possibly a murder," says the other woman's voice. It must be my old friend Caroline. But why Violet brought these people to my house is a complete mystery to me. Not for the first time, I would like to murder my little sister. "The address? I don't know the number, but it's Sequoia Street, just a couple of blocks."

"258 Sequoia Street," says Violet.

"Stop!" I fling the comforter off my face as I sit up in bed—just in time to see their horrified faces. Caroline drops the cell phone and clutches her chest as if she's experiencing a heart attack. Meanwhile Eddie collapses onto my chair, which is piled high with clothing, including a brassiere that's dangling across the arm.

Violet just stands there with wide eyes and a gaping mouth. "You're not dead!" she finally gasps.

I glare at all of them. "No, unfortunately, I am still very much alive."

"I think I'm having a heart attack," says Caroline.

"Here." Eddie hurries to stand, helping her to the clothing-covered chair. "You sit here."

"Oh my." Caroline takes in a slow, deep breath.

"You are okay?" Roberto asks Caroline.

"Yes...just shocked." Caroline turns and looks at me with a puzzled expression. "But how about you, Claudette? Are you all right? Have you been injured? Should we call for medical assist—"

"No," I snap, "I have not been injured!"

Roberto bends down and picks up his phone, and looking embarrassed, he excuses himself and leaves the room. Too bad the others aren't as polite.

"But there *has* been a break-in?" Eddie stands by my bed now, peering down at me, as if I'm a specimen from some strange scientific experiment gone badly.

"The only break-in has been the result of you people," I tell them.

"But the front door was wide open," says Caroline.

"And the window was broken," adds Violet, "and—"

"And everything was messed up," says Eddie. "Things strewn all about as if an intruder was—"

"As I already explained, *there was no break-in.* And I would appreciate it if you trespassing interlopers would please leave me alone!" I stare at them, trying to absorb the fact that they are all in my bedroom. "Just why did you come here in the first place?"

"We wanted to invite you to come to McLachlan Manor for Thanksgiving dinner tomorrow." Caroline smiles.

"Not *all* of us," says Violet. "I only came along because we were going to see the Festival of Trees."

"We were going to invite you to that as well," says Caroline.

"*They* were," Violet adds, as if to make her position perfectly clear.

"So…would you like to get ready and come along?" Eddie asks in a tone that suggests he knows this is not likely.

"Thank you, but no thank you." I glare at my sister. "To *both* invitations, tomorrow and today."

"*What is wrong with you?*" demands Violet.

"What is wrong with *you*?" I shoot back at her. "I'm obviously having some difficulties right now, and yet you walk right into my home and you invade my private space. Did you simply come here to torment me?"

"No, of course not." Eddie shakes his head.

"But everything looked so strange," says Caroline. "We didn't know what to think. We assumed something was wrong."

"Well, now you know that's not the case. No one broke in. I am not dead. My only problem at the moment is that I want to be alone!"

"Not so quick." Violet frowns. "You scared us half to death, Claudette." She picks up the empty wine bottle and dangles it back and forth in front of me in an accusatory way. "You obviously have some problems."

"We're your friends, Claudette," Caroline says in a gentler voice. "Maybe we can help."

"Please, tell us," urges Eddie. "What is going on here?"

"And why are you wearing that ridiculous hat?" Violet drops the wine bottle back onto my bed. "And those silly purple gloves?"

"Because I was *freezing* to death!"

"Why didn't you just turn on the heat?"

"Because it wasn't working."

"Had you considered ordering some heating oil?"

I don't answer, but I do narrow my eyes at her.

"Well, that must be the problem with the heat." She wrinkles her nose, as if she's disgusted. "And what is that horrid smell in the bathroom? We thought we were about to discover your dead and decaying body in there."

"Too bad you didn't." I lean back against the pillows, folding my arms across my chest, wishing they would all just leave.

"What happened in there?" asks Caroline.

"Plumbing problem."

"Why didn't you call a plumber?" demands Violet.

I lean forward and screech at my sister. "None of your blasted business!"

"*Well!*" Violet takes a couple of steps backward.

Caroline stands now. Using her cane, she comes over to my bed and looks sadly down at me. "You are obviously having some problems, Claudette."

"*Obviously.*" I roll my eyes dramatically. "But they are *my* problems, thank you very much."

Caroline turns to my sister. "Has there been any concern about Alzheimer's?"

Violet shrugs. "It wouldn't surprise me a bit if she was losing her mind."

"I am not losing my mind! But I am losing my patience and would appreciate it if you would all leave. Now!" I pull the covers back and get out of bed, standing before them as if I am prepared to physically throw them out.

"What on earth are you wearing?" Violet holds her hand to her mouth as if to suppress laughter.

"As I said, I was cold," I growl at her. "Now if you will—"

She lets loose with a loud, snorting laugh. "I've never seen my fashionable sister looking so—"

"Violet," Caroline interrupts her.

I walk directly toward my sister, holding my purple gloved hands out as if I plan to wrap them tightly around her neck. And I must have a slightly crazed expression in my eyes, but I don't care. My goal is to frighten her.

"I think we should go. Come on, Violet." Eddie tugs her toward the door.

"Yes," says Caroline. "Let's go now."

And just like that, they are gone. I slam the door behind them and begin to stomp around my room, swearing profusely. I have never been a violent woman and never the sort of person to use such coarse language. Gavin frowned upon such behavior. But at the moment, I cannot control myself. I am so angry, so infuriated, so enraged... I honestly think if they hadn't taken Violet out of here, I might have strangled her with my own two gloves.

I can hear them talking in the living room. Why are they still in my house? Why can't they leave me alone? And then I hear the sound of a siren, growing louder, closer...and then it stops directly in front of my house. More voices. More questions. I pull my red ski hat down over my ears, trying not to hear the commotion out there. It's like a never-ending nightmare. Or perhaps I have died and this is hell. I would not be surprised.

Perhaps these people are simply trying to drive me mad. Perhaps my sister has concocted this evil plot. Maybe she sneaked over here when I was gone and turned off the furnace, stopped up the plumbing, plugged the chimney—all part of her devious plan to drive me out of this house so she can have it all for herself.

I sit on my bed and consider my new theory. The more I think about it, the more it seems plausible, the more it makes sense. My sister has always been jealous. She probably is out to get me. I remember the old *What Ever Happened to Baby Jane?* film that Billie starred in with the marvelous Bette Davis. Jane, played by Bette, was insanely jealous of her older sister's acting career. The aging sisters were living together, and Jane was torturing her older sister, Blanche, trying to drive the poor woman crazy. It all makes sense and—

"Ms. Fioré?"

I jump at the sound of a male voice and a knocking on the bedroom door.

"Can we talk to you?"

"What do you want?" I demand.

"We need to come in and see if you're okay," he says.

I make a groaning sound. "Fine. Let's get this over with."

A policeman and paramedic step into my bedroom, and I just shake my head.

"I'd like to do a quick medical check on you, if you don't mind," says the dark-haired paramedic. He's actually a nice-looking young man with an attractive profile, so I agree. I let him poke around on me, checking my pulse, heart rate, breathing, and such.

"So, am I alive?"

He grins. "You seem to be alive and healthy."

The policeman clears his throat. "I'm Officer Bradford, ma'am. And I need to ask you a few questions."

"Yes?"

"Did you experience a burglary?"

I let out a loud sigh. "No, as I told the others, I did not."

"Can you explain why the glass in the door is broken? Why it looks as if someone has gone through your things?"

I tell him the embarrassing story of having no heat, going out for firewood, and being locked out. I even explain the fireplace disaster.

He nods and makes notes.

"If you don't believe me, go and look around."

"And the bathroom situation?"

"The plumbing seems to have quit working."

"How long ago did this occur?"

"It all happened last night," I say impatiently.

"Wow," says the paramedic. "You had a bad night, didn't you?"

"Yes. It was rather horrific."

"Why didn't you call for help?" asks Officer Bradford.

"Because my phone was not working."

He frowns. "Sounds like not much is working for you, Ms. Fioré."

"Certainly seems that way, doesn't it?" I frown at him, unsure as to whether this man can be trusted or not. "Have you ever seen that Alfred Hitchcock film *What Ever Happened to Baby Jane?*"

"Oh yeah," he says. "I love Hitchcock movies, and that one was a real piece of work. I was a kid when I saw it, and for a long time, Bette Davis gave me nightmares."

"My good friend Billie, otherwise known as Joan Crawford, played the older sister, Blanche…the one who was mistreated by her younger sister."

"You were friends with Joan Crawford?"

"Yes. And despite that horrible book that her ungrateful daughter Christina wrote, which was a pack of lies by the way, Billie was a wonderful person."

"You don't say…"

"Anyway," I say in a quieter tone. "I think what happened in that movie may be similar to what is happening here."

Officer Bradford looks slightly confused. "What do you mean exactly?"

"I *mean*…my younger sister, Violet, has always been extremely jealous of me. I had my acting career, my marriage. I was wealthy and beautiful, living the good life in Beverly Hills. Gavin and I traveled all over; we were friends with some of the best people in Hollywood…"

He nods. "Yes, I know of your husband. He was a great director."

"So do you remember how Baby Jane sabotaged her older sister in that movie? She tried to make poor Blanche go crazy so she could put her away?"

He nods again. "I still remember the dead rat scene."

"Well, I think it's entirely possible that my younger sister, who has been extremely jealous that I inherited our mother's home… I think it's possible she sneaked over here while I was gone doing errands yesterday. I think she may have turned off the heating oil, done something to block the plumbing, and perhaps even stopped up the fireplace which nearly asphyxiated me. Do you understand what I mean?"

"I don't know for sure, ma'am…"

"Think about it. All that happens in one single night— what are the chances?"

"She makes a good point," says the paramedic.

Officer Bradford makes more notes. "Will it make you feel better if I look into this?"

"Yes, immensely." I give him my best smile, which I fear could be lost due to the effect of my strange ensemble. I've noticed them looking at me curiously. "I don't normally dress like this," I say with a slight laugh. "But it was so cold last night, and with no heat, I really thought I was going to freeze to death."

"It's a wonder you didn't," says the paramedic. "You better be sure to get that heat back on today. It's supposed to be even colder tonight."

"But you say your phone doesn't work either?" asks Officer Bradford.

"No." I wonder if Violet is responsible for that as well, but keep this suspicion to myself. No need to overwhelm him with too much information.

"Well, I'm going to send someone out to help you," the officer says.

"Really? Who might that be?"

"We have a nice gal in town; she heads up Senior Services. Her name is Melinda Maxwell. I'll give her a call and see if she or one of her volunteers can come to your house and help you with your phone and everything else."

"Just in case," says the paramedic, "do you have anywhere else you can stay?"

"In case of what?"

"In case your heating and plumbing problems aren't resolved. Do you have a neighbor or relative who can take you in?"

I consider this. "Not really."

"Maybe you can book a room at the motel," suggests Officer Bradford.

"Perhaps." I nod.

"Do you have transportation?"

"The Jaguar in the driveway belongs to me."

"Sweet." The paramedic smiles.

"And a current driver's license?"

"Of course." I frown at Officer Bradford. "You can see it for yourself if you don't believe me."

"That's okay. This isn't a traffic violation."

"And you will look into it—what I told you about?"

"Your Baby Jane theory?"

"Yes."

"Sure." He closes his notebook. "And if I find anything that supports your story, I'll get a detective to investigate it with me. Those are serious accusations, Ms. Fioré."

"I'm well aware of that."

"And under the circumstances, the duress of your situation last night, it would be understandable if you weren't thinking completely clearly today."

I glare at him. "Are you suggesting that I might be crazy?"

"No, no. Not crazy. But a little stressed."

The paramedic places a hand on my shoulder. "It's only natural that you would be stressed, ma'am. You've been through a lot."

"I'll say."

"Well, take care," says Officer Bradford. "Someone will be checking on you shortly."

"And stay warm."

"I'll do my best."

"I'll take a quick look at that fireplace," says the paramedic. "Maybe we can even get it working, take the chill off."

"That would be lovely," I tell the handsome young man. "Thank you ever so much."

I listen as they return to the living room. Apparently my sister and her gang of thugs are still out there. Their voices are lowered, and I suspect they're discussing my mental condition.

I just hope Officer Bradford doesn't tip his hand regarding my suspicions of my sister.

22

After about forty minutes, my house quiets down, and I think all of my "guests" have finally departed. I cannot imagine what they found to talk about for so long, besides me and my unfortunate state of affairs, but then I refused to leave the sanctuary of my bedroom and join the party to find out.

Now, still dressed in my layers to protect myself from the cold, I tiptoe out of my room, unsure as to whether any lurkers are staying behind. As I walk through the kitchen, I hear a noise from the living room and wonder if I really am alone. I hear another popping sound and realize it could be a fire.

I go out to the living room to see that a nice fire is burning in the fireplace, crackling and popping the way I wanted it to do last night. Not only that, but a fire screen is set up. Oh, it's a bit rusty and dusty and old looking, and I suspect it came from the woodshed, but at least it should keep the embers safely enclosed. There is also a note on the mantle, secured with one of my silver candlesticks, informing me that the reason for my smoke problems was a closed flue, which is now open.

Despite the fire, it's still cold in here. Someone taped a piece of cardboard over the broken window in the front door. I suppose that will help to keep some of this heat in. Just the same, I'm not ready to remove any layers yet.

I need to use the bathroom but cannot bear the thought of going back into that cesspool. And yet I really have to go. If Bea were home, I would actually set aside my pride and ask to borrow her facility. I think about what pioneers did back in the "good old days," and I suppose I could find something to work as a temporary commode. It would certainly be better than wetting myself.

It takes me several minutes of searching in the house, and I refuse to go outside to the shed. Finally I decide on a Crock-Pot Michael stored in the laundry room. I honestly do not see that I'd ever have a use for such an appliance anyway. Well, other than this. And after I use it today, I will dispose of it.

I consider taking it to the bedroom, but I don't want to risk spilling anything on the carpets in there. So I settle it in the center of the kitchen and, after peeling down my layers of pants, I attempt to hold on to the edge of the counter to balance myself. However, squatting doesn't come as easily as it once did, and I decide it might be best to elevate the Crock-Pot. I notice a nearby plastic crate, one that had clothing in it, which will be just the thing. Soon I'm all set.

With the Crock-Pot balanced on the crate, I am able to hit my mark with no problem. I'm feeling pleased with myself when I realize I forgot to bring toilet tissue. Oh, what have I been reduced to? I try not to think what some of my old friends would say if they could see me now. How tongues would wag and phones would jingle.

Just as I'm finishing up, someone knocks on the front door, and this is followed by the incessant ringing of the doorbell. I jerk on my layers of pants, not even getting them fully zipped, then rush to see who is at the door. I just hope that it's not unlocked this time. I cannot bear any more uninvited visitors barging in on me again. I especially hope it's not Violet or her friends. I do not care to see my sister or any of them anytime soon, if ever.

I peek out to see what appears to be a well-dressed and fairly nice-looking woman standing on my porch. She's probably in her thirties and carrying what appears to be a Gucci purse as well as a black briefcase. I inch open the door to see what she wants. Hopefully, she's not selling anything.

"Hello." She smiles and hands me a business card. "I'm Melinda Maxwell from Senior Services."

I examine the card, and it looks to be authentic, so I open the door wider. "Yes?"

"You must be Mrs. Ford."

"Ford?"

She frowns. "Yes, I believe that's the name I was given. Mrs. Ford?"

"*Fioré.*"

"Oh, well, then. Mrs. *Fioré*...I'd like to come in and have a nice little visit with you, if you don't mind."

It could be my imagination, but it seems she is using baby talk with me. As if she thinks this is how you address "elderly" people. I do not care for it. In fact, I find it highly offensive, not to mention affected, and I'm tempted to tell her so in no uncertain terms. But then I think better of this and invite her in.

"Thank you." She comes into my house and looks around my still messy living room, as if taking some sort of mental inventory.

"Things are rather messy," I explain. "I had a rather disturbing day yesterday... I'm sure you heard."

"Only yesterday?"

I frown at her. "What do you mean?"

"Oh, simply that, uh, people sometimes get confused as to time frames and when something really happened. What you think was only yesterday may have actually started, say, a month ago." She smiles again. But now I see that it's as phony as her fake Gucci handbag.

"Perhaps," I say in a cool voice. "But since I have been in this house for less than two weeks, I do not see how that is possible, Ms. Maxwell."

She waves her hand. "Call me Melinda, please. And I was just using that time period as an example."

"I see..."

She glances at the fireplace. "That's cozy. Did you make that fire?"

"No, I did not."

"Oh. Who did?"

I want to ask her if she has any intelligent questions to ask me but decide to bide my time with this woman. "I don't happen to know who made it."

She nods, looking at the shards of shattered glass still in and about the fireplace. "Right…"

"I mean, it might've been the policeman—I don't recall his name. No, actually, I believe it was the paramedic. It's been a rather hectic morning."

"So I've heard."

"Would you like to sit down?" I finally ask, thinking that we might as well get this wrapped up as soon as possible since this woman is as aggravating as a broken heel on the way to a premiere.

"No, actually, I'd like to look around, if you don't mind."

"Suppose I do mind?"

She smiles. "I'd like to look around anyway."

"Why is that? Are you going to write up a report on me?"

"Oh, Mrs. Fioré, you should be careful. You don't want paranoia to kick in."

"Well, am I wrong?"

"If you must know, I'm here at the police department's request. I need to do an evaluation."

"Why?" I glare at her. "Do you think I'm crazy?"

"I don't even know you." Again with the smile. "That's why I'm here, Mrs. Fioré. I want to get to know you. One of the ways

I get to know my senior clients is by looking around. I see how they're getting along and whether or not they're in need of assistance."

"Fine," I snap, tired of this cat-and-mouse game. "But you might as well know the place is a complete disaster. Everything that could go wrong did go wrong last night. And it wasn't my fault either. I did all I could to make this work. But I believe I have been sabotaged."

Her eyebrows rise. "Sabotaged? Really?"

I simply throw my hands up. Perhaps I should keep my mouth shut around this woman.

She nods toward the kitchen. "May I look around?"

"I doubt I can stop you."

She sort of laughs, then proceeds into my kitchen where her laughter comes to an abrupt halt. "Oh my!"

I look around the kitchen too, suddenly seeing it as she must see it—as my sister and her friends and the public servants must've seen it—broken dishes on the floor, scattered clothing all around, random household items dumped from the cardboard box I used as kindling, my Armani pantsuit with horrible red wine stains, a large knife nearby. But then I see what her eyes are really focused upon—my makeshift commode.

"What is *that*?" She points to the structure.

"You mean the Crock-Pot and the crate?"

"Are you using *that* as a toilet?"

"Perhaps you didn't hear that I had a plumbing problem."

"Really?"

"Yes. Last night my toilet backed up, all over the bathroom. I haven't had a chance to clean it up."

"Is the bathroom this way?" She heads down the hallway.

Before I can direct her, she opens the door to the guest room/office. "Well, now, whose room is this?"

"No one's."

"Oh."

Then she moves on to the bathroom, opens the door, and glances around. Making a face, she quickly closes it. "That is disgusting."

"Tell me something I don't know."

"What's this other room?" She reaches for my bedroom door, but before I can answer, she opens it and enters. Like my sister, she picks up the wine bottle and holds it out. "Do we have a drinking problem?"

"I don't know, do *we*?"

"Do you always take a bottle of wine to bed with you?"

"Only when the plumbing backs up, the house nearly burns down, and I expect to suffer from hypothermia before morning."

"I see..."

"Yes, I'm sure you do."

She shakes her head. "You're not much of a housekeeper, are you?"

"No, actually, I am not. I haven't kept house since I was a child. I married a very wealthy man, lived in a beautiful mansion, and always had servants who did the cleaning and cooking for me."

"Really?" She looks at me with skepticism. "Sounds like a dream life."

"Yes, it was…"

"So, what happened? If what you're saying is true, how did you end up like this?"

I sit on my bed and sigh. "I wish I knew."

"Surely, you must know. If you really were as wealthy as you say, you must know what happened to change things for you. Tell me, I'd like to hear your story." She actually pushes my clothes off my chair and sits down.

"I got old."

"Oh yes. Getting old can be difficult. But it's not the end of the world, Mrs. Fioré."

"And you know that for a fact, do you?"

She smiles again, and I swear I'd like to rip the lips from her face. "My degree is in gerontology. You may not know what that is, but it happens to be the—"

"Just because you've studied aging doesn't mean you understand it."

She blinks. "Are you trying to tell me that you understand it?"

"I am *experiencing* it."

"Does that mean you *understand* it?"

I consider this. The truth is, I don't understand it. I don't wish to understand it. But I refuse to give her the satisfaction of hearing that confession.

"Okay, I think we need to get down to the basics here." She looks around my room. "But perhaps it would be more comfortable in the living room."

"Not to mention warmer."

"Yes." She nods. "Good point."

Oh boy, I made a point!

Soon we are both seated in the living room, and she opens her black briefcase and removes a notebook. "I have some questions."

"Is this a test?"

"No, Mrs. Fioré," she says in that baby-talk voice again, "it's just our way of finding out how we can best serve you."

"*Please,* I am not a child, and I am not senile. I would appreciate it if you would address me as an intelligent adult."

She nods and looks down at her notebook. "First of all, is it true you have no source of heat…other than the fireplace?"

So, for what feels like the umpteenth time, I explain about the furnace. "It had been working perfectly fine." I remove my purple gloves and set them aside. "Until yesterday. That's when everything fell apart. I'm sure you may think I'm experiencing paranoia, but I cannot help but think there was a human hand involved."

"Why do you think that?"

"Well, just consider it. I'm away from home during the day. I return to no heat, stopped-up plumbing, a fireplace that doesn't work properly… Does that seem like a coincidence to you?"

"I'd say it's a stretch of bad luck. But why didn't you call for help? A plumber? The oil company?"

"Because my phone wasn't working."

Now I seem to have gotten her attention. "You mean your phone line is down as well?"

"Not my phone line. My cell phone. I had it all charged, but it would not connect. I tried and tried, but I just couldn't put a call through."

"Where is your phone? Maybe I can give it a try."

I nod to the fireplace.

"You *burned* it?"

"Something like that."

"Oh…" She studies me carefully, and I can tell she's questioning my mental capacity. I must either win her confidence or risk being written up as a lunatic, which could mean they would see fit to have me locked away in a place like Laurel Hills or worse. I cannot have that.

"As you said earlier, you do not *know* me. And what you're seeing right now is not the Claudette Fioré I used to be. To start with, the IRS recently forced the sale of my beautiful home in Beverly Hills. They seized most of my assets, and I had to relocate to Silverton because this was all I had. You see, I inherited my childhood home, and although it's not much, it was better than being homeless. But I'm not accustomed to living in deprivation or being without my household staff. My stepson helped me set up housekeeping, and believe it or not, this place looked rather good before he left less than a week ago."

She glances around again. "I did notice that you do have some nice things."

I nod. "But even so, I am living in an impoverished way."

"And what you're telling me is the truth, Mrs. Fioré? You really did live in Beverly Hills? You really were wealthy?"

"Why would I make that up?"

She laughs. "Oh, you'd be surprised at the things elderly people, in need of attention or suffering from dementia, will make up."

"Look at this." I wave to the abstract behind me. "That is an original Sean Scully. I don't know if you know anything about art, but it is quite valuable."

Melinda frowns up at the painting. "I happen to be quite fond of abstract art, Mrs. Fioré, and I certainly know about Sean Scully. But I can't believe that's an original. A good reproduction, perhaps, but *not* an original." Then she laughs.

"Your fake Gucci purse may be a *reproduction*. Not a good reproduction, mind you, since I spotted it the minute you walked in. But that painting, like most of the art in my home, is the real thing."

She stands up, goes over to the painting, and studies it carefully. Then she turns and peers at me. "It's authentic?"

"Unlike *some* people, I do not care for imitations."

She points to my hand. "I suppose you're going to tell me that diamond ring is real too?"

I roll my eyes. "My husband got it for our fortieth anniversary. He was extremely wealthy. Why would I wear a fake?"

"Because it's huge. No way can it be real."

"Last time I checked, it was insured for half a million."

Melinda shakes her head. "And yet you are living in squalor, Mrs. Fioré, using your kitchen as a toilet, and you have human feces on the floor of your bathroom. Doesn't any of this strike you as odd?"

"Terribly odd."

"Why don't you hire household help?"

"Because I must live on a budget now. A very small budget."

"But you could sell something." She points to my hand. "I'm sure that ring alone could pay for maid service for the rest of your life."

"Sell my ring?"

"Or some art. If they really are originals, you'd only need to sell a few and you'd be set for some time."

"My art?" I say sadly, looking up at the Scully. "And then what would I have left?"

"You might have a clean house and plumbing that works."

"I suppose…"

"Look, Mrs. Fioré, I can't help you if you won't let me. Or if you're unwilling to help yourself. If that's the case, we would need to find another living situation for you. But if your paintings and jewelry are authentic and as valuable as you say, then I'm wasting my time here. I have truly impoverished people who actually need Social Services." She studies me closely. "Unless, of course, you have some other challenges, such as the onset of

Alzheimer's, dementia, or some other mental health issue. Is there anything else you'd like to discuss?"

I just shake my head. This woman may think she understands old people, but she does not understand me. I hold up my hands in true desperation. "I *do* need help, Melinda. This is the truth… I do not know how to do the simplest of things. I do not have a phone. I do not have heat. My plumbing does not work. And until I can call my accountant, I am temporarily broke. Now, if you really think I should go downtown and pawn my wedding ring to—"

"No, no, I'm not suggesting that." She actually seems to give this some thought. "Okay, Mrs. Fioré, this is what we'll do. Since tomorrow's Thanksgiving and it'll be hard to get help, I'll call the phone company right away. I'll tell them to get in here today and that it's an emergency."

"It certainly feels like an emergency to me."

She nods and writes something down. "Yes, I'm sure it does." Then she looks up at me. "And then I'll call a plumber and tell him it's an emergency as well."

"Thank you."

"And I'll get the oil company out here too."

"I would appreciate that."

"Anything else?"

"I think that should help immensely, thank you."

She puts her notebook back in the briefcase. "And if I'm going to get these people out here today, I'll have to jump on it."

She stands and hooks her handbag over her arm. "You really knew this was a fake?"

I nod. "But if it's any comfort to you, I am rather an expert at these things." I look down at my sorry looking outfit. "Although I'm sure you wouldn't know by looking at me just now…"

"No, but I did notice a nice-looking Kelly bag in your bedroom and several other items I wouldn't mind having."

I smile at her. "Maybe I should have a boudoir sale."

"Hey, if you do, let me know."

As Melinda leaves, I think it's possible that I misjudged her earlier. She actually seems somewhat decent, and I find myself wanting to trust her. I just hope she's sincere about getting me the help I so desperately need.

It has not been easy to admit how helpless I really am. On the other hand, I do not think I can possibly face another night like the one I experienced last night.

23

As soon as Melinda leaves, I straighten my living room. It's true that I don't know the first thing about housekeeping, but it's also true that I'm somewhat lazy, not that I would care to admit this to anyone. But when it comes to menial labor, I am rather unmotivated. However, I was never lazy when it came to other physical exertions, like yoga, golf, tennis, boating...but then those activities were enjoyable.

As I pick up items of clothing, trying to decide the best places to put them (do I keep them or toss them out?), I realize that I'm getting warmer. I suppose this is from moving about. But the fire has burned down to glowing embers. Fortunately someone, probably that attractive paramedic, has set extra firewood on the hearth. So I throw on a few more logs and continue with my cleaning.

As I continue puttering about, putting things where they belong, I observe something quite ironic, something that actually surprises me. Putting a room back in order leaves one with a feeling of something... I believe it's *accomplishment.* I try to remember who told me this tidbit about housekeeping—that it is its own reward. I think it was Busybody Bea! Perhaps I'm starting to grasp this concept.

I take a break and fix myself some coffee and a bite of breakfast. But as I sit at the table in my still messy kitchen with my makeshift toilet still in the center of the room, I wonder if Melinda will really follow through with her promises. Perhaps I should consider getting myself a room at that ratty old Motel 6 on the edge of town. Then, as I'm rinsing my cup and plate, someone knocks at the door. I peek out the front window to see a red van, with the black silhouette of a rooster and the words *Rooster Rooter* painted on the side, parked out front. And when I go to the door, a man in brown coveralls is standing on my porch.

"Morning, ma'am. I hear you got plumbing problems."

"Yes!" I say as if I am happy about that. "Come in!" I open the door wider and let him in.

"Can you tell me what's going on exactly?"

"Well, first I flushed the toilet, and it didn't go down like it should." I grimace to remember. "In fact, it went all over the bathroom floor. Then I took a shower, and the water didn't go down at all. It seems things are stopped up."

"Uh-huh. Sounds like a drain problem to me."

"Well, my stepson helped me move into this house recently, and he mentioned that I should get a plumber to look at the pipes, or something to that effect. Someone told him that if a house sits too long, there could be plumbing problems."

"That sounds right." He nods. "I'll go take a look."

"The bathroom is this way," I tell him, wishing it wasn't in such bad shape.

"No, my work is mostly outside, ma'am."

"Oh."

"I'll root out your sewer line, and we'll see if that solves the problem."

He heads outside and I go and try to figure out how to clean the horrible mess still in my bathroom—just in case he needs to go in there. But I just stand there in the doorway holding my breath and feeling utterly helpless. Where does one even begin?

Finally, I close the door and return to the kitchen to ponder my dilemma. Seeing my makeshift toilet only makes me feel worse. This has to go. I carefully carry the Crock-Pot outside, empty its contents in the shrubbery, and set it beside the trash can, which is already full to overflowing.

I feel slightly better when I go back in the house and wash my hands. At least that's gone now. The memory of Melinda standing here and staring at it is more than I can bear. I shudder to think of all that I've been through in the past twenty-four hours. My heart must be in excellent condition.

Then, seeing the large plastic crate still on the kitchen floor gives me an idea. Perhaps I can use this to transport the ruined towels from my bathroom out to the trash. But then I remember the smell in there. I'm not sure I can possibly endure it without losing my breakfast. What I need is a gas mask.

I pace back and forth until I finally think I have a solution. I get a silk scarf, which I spray with cologne and then tie around my face like a bandit's mask. I glance at my image in the mirror and just shake my head. Oh, if my friends could see me now.

I hurry to get the crate and prepare to do the nasty task. But I cannot bear to touch those soiled towels. If only I had some rubber gloves. Then I spot the ugly purple suede gloves. Who cares if I ruin those things? So with my scarf and my purple gloves, I roll up my sleeves and attack that bathroom. First I remove the rug, using the crate to transport it, carrying it through the house at arm's length. I dump the ruined carpet next to the trash can. Then, one at a time, I do the same with the soggy, putrid towels and clothes, until I'm dumping the last one, lamenting over the fact that these thick white towels— made of the finest Egyptian cotton and of a quality I will not see again anytime soon—are history.

"What on earth are you doing?"

I turn to see a woman staring at me with an expression that suggests she has just spotted an alien from Mars. She is nicely dressed in a Harris tweed A-line skirt, soft brown leather boots, a well-cut tan suede jacket, and a pretty plaid silk scarf. Her hair is hidden by a brown felt hat, complete with a jaunty little feather. And although she's dressed in a rather stylish and youthful way, I can tell she is actually quite old. Perhaps even older than I.

Naturally, seeing this well-dressed woman in my backyard,

while I am still garbed like the neighborhood bag lady bandit and dumping trash that smells like raw sewage, makes me rather uncomfortable.

Even so, I stand up straight and hold my head high, which reminds me that besides the strange layers of clothes, soiled purple gloves, and bandit scarf, I still have on the horrid red ski hat as well. A pretty picture. Despite all this, I manage to demand, "Who are you?" in a rather haughty voice.

"Sorry, I shouldn't have snuck up on you like that. But I knocked on the front door and no one answered. The nice plumber said that he'd seen you doing something out back." She smiles. "My name is Irene Hawthorne. Melinda from Senior Services asked me to come over to visit you. I volunteer for them."

I frown at her as I attempt to peel off the slightly damp and smelly suede gloves, which I toss into my steadily growing trash pile next to the garbage can. Then I reach up and carefully remove the silk scarf, wipe my hands on it, wad it up, and toss it on top of the pile too.

"You're throwing that pretty scarf away?"

I nod and pull off the dreadful ski hat and dump that as well. "Good riddance." I step away from the nasty pile, as if it might spring up and attack me. Then I look at this woman, Irene Somebody. "I do not know why Melinda asked you to come visit me. But as you can see, this isn't a good day for entertaining guests."

She laughs. "Well, I didn't expect to be entertained, Mrs. Fioré. I thought perhaps I could lend a hand."

I look at her attractive ensemble, perfect for a country drive, casual lunch, or a walk in the park, then shake my head. "I don't think you understand." I point to the pile of towels, gloves, scarf, and hat, which in a strangely grotesque way resemble a melted snowman. I blink then look back at her. "I have had plumbing problems."

"I assumed that was why the plumber was here."

"Yes. Hopefully he will resolve my problem. In the meantime, I still have something of a mess to clean up."

"And you don't want help?"

I study her. "Of course I'd love help. If you know of a house-keeping service that can come out here right now, I'd—"

"I am quite good at housekeeping."

"I'm sure you are, but you're not really dressed for—"

"How about if you let me be the judge of that?"

Well, this just irks me. Who does this woman think she is anyway? She comes here, nicely dressed, then has the audacity to think she can clean my bathroom. Perhaps I should let her.

"Fine. Follow me." I lead her into my house, going directly to the still putrid-smelling bathroom. "Do you feel up to cleaning that?"

She sort of laughs, then actually wrinkles her nose. "That is a bit nasty, isn't it?"

"I didn't think you'd be interested."

"Oh, but that's where you're wrong. *I am.*" And already she's removing her suede jacket, which she hangs over her arm. "Lead me to the cleaning things."

"Cleaning things?"

"You know...cleansers, mops...that sort of thing."

"There are a few things under the sink in the kitchen. And I think I saw a mop in the laundry room."

"That's a start." She looks down at the runner in the hall-way. "Have you been tromping back and forth over this carpet and through your house?"

"Well, yes, I suppose so."

"Now it will need to be cleaned too."

"Oh..."

"Too bad you didn't use a different route."

"A different route?"

She points to the window. "If it had been me, I'd have simply tossed them out that window."

I sigh. "I never thought of that."

She smiles. "That's just my point, Mrs. Fioré. And exactly why I came to help you. Sometimes two minds are better than one."

"Right." I force a smile. "And, please, why don't you call me Claudette?"

She nods, then sets off to search through my cupboards and laundry room, producing cleaning things I didn't even know I had, as well as a brand-new mop. Michael must've been the one to put these things together. Too bad he didn't have time to give me some instruction before he left. Then Irene puts me to work spraying some sort of foaming cleaner onto the hallway carpet, and she starts mopping the bathroom floor.

"Excuse me," calls a man. I go out to the living room to see the plumber standing at the door. "I think you should be good to flow now."

"Good to flow?"

"You know, the water—it should be flowing just fine. Why don't you flush the toilet a couple of times just to make sure."

So I go back to the bathroom. "The plumber said to flush the toilet," I tell Irene. She's over by the shower, just dipping her mop into the bucket of water.

"Yes?"

"Should I do it?"

"Well, of course."

"What if it overflows again?"

She chuckles. "Then we shall just clean it up again."

So I push the handle and watch as the water miraculously goes down. "It works!" I say, victorious. I wait for the bowl to fill, then flush it again. "It still works."

"Hurray." Irene returns to mopping.

"It works!" I proclaim to the plumber.

He's writing something on a small pad. Then he tears off a piece of paper and hands it to me. "Here you go."

"What's this?" I peer down to a line that reads Amount Due.

"A bill, of course."

"But I don't have any cash on me."

"It's okay. The lady at Senior Services said you'd send me a check once you got your banking and everything set up."

"Oh yes. Of course." I smile. "Thank you."

"You have a happy Thanksgiving now."

"You too," I call as he heads back to his rooster van.

By one thirty, Irene and I have made real progress. The entire house smells amazingly clean, and the only chore left to do, besides my messy bedroom, is to wash the dishes and clean the kitchen.

"I do not know how to thank you." I peel off another layer of clothes and toss them into the laundry room on a growing pile I intend to throw in the trash. The heat still isn't on, but all this work has warmed me some. Plus, we've managed to keep the fire going.

She just smiles. "I suppose you don't remember me, Claudette."

"What?" I peer at her more closely. "Have we met before?"

"Yes, as a matter of fact, we have."

"Where?"

"You really *don't* remember, do you?"

I strain my memory, trying to remember where I've seen this woman. Admittedly, she is attractive and rather stylish. "Did you live in Beverly Hills?"

She laughs. "Not even close. I used to be Irene Yorker. I went to school with you right here in Silverton."

My eyes widen. *Irene Porker*—the fat girl we teased relentlessly in school? I swallow hard. "Irene Yorker?" I repeat, careful to get the last name correct.

"Yes. You might not remember me... I was very chubby, and some kids called me Irene *Porker*." She smiles sadly. "Funny, even after all these years, it still stings a bit to think of that."

"I do remember you." Now I'm trying to remember if I ever actually teased her—to her face, that is. I'm absolutely certain I said horribly mean things behind her back. And while no one ever considered me a particularly kind or caring person in school, I did have a sense of decorum. My mother made sure that Violet and I practiced good manners. When we were young, she taught us to behave ourselves and "act like ladies." Especially in public.

In fact, that was one of the traits that first attracted Gavin to me. He believed I was truly a lady—something that couldn't be said for all actresses back then, or even now, for that matter. Oh, he might've thought otherwise, from time to time, after we married, but I usually tried to maintain a certain sensibility, and in most situations, I could maintain the appearance of good etiquette. "But you've changed," I continue. "Of course, we all have changed. Age does that."

"I lost the weight after high school," she says. "It was in college and my first time living away from home. I changed my eating habits, and the pounds just seemed to drop away."

I nod. "As I recall, your family tended to be heavy."

She laughs. "That's an understatement, if there ever was one. They were all horribly obese. My mother grew up in the South, and she loved to cook, and she fried everything."

"That would make it difficult."

"Yes, I can remember being called names like Bacon Fat because I came to school smelling like bacon grease."

I chuckle. "That's probably because everyone was jealous that you'd had bacon for breakfast and we were lucky to have oatmeal."

"But oatmeal would've been healthier."

"Didn't your dad run the grocery store and the meat lockers?"

"Yes. It might've been the Great Depression for other people, but the Yorkers always had plenty of food."

"Speaking of food, I'm starving." I'm about to invite Irene to go out for lunch when I remember that I'm broke.

"Do you have anything we can fix here?"

I consider this. "Well, I did get groceries a couple of days ago." Then I look down at my still grimy clothes. "Perhaps I should clean up a bit first."

"Why don't you go do that? I'll see if I can scrape us together something."

"You don't mind?"

"Not at all. Go ahead, Claudette. Take your time… Take a shower, if you like."

"A shower?" I sigh. "That sounds lovely."

So I do take a shower, a long lovely shower, using the last remaining Egyptian cotton towel. And I take my time to get dressed, fuss with my hair, and put on makeup. Fortunately I didn't ruin all of my winter clothes. I put on my gray Ralph

Lauren tweed trousers, a burgundy cashmere sweater set, and pearls. When I go out to the kitchen, I almost feel like myself again.

"You've cleaned up in here," I say when I notice the clear sink and countertops.

"I find that I'm a better cook with clean surfaces." She directs me to the table, which is all set. "I was just finishing up this salad to go with our soup and sandwiches."

"This looks delicious," I tell her as I sit down.

"Well, they were your ingredients."

"That might be true, but I never could've put them together like this." I examine the salad, which looks like it could've been from one of Beverly Hills' best restaurants.

"Do you mind if I ask a blessing?" she says just as I'm reaching for my fork.

I pull my hand back. "Not at all."

Then she bows her head. "Dear heavenly Father, thank you for all your good provisions. Thank you for loving us and taking care of us. And thank you for new friends. Now, please, bless this food to our use. Amen." She looks up and smiles.

"That was nice. My late husband had taken to saying a blessing before meals. It was a practice he started just a few months before he passed away. At first I wasn't quite sure what to think of it, since we'd been married for nearly sixty years and he'd never been the least bit religious. But then I got rather used to it... It had something of a calming effect on me. Perhaps it was a digestion aid. But then Gavin died, and I haven't heard anyone say a blessing since."

"I grew up in a churchgoing family," she says. "So I don't remember a time when they didn't ask a blessing. But I rebelled against it for a while in my adulthood."

"Really?"

"Oh yes. In college I decided that I was far too smart and sophisticated for my old-fashioned, fat-eating family." She chuckles. "I'm glad they didn't give up on me so easily."

As we partake in what proves to be a rather tasty lunch, Irene tells me about how she got her teaching degree, then married and had children, and then returned to college for a higher degree. But I have difficulty focusing because I keep wondering, *How can this woman possibly be the same Irene (Porker), the smelly fat girl that no one wanted to sit with during lunchtime?*

24

After lunch, Irene gives me a step-by-step lesson on how to operate the washer and dryer. "It looks like it might take you a few days to get on top of this." She nods to the heap of clothes on the floor. "The main thing to remember when you're doing your wash, Claudette, is *do not leave wet laundry in the washer.*"

"Why?"

"Because your things will mildew and then it's very difficult to get that smell out. Also, you might want to get some laundry baskets to keep your things off the floor."

"Oh…" I sigh deeply. "So much to do, so much to remember… Do you think I'll ever be able to do this on my own?"

"It might take some time, but if you don't give up, you'll get the hang of it. In the meantime, I recommend you make and use lists."

"More lists?"

"You already have lists?"

"Well, my stepson gave me some lists before he left."

"And you've been using them?"

"Well, somewhat…" I almost laugh. "It's just too bad I didn't take his lists more seriously—I wouldn't have gotten into so much trouble with things like plumbing and heating yesterday."

"Speaking of heating, what sort of backup do you have in here, besides the fireplace, I mean?"

"That's just the problem. I have no backup."

"You should go to the hardware store and pick up a couple of space heaters. They have these small ceramic units that are highly efficient and don't take up much room."

"Wait a minute," I tell her as I head back in the house. "I think I should write this down."

After I make myself a new list, I ask Irene how she got so smart about these things, and she just laughs. "When you don't live the lifestyles of the rich and famous, you learn to do things for yourself, Claudette."

"Yes, I suppose." It's the first reference Irene has made to my former life. I was actually starting to wonder if she was even aware of who I was or who I had been married to…and it was somewhat disappointing.

We're standing by the front door now, and she's putting on her coat and getting ready to leave. But she pauses to look at the photo montage Michael arranged for me on the wall by the door.

"Is that your late husband?" She points to a shot of Gavin and me taken in the Mediterranean.

"Yes…" I gaze with longing at the photo taken back in the sixties. I was still quite a beauty back then, still looked good in a swimsuit. "We were in Monte Carlo… I'd just turned forty and felt that life as I knew it was about to end."

She chuckles. "Isn't life ironic?"

"Yes. Here I am more than forty years older, thinking how young I looked."

She points to another. "Is that Joan Crawford with you in that shot?"

"Yes, although I called her Billie." I sigh.

"And is that Rita Hayworth?"

"Yes. Gavin was doing a film with her."

"You've had an exciting life, Claudette, lots of colorful friends."

"If only I could turn back the clock."

"And do what?" She peers curiously at me. "Just live the same thing all over again? Or would you do it differently?"

I consider this. The truth is, I don't really know. Most of me would like to simply go back and do the same thing all over again—just for the pure fun of it. But I suppose a part of me has some regrets.

"I know this adjustment period is difficult for you, but you should remember that you need friends."

"*Friends?*" I say vaguely as I look longingly at the photo of Gavin and me taken shortly after our wedding. We're toasting with champagne with Lana Turner and John Garfield at a party following the premiere of *The Postman Always Rings Twice*. We all looked so young and glamorous and alive. Oh, weren't those the days?

"Well, I'm your friend, of course," says Irene, bringing me back to the present. "And speaking of making new friends, why don't you come to my house for Thanksgiving tomorrow?"

I stare at Irene as I consider her invitation. Naturally it pales in comparison to the parties and events I've enjoyed over my lifetime. Really, would I ever have imagined myself celebrating a holiday with Irene Porker from Silverton? I don't think so. "Thank you so much. But I think I am still a bit stressed over yesterday, and I still have so much to do…"

"I understand, Claudette, but don't forget that you need to let people into your world. If you set yourself apart, you set yourself up for trouble. Isolation isn't good for anyone, but it's particularly bad for older people. We really do need each other."

I remember Bea's little speech about being neighborly. I also remember Page Turner's invitation to join a book club. And now I have Irene's offer of friendship and Thanksgiving dinner. Still, I do not feel ready… I'm not sure if it's my reluctance to completely let go of my old life or just the assumption that these small-town people will simply bore me.

Irene opens the door. "Oh, wonderful! It looks like the phone company is connecting your line right now. Now you can call for help if you need it." She reaches into her purse and hands me a business card. "Senior Services encourages us to give these to the people we're helping. But I've written my home phone number on the back. Feel free to call me, Claudette. And if you reconsider Thanksgiving tomorrow, you'll be most welcome."

"Thank you. And thank you for your help today. I really do appreciate it."

"You take care now."

I stand watching as she drives away in a white minivan, of all things. I cannot imagine why someone her age would choose to drive such an unattractive vehicle. But then she is, after all, Irene Yorker who used to be Porker. Perhaps she's not as changed as she seems.

It's foggy and dreary outside, and it's still freezing cold. I go back to the kitchen and look over my lists, both the ones Michael made for me and my new one. Yes, now I must call Jackie and get my finances squared away so I actually have some money, perhaps even before the business day ends.

But I don't have a phone, neither a cell phone or one that plugs into the wall. I consider going to Radio Shack again, but I haven't gotten their charge card in the mail yet and I'm not sure if they will allow me to use credit again.

Then I remember the account at the hardware store and wonder if they might possibly have phones. I add *phone* to my list and decide it's time to venture out of my house once more. But fully aware of the freezing temperature outside, I must do this thing right. First I put on my black Versace boots, then slip into my full-length Tucci coat, taking a moment to fondle the buttery smooth, black lambskin leather. I suppose this is something to be thankful for here in Silverton... I seldom had the opportunity to wear these things in Southern California.

I search in my drawer until I find a pair of soft kid gloves, also in black. This reminds me of my fur coats, still in storage, and I wonder if there might be any way to have them sent to me. I will have to put that on another list.

I top off all this black leather by wrapping a soft aquamarine cashmere scarf around my neck. I've been told that older women shouldn't wear black unless they soften it a bit with pastels, and I think this scarf does the trick. Although I do wish I had a nice hat to go with this, something to cover my frightening looking hair. Perhaps one that's similar to the one Irene was wearing today, perhaps in gray. I consider asking her where she got it but can't force myself to sink to that level. It's one thing to allow her to give me housekeeping tips, but to go to Irene Porker for fashion advice—well, that is simply too much.

As I expected, it's bitter cold outside, and not only is the sidewalk a bit slick with ice, but my windshield is frosted as well. I attempt to use my nice gloves to scrape off the layer of ice, but it's not working.

"Need a hand there, lady?" asks the telephone man as he throws something into his van. "I got a scraper."

"Thank you," I call back to him. "I'm from Southern California, and this is all very foreign to me."

He chuckles as he comes over. "Don't know why you'd wanna leave all that warm sunshine down there to move up here."

"Trust me, I keep asking myself that very same question."

In mere seconds he not only has my windshield cleared but all the other windows as well. "Thank you." I say sincerely, "I feel I should give you a tip."

He just grins. "Consider it my Thanksgiving treat to you, ma'am. And your phone should be working just fine now; it's all hooked up and ready to go. I just set a couple of phone books and some phone company information on the porch."

I thank him again and wish him a happy Thanksgiving, and he hops into his van and drives away. Perhaps I've been a bit too harsh on this town. People in Silverton really seem quite nice.

I get in my car and turn the key, but nothing happens. Something is wrong with my car. I try the key again. Still nothing—absolutely nothing. Then I consider this cold weather. Was there something I should've done to my car, something to protect it from the freezing temperatures?

I get out and look up and down the street, almost as if I expect someone to happen along and help me. This is ridiculous. I will simply walk to town and to the hardware store, where I will purchase my phone and come home. But these lovely Versace boots are probably not the smartest thing for walking on ice, especially with the heels. I go back into the house and change into a pair of sensible gray loafers. Not quite as elegant as my pretty boots, but then neither is a broken leg.

By the time I reach the hardware store, it is nearly four o'clock and I discover that they will be closing at five. Feeling slightly anxious, not to mention rushed, I get a cart, take out my list, and make the rounds, filling my cart with three laundry baskets, two telephones, and four of the small heaters Irene told me about. I even get an ice scraper. And while I'm in the automotive section, I see a man buying what turns out to be antifreeze. I tell him about my own car problem and being from a warmer climate.

"Oh yeah," he says. "You better get some antifreeze into that car ASAP."

"Do I do it *myself*?"

"I always do. But if you don't know what you're doing, you better get someone to help you. Maybe a neighbor or at the gas station."

I thank him and put a jug of antifreeze in my cart. Then I notice two women talking about the weather. "My walk was so slick that the mailman almost slipped this morning," one tells the other. "He told me I better get some rock salt on it or come to the post office and pick up my mail myself." She hoists a big bag of something into her cart.

"That's a good idea." The other woman picks up a bag and slips it onto the lower shelf of her cart.

After the women move on, I get a bag for myself. I'm not completely sure what I'll do with it; so I hope there will be instructions on it. The bag is quite heavy, but I follow the second woman's example and slide it onto the bottom shelf of the cart. I hadn't even noticed that handy space down there.

I wander around the store a bit more. I'm surprised to discover it's rather comforting being in a hardware store like this. They have so many practical things that one really needs and people who actually know how to put them to use. It's also a good feeling to know I have credit here and that, although I am broke, I can still make these purchases today.

Just a few minutes before five, I make my way to the checkout. I feel quite pleased with myself and my collection of merchandise. I inform the clerk that I have an account. For a brief moment I worry that something is going to go wrong and she's going to tell me, "No, you do not," and send me on my way. But she rings it all up, prints out a paper, which I sign, and then she asks if I need someone to help me load this into my car.

That's when it hits me: I did not drive a car. My revised plan had been to simply purchase a phone and carry it home on foot. But somewhere along the way, I forgot all about this and imagined that my car was out in front of the store.

"Ma'am?" asks the clerk. "Do you need any help out?"

I put my hand to my mouth. "I am so embarrassed. I completely forgot that I walked to town. You see, my car had a mechanical problem, and I needed to purchase a telephone." I look at my very full cart and then back at her. "You don't suppose I could wheel this home and return it tomorrow?"

She frowns. "For one thing, we don't allow carts off the premises, and besides, we're closed tomorrow."

I nod. "Right. Thanksgiving." I consider my dilemma and wonder if I really am developing Alzheimer's or some other form of dementia. "Perhaps I could simply take one of the telephones with me and then return for the rest of my things after the holiday?" Then I frown as I remember how cold my house was last night. "Although I really could use those heaters… You see, I just moved to town and my heating oil hasn't been delivered."

"Tom?" yells the clerk.

"I'm so sorry," I say, noticing the customers waiting in line behind me.

I begin to push my cart away from the register and toward the door. However, I don't know what to do now. I can't very well make off with their cart after she explicitly told me that's not allowed. Still, it's hard to imagine her calling the police and having an old lady arrested for borrowing a cart just so she could get her heaters home and avoid freezing to death.

Then I notice the clerk talking to a man, pointing at me. She's probably telling him I'm crazy and that they should call the authorities before I steal their cart. The other customers are looking at me as well. I can't read their expressions. Perhaps they're looking with amusement, or maybe even pity. I don't think I care to know. I'm tempted to simply take my phone from the bag and march out of here, leaving the rest of my merchandise for them to sort out, when the man, presumably Tom, comes over to me.

"I'm sorry we can't let you take the cart from store property." He glances outside and frowns. "Even if we could, it's pretty dark out there and it might be dangerous to walk with a cart. Plus, there's ice to consider."

"That's fine," I say crisply. "If I could simply take one of the telephones I purchased, I can return later to pick up the remaining items."

"I have a better idea." He checks his watch. "How about if I give you a lift home? My shift is over now anyway, and I'm guessing you don't live too far away if you walked here."

Normally I do not take rides from strangers. But my life has not been normal for weeks now. "Thank you. I would greatly appreciate that."

"Let me go punch out and get my coat, and I'll be right back."

Soon the last of the customers have been checked out, and some of the lights are being turned out. "Okay…" Tom returns with his jacket and cap on. "You ready to roll?"

Then he loads up my things into the back of his pickup and helps me into the cab of his truck, which is rather high. It smells like gasoline in here, and I'm thankful we don't have far to go. As he drives down Main Street, I tell him my name and where I live. Within minutes he pulls into my driveway behind my car.

"Hey, nice Jag." He opens the cab door. "Let me help you outta the truck, Mrs. Fioré. I know it's a pretty tall step. My wife gives me a bad time about it, but I can't help it. I just happen to like big tires."

"Thank you," I say as he helps me down.

"And I'll give you a hand with your stuff; it's pretty heavy. Why don't you go on ahead, turn on the lights, and unlock the door."

I feel slightly uneasy and a bit vulnerable as I carefully make my way up the darkened path to the porch. I've never worried too much about being a woman alone, but I suppose one can't be too careful. Still, as I unlock the door, I think that he does seem like a nice young man…and I don't see what choice I have. I turn on the porch light. How would I even attempt to defend myself if he turned out to be a mugger or worse?

"I'll just set this first bag on this bench here," he says, "and go back for the rest."

I consider offering to help but am not sure I want to risk that icy walk again. The next trip he brings the stacked laundry baskets with items in them.

"I notice you got some antifreeze here, Mrs. Fioré. Was that for the Jag?"

"Yes." Then I explain my engine problems.

He lets out a low whistle. "Wow, I hope it's nothing serious. If you want, I could put this in tonight. I got a flashlight in my truck. They say it's gonna get even colder."

"Oh, would you?"

"No problem. Just get me your keys while I unload the rest of the stuff."

I carry one bag into the house and retrieve my car keys. For a brief instant I imagine him stealing my car, but then I realize he would have to leave his truck behind to do so. Also, I have a phone and I could call the police if necessary.

"That's all of it," he says when I meet him on the porch.

"Here are the keys, Tom."

"Shouldn't take long."

I carry everything, except the heavy bag of rock salt, into the house. Then I stand by the front window and watch him. He's under the hood with his flashlight, apparently pouring that stuff into the right hole or slot or wherever it goes. I certainly hope he knows what he's doing. Still, it's not as if the car was running this morning anyway.

Then he goes around and opens the driver's door and gets inside. Well, I don't know what to think, but he cannot back out with his pickup blocking the driveway. The next thing I know, he gets into his pickup, moves it back, then drives it right onto the front lawn, parking it directly beside my car. Well, this is too much. Tom really does plan to steal my car after all.

I'm just about to run and get my phone out of the box and plug it in when I notice he's opening the hood of his pickup. Then he pulls out some long ropelike things and goes back and forth between my car and his pickup. I cannot imagine what he is trying to do. I wait and watch, convincing myself that he doesn't really intend to steal my car, and finally he gets back into my car and somehow manages to make it run. The headlights come on, dimly at first and then brighter. Well, now.

He hops out and jogs up to my front door. "I'm charging your battery, Mrs. Fioré. It'll take a few minutes to get it charged up good. That's what the problem was this morning. My guess is your car's not used to this cold weather. Too bad you don't have a garage to keep that pretty baby in."

I nod. "Yes. I feel the same way."

"You got room on this lot to build yourself one." He rubs his hands together. "My brother-in-law is a builder. I could give you his number."

"Yes. Why don't you come inside and get warmed up a little. Not that it's terribly warm in here, but I can try out one of these little heaters."

"You get your heater going, and I'm gonna put some of this rock salt out on your walkway; it's slicker than snot on a doorknob out there."

So I remove a small boxlike heater from its packaging, search for an outlet, and finally get the heater set up near the fireplace. I turn the knob and, just like magic, heated air comes pouring out. I feel like cheering. I hear Tom's boots on the porch and go to let him in. "The heater works."

"Well, it'd better or you should take it back." He walks over to it and warms himself. "You know what you should get, Mrs. Fioré." He points at my fireplace.

"More firewood?"

"Maybe…but that's not what I was thinking. We have these units at the store that slip right into a fireplace, but they're electric. They look like a real fire and put out real heat, but you don't have all the mess and ashes and smoke to go with it. Plus, you can close up the flue so you're not sucking all the heat out of your house."

"Close up the flue?"

He bends over, takes out his flashlight, and peers up into the fireplace. "See this piece of metal right here?"

I bend down next to him and look up to where he's shining the light. "I think I see it."

"If you keep it closed, except when you want a fire, your house will stay warmer." He pulls on the metal, and I hear a *clunk* and some soot falls down. "Just like that."

"I see." I slowly stand up. "Thank you."

"No problem. Just don't forget and start a fire with your flue closed, or you'll really have problems."

I nod as if this is news to me.

"Nice place you got here." He glances around my living room. "Really cool stuff too."

"Thank you." Now I feel as if I should do something to thank this young man. Does he expect some sort of payment?

"Wow, are these real photos or just posters?" He's studying the photo montage now.

I go over and stand with him. "They're the real thing." Then I tell him about Gavin and his work, and although Tom doesn't recognize the name, he's familiar with some of the movies Gavin directed. And he's impressed. I point out Gavin and myself in the photos, and Tom turns to me and says, "So you were, like, famous?"

"My husband was...although I did have a brief acting career...but mostly I was famous by association." I'm somewhat stunned to have admitted this much. But then, really, who is Tom going to tell?

"Well, that is really cool. I can't wait to tell my wife."

"I'd like to pay you for helping me tonight, but I don't have any cash on me at the moment."

"Oh, that's okay. I just helped you 'cuz it was the right thing to do."

The right thing to do. I wonder how he so easily determines what "the right thing to do" is.

He points to a shot of Gavin and John Wayne. "So you even knew the Duke?"

"Oh yes. He came to our house quite a bit. That shot was taken on the set of *The Searchers*."

"Your husband directed *The Searchers*?" His brown eyes are huge now.

I chuckle. "No, no… John Ford directed that one. But Gavin helped a bit on it. He and John were friends."

Tom just shakes his head in wonder. "Wow, this is the closest I've been to anyone famous."

Then I do something that surprises even me. I remove the photo from the wall and hand it to him. "Here. You keep this."

"No way, Mrs. Fioré. You can't be serious."

"I am serious. I want you to have this for helping me tonight."

"But it's your husband and—"

"I have many, many photos of my husband. And to be perfectly honest, John Wayne wasn't my favorite. I suppose I never forgave him for that time he threw my punch bowl into the swimming pool."

"He what?"

I laugh. "Oh, it's foolish, I know, and I really shouldn't hold it against him, but we were having a very nice cocktail party, and John was enjoying quite a bit of Tequila Conmemorativo—his favorite drink—and he got a little carried away with a story he was telling. And the next thing we knew, he had slung the punch bowl, along with the punch, right into the swimming pool."

Tom laughs, then tries to hand the framed photo back to me. "I can't take this."

I hold up my hands. "Yes, you can."

"But why?"

I consider this. "Because it's *the right thing to do.*"

He thanks me for the photo, then goes out to check on my car. After he's removed his equipment, he knocks on my door again. "I'm not sure if that charge'll hold till morning, Mrs. Fioré. You might want to take your car out for a little drive to keep the battery going."

"I really don't like to drive at night. What happens if I don't?"

"Could be dead in the morning."

"Oh…"

"I could take it for a little spin, I mean, if you trust me. I don't blame you if you don't. But if you want to make sure the car's charged up good, it'd be the best thing to do." He grins. "And I've never driven a Jag before."

I wave my hand at him. "You go ahead, Tom. Your truck will be here. If you don't come back, I shouldn't have too much trouble tracking you down."

"That's for sure." He laughs. "My wife would kill me if I stole a car. We're expecting our first baby in February, and I don't think she'd appreciate having a felon for the daddy."

So I watch as an almost complete stranger drives off into the freezing, foggy night with my car. I'm sure some people would call me incredibly naive or simply stupid, but I trust Tom.

25

I feel strangely empowered now. As if I have a smidgeon of control over my recently disrupted life…or perhaps, as Michael suggested, someone more powerful is watching out for me.

With authority and purpose, I open more heater boxes, placing one unit in my bedroom, one in the bathroom, and one in the kitchen. Then I put my other hardware store purchases away and plug in my new telephones. I place the black one in the living room and the white one in the bedroom, testing them to make sure they both work. I'm fully aware that this is an everyday thing for most people, but when I hear the dial tone, I feel as if I've just climbed a mountain.

Unfortunately it's probably too late to call my accountant. Just the same, I try Jackie's number. When I get his answering machine, I leave a message, asking him to call me at my new number. "At your earliest convenience, please."

I feel quite pleased with myself when I hang up. Although I felt like screaming and demanding that he send money immediately, I was actually rather polite. Hopefully that will get his attention. Then I call Michael.

"Hello, darling! It's so good to hear your voice. How is everything in Silverton?"

"It's been interesting. But I think I might survive."

He laughs. "Oh, you are a survivor, Claudette, if ever there was one."

"I wouldn't go *that* far."

"Well, I'd love to chat, but we have guests. Richard's sister and her husband and kids came out for Thanksgiving, and we were just about to head down to the beach for a sunset picnic."

"Sounds lovely."

"Oh, it is. I wish you could join us. It's been glorious weather."

"I wish I could too. It's freezing cold here."

"Well, stay warm, darling, and have a good Thanksgiving."

"Yes. You too."

I hang up and look out the window in time to see headlights pulling into the driveway. I meet Tom at the door, and he hands my keys over. "She's a great little car, Mrs. Fioré." Then he gives me a business card as well. "I hope you don't mind, but I stopped by my brother-in-law's house and showed off your car. I told him you might be in the market for a garage to keep her in. He sent you his card."

"Thank you."

"Thanks again for that photo of the Duke. I can't wait to show my wife."

"You are very welcome, Tom. Thank you once again for all your help tonight."

I close the front door and walk through my living room,

looking at the photos and various pieces of original art that grace my walls, studying them closely as if seeing them for the first time. I suppose I have taken these things, as well as their monetary value, for granted. I remember Melinda's challenge to me earlier today, that if I could part with some of these pieces, I might be able live a bit more comfortably. I consider Tom's suggestion of a garage. Surely, a garage might be more useful to me, not to mention my car, than one of these paintings. And yet how does one go about selling a valuable piece of art? I wouldn't even know where to begin.

I decide to be like Scarlett O'Hara and just think about that tomorrow. Right now, I am hungry. And I have a load of wet laundry that needs to be placed in the dryer. I hope it hasn't gotten smelly with mildew yet. To my relief, the clothes seem fine as I take them out piece by piece and place them in the dryer with one of Michael's magical dryer sheets.

"There." I close the door and turn the dial to sixty minutes, just like Irene showed me. And then I hear the dryer running, and I figure I must've done something right.

After fixing myself a light dinner, I am exhausted. I should wash the dishes, but I'm afraid I might break more than I clean. They will have to wait until morning. And yet it seems too early to go to bed. I wish I could sit down and lose myself in front of an old movie, but the television is still not connected to cable.

I wander back to my bedroom, which is still rather messy. That too will have to wait until tomorrow. When I would get impatient about something not getting done, Gavin used to remind me that "Rome wasn't built in a day." Of course, I was usually impatient with someone else's lack of initiative…not my own. Nevertheless, the saying probably still applies.

Thinking of Gavin reminds me of that box of letters my mother saved over the years. From a glance I could see that a number of them were written by Gavin. I know he and Mother got along wonderfully—sometimes so much so that I would become jealous. But, really, what could he have possibly written to her?

I retrieve the box of letters, take them to the living room, and begin to sort through them. It might make more sense if I read the older ones first, a bit like reading someone's journal. I separate Gavin's letters from the occasional postcard or greeting card sent by me. I feel slightly embarrassed to see my brief notes…not even complete sentences, and many times I simply signed my name. How personal.

I start with the oldest letter I can find. It was written in 1981, shortly after we returned from Mother's seventy-fifth birthday party.

Dear Mother,

It feels a bit odd to call you Mother, but since you so sweetly asked me, I will comply. It was fantastic to meet you last week. I had no idea that Claudette's mother was such a lovely person. I know, from what little I manage to dredge from my wife, that you've had more than your

share of struggles. And yet when I met you, you were so
gracious, so kind—I didn't see a trace of bitterness in
you. And I have to say that impressed me. It impressed
me a lot. But not only impress me, it gave me a new
sense of hope for my wife. I don't want to sound like I'm
complaining, but I'm sure you must know: Claudette
can be difficult. And I suppose, in all fairness, I have
spoiled her some over the years. I feel that I can trust
you, Mother, when I admit that my marriage hasn't been
all roses. We've had a few thorns. And yet I am commit-
ted to do my best by your daughter. And despite these
moments of emotional betrayal, I do believe she loves
me—in her own way. But I would appreciate any sage
advice, any motherly bits of wisdom you might share.
And if not, I remain yours just the same.

    Gavin

As I attempt to slip the pages back into the envelope, my
hands are actually trembling. So Gavin did know about my relationship with Phillip. Yet he never said a word about it to me.
In my defense, I never slept with Phillip. Of course, I wouldn't
have slept with anyone by the time I was past my midfifties. I
just didn't have that kind of confidence. But Gavin was right; I
was involved in an emotional affair.

Still, I am stunned to think that Gavin told my mother
about this. Oh, certainly, he didn't go into detail, but he did tip

his hand. I couldn't be more surprised. I hurry to read the next letter. It's dated a few months later.

Dear Mother,

Thank you for your wise words in regard to our Claudette. I must agree with you that despite that tough veneer she so cleverly reveals to the world, there is a scared, insecure girl underneath. I appreciate that reminder. On a happier note, I do believe she has tired of her game. And, in her way, I think she is trying to show me she's sorry. To be fair, I must blame myself a bit for some of the problems our marriage has suffered. Early on I was more married to my work than to my wife. I neglected her. And of course, my payoff was always monetary. I felt that things, expensive things, could make up for what I was unable to give. I also blame myself because of our age difference. When we married I told myself that sixteen years wasn't so much…but in so many ways Claudette has always been young for her age; whereas I have probably been old and stodgy. Still, I look forward to my remaining years with her. I hope to help make up for previous years, perhaps to build something solid and honorable.

All my love,
Gavin

P.S. Please, don't mention the gift to Claudette. And please know that I enjoy being able to help you financially. I sometimes feel there is little I can do to help anyone personally. It gives me great pleasure to make your life more comfortable. So much so that I'm setting up something permanent with my accountant.

I read over the part about where Gavin regretted being married to his job. I do remember when this realization seemed to hit him. At the time I worried that it was because he had gotten some grim diagnosis and was dying. He was, after all, in his seventies then. For all I knew, our time together was limited.

Things did begin to change between us in the eighties. It was as if we truly became friends. We had good times on vacations. We willingly spent time doing things together. He talked me into taking up golf. Despite the fact that I was getting older and more obsessed over the whole aging process, those really were the golden years. And whenever I wanted the latest procedure, insisting I would only be happy if I could remain young, Gavin never argued. No matter the cost, he never balked. All he would say is, "I think you look lovely as you are, darling, but the choice is up to you."

Still, I don't think he minded having a somewhat youthful-looking woman on his arm in those days. Oh, certainly no one would've called me a trophy wife at that stage of the game. But I don't think he was ever ashamed to be seen with me either.

I look at the stack of letters and wonder how much I can take. Already I am filled with a mixture of feelings. A part of me is slightly chagrined that Gavin was so open and honest with my mother. But another part misses Gavin more than ever, regretting how much I took for granted…how much I completely overlooked. Gavin really was a good man.

I read through a few more and am relieved that they don't delve too deeply into personal or painful things. Oh, there are glimpses of his sorrows and disappointments, things he tells her that he never told me. Or maybe he did tell me; maybe I just wasn't listening. The next letter fills me with both anger and guilt.

Dear Mother,

I have finally come to accept the fact that Claudette is an extremely jealous woman. Did you know this about your daughter? As you're aware, I was married to Gala Morrow before I met Claudette. We were married less than ten years and then Gala died in 1940. She was only thirty-seven, and I was devastated and never expected to remarry. In fact, I didn't date for several years. Then, six years after losing Gala, I married your daughter. I told myself that I was over Gala, but I don't think that was honest. Gala was my first love. How do you get over that? So I've insisted on keeping her photos in our home. Today Claudette threw a horrible fit. She accused me of loving Gala more than her. Of course, I denied this. But now as I sit at my desk, late into the night with perhaps too much Glenmorangie flowing through my veins, just staring at a photo of my dear Gala, I know that it's true. I did love Gala more than Claudette. But what am I to do about this now? Should I confess my falseness to Claudette? Should I remove Gala's photos from our home? I have come to trust your wisdom, dear Mother, please advise me now.

All my love,

Gavin

I refold the letter, return it to its envelope, and wonder how my mother reacted to this confession. How did she answer his questions? Still, based on history, I'm sure I can make an educated guess as to her response. Gavin never did confess to me that he loved Gala more than me. Not that I didn't know this already. And yet he didn't remove her photos either. Somehow I'm sure this was upon the advice of my mother. Suddenly I feel enraged at her. What right did she have to interfere with my marriage like this? What had ever made her an expert in marriage? or relationships? or even love, for that matter? And why on earth did Gavin turn to her for marital advice?

I am too angry to continue reading. Instead, I go to my room, and upon seeing the mess that's still there, I start throwing clothes and shoes and magazines and things around until it looks even worse. Then I just stand there, staring at the chaos of my creation, and I begin to cry. What is the matter with me?

Slowly, I go around, picking up the items I have so carelessly slung about. I throw some things away, hang some things up, fold others, make a pile of clothes that need laundering. I even remember the laundry baskets and put them to use. Eventually, other than my unmade bed, which has not been made since Michael left, the room is back in order. I feel pleased with my efforts, so I take it even one more step. I will change the linens on my bed.

Naturally this takes much longer than expected. And it is thoroughly exhausting. But finally, close to midnight, I am done. My bedroom looks almost as nice as it did the first time Michael showed it to me. The only thing missing is the vase of pink rosebuds he had placed on the bedside table. Proud of my work, I carry the used sheets to the laundry room and set them on the washer. That can wait until tomorrow.

Hungry from this evening's unexpected exercise, I decide I should make myself a late-night snack. I look in my refrigerator, trying to decide what to have…and then I remember how sometimes, back in the earlier years of marriage, Gavin and I would have a late-night snack. Usually it was much later than this, more like three in the morning. Gavin would whip up what he called a "scrambled omelet," because he didn't know how to make an official omelet. He would take out a bowl and stir up a bunch of eggs, adding things like shredded cheese and chives or mushrooms. Then he would melt butter in an omelet pan and stir them over the heat until they were done. I think it's time for me to attempt something like this.

I slowly go through the steps of chopping and shredding and breaking eggs, thinking of how Gavin did this and that. And it's odd, but it almost begins to feel as if he is here with me. Perhaps he's looking over my shoulder as I stir this yellowy mixture in the pan, unsure as to whether it's actually going to turn out to be edible or not. And then, presto, it begins to cook and slowly gets thicker until finally I can tell it's done. I'm so excited at this success that I feel like a child. I giddily spoon some of my scrambled omelet onto a plate. And then I remember seasonings. Gavin always added salt and pepper, and so do I. Then I pour myself a goblet of orange juice and sit down.

I hold up my glass in a toast, saying, "To you, Gavin," and then I eat. To my delight, it is rather good, and I eat every bit of it. Perhaps not as good as Gavin's, but it's a beginning. I'm just finishing up my juice when I smell something burning. I look over to see that the stove is still on and the omelet pan is smoking. I turn off the element and move the pan. Oh well, at least I didn't go to bed with it like that. I didn't burn down the house. Not yet anyway. As I get ready for bed, I wonder how long it will take for me to get good at this. Or is it even possible?

I sleep in quite late, but I believe it's the best I've slept since moving to Silverton. Perhaps one of the best night's rests since Gavin died. It's almost noon when I get up, and I feel surprisingly refreshed as I put on my dressing gown and slippers. Then I go check to see that the other heaters are still running. While it's not as cold in here as yesterday, it's still a bit nippy, and I can tell that the oil furnace is going to be a necessity if I am to survive this winter.

Thinking of the oil furnace reminds me of my suspicions regarding my sister yesterday—my *What Ever Happened to Baby Jane?* theory. It seemed very real to me at the time, especially considering my dire straits and Violet's antagonistic attitude toward me. However, I am not so sure today. It's possible I over-reacted. Still, I don't mind if the police look into it.

Thankfully no one is beating on my door this morning. Then I remember that today is Thanksgiving and people are probably busy getting ready to spend time with family and friends. How many, right now, are cooking up calorie-laden foods? How many are preparing to gorge themselves on turkey and stuffing, raising their cholesterol levels with too many help-ings of mashed potatoes and gravy? Well, good for them. I don't mind missing out on this occasion.

Besides, I tell myself as I make espresso, I did have two invi-tations. Caroline—not Violet, of course—invited me out to McLachlan Manor, and then Irene invited me to her house, telling me I could change my mind if I liked. However, I don't believe I will change my mind. For some reason, that seems a bit pathetic. It would be like admitting to her and everyone there that I'm lonely. And although I have done almost everything possible to humiliate myself these past few days, it's about time to start drawing the line.

I rather relish the idea of being in my house today. Only twenty-four hours ago this place was a house of horrors. Now it feels peaceful and somewhat orderly... My goal is to keep it that way. After a light breakfast, I wash the dishes from yesterday and today. Then I put a load of laundry into the washing machine, and as Irene advised me, I'm careful not to overload it. After that, I take more of Irene's advice and go over my lists and even make a new one. Things I will do tomorrow.

But by midafternoon, I feel a bit out of sorts. I try not to think about other people, those who are gathering with friends and family right now. Perhaps there's the sound of a ball game playing in the background, the tinkling of glasses, the ringing of laughter, pumpkin pie with whipped cream for dessert. I long for some distraction from these thoughts—a television, some kind of chatter or noise to fill up the quiet space of my small house. But there seems to be no escape. I suppose there's no getting around this.

I am lonely. And I feel a fool for declining Irene's invitation.

So what if she or her friends make the assumption that I'm lonely? Why am I such an old fool? Lonely. Old. Fool.

26

On Friday I attempt to call my accountant again. This time I listen a bit more carefully to the recording to discover that his office will be "closed during the holiday and won't be open again until Monday." I don't leave a message this time. Instead I slam down the receiver. What right does Jackie have to tie up my funds until Monday? For all he knows I could be starving, freezing… Come to think of it, wasn't that nearly the case? I had really been hoping to have some funds transferred up here so I could get a few groceries today. Unfortunately that doesn't appear to be possible.

I go over my lists again. I call the heating oil company and am informed that an order for oil has already been placed by a woman from Senior Services and that a delivery truck should be by later today. Then I decide to pay a visit to the local bank. At least I can open an account and have it all ready for when I speak to Jackie, which I hope will be Monday.

Once again I dress carefully. I suppose I'm hoping to impress the people at the bank. After all, I may have to ask them for a loan or something to temporarily get me by this little financial dry spell. It's hard to believe that I have less than seven dollars to my name at the moment. I look at the art on my walls and remember what the Senior Services volunteer said about selling something. And then I remember there is that art gallery by Maurice's restaurant. Perhaps they would have some interest. I think I'll pay them a visit as well.

My stop at the bank is disappointing. Not only am I unable to discuss a loan, since their loan officer is gone, but I cannot even open an account. "You have to have *money* to set up an account," she tells me as if I'm a simpleton. Goodness, I don't know when I've suffered such humiliation—publicly anyway. So I crisply tell the ignorant girl, who is dressed in blue jeans, of all things, that I am waiting for funds to arrive and that I simply want to get an account in order to have a deposit made.

"Perhaps I shall look for another banking establishment to handle my financial affairs." I hook my purse strap over my arm and make a hasty exit. Unfortunately that bank is the only one in town. Still, I hope I've worried her a bit. As I get into my car, I wish I'd mentioned something about speaking to her manager next week when my funds do arrive—perhaps that would've put that disrespectful upstart in her place.

Feeling slightly more desperate than when I set out this morning, I drive on up to the Phoenix Gallery, park my car in front, and go inside. Classical music is playing, and there is a good smell in here—a combination of oil paint, pine trees, and something else—coffee perhaps. Although the building seemed small on the exterior, it feels spacious inside with its high ceilings and wooden floors. The lighting for a small gallery seems well done, and the selection of art, while slightly minimalist, isn't half bad. Especially for a small town. Of course, I don't recognize the names of these artists, but the quality of the work, much of it abstract, contemporary, and modern, is something I wouldn't be ashamed to hang on my own walls. Although a recognizable name on the canvas would make the prospects more tempting. Not that I can afford to purchase anything right now.

"Good afternoon, ma'am," says a man who appears to be fortyish. He has a goatee and short-cropped dark hair. "Anything I can help you with today?"

"I'm new in town," I begin, thinking that's not exactly true, but I don't care to explain my roots to someone I don't even know. "I heard about your gallery and I thought it was time to come see it for myself."

He smiles and extends his hand. "Welcome to Silverton. I'm Garth Rawlins, the owner of the Phoenix."

I nod with appreciation. "I'm Claudette Fioré, and this is a lovely little gallery."

"Thank you. Where did you relocate from, Ms. Fioré?"

"Southern California..."

"Ah yes, well, then this must seem like a very small gallery to you."

"But it's marvelous for Silverton. I was actually quite surprised to find the town has an art gallery at all."

"So what brought you to Silverton?"

I quickly explain that I grew up here and have returned to my family home. "I think I'll appreciate the slower pace," I say, getting more and more comfortable with my little white lie. "It's nice to be able to walk to town... And I feel safer here... although the weather seems a bit extreme."

"It's not usually this cold."

"I noticed you have a good selection of contemporary art," I say. "I don't recognize the names, but they seem talented enough." Then realization hits me. "Oh, did you say your name is Garth Rawlins?"

He nods.

"So some of these paintings are yours?"

"Yes." He seems uncomfortable. "I suppose my gallery is a little self-serving."

I walk over to one of the abstracts I had already admired— a large piece in blocks of burgundy, orange, and gold. "This is very nice. Those colors would be absolutely perfect in my house."

He brightens. "Really? I have a policy where I allow clients to take something home and try it for three days. If you don't like it, bring it back and try something else."

"Unfortunately I have more than enough art in my house."

He looks disappointed, and I feel badly for having strung him along. "But if I did have room, I would certainly consider your work."

"Yes, I get a lot of that. Sometimes I wonder if it was a mistake to set up a gallery in this town."

"What made you choose Silverton?"

He shrugs. "I passed through here one day in the summer a

few years ago. For some reason I thought the town was charming...maybe because it was a sunny day. I had started a gallery in Bodega Bay, but there was a fire... The gallery burned to the ground—including my work."

"Oh, how heartbreaking."

"It was even more heartbreaking when my insurance company took more than a year to pay me a settlement. They actually thought I'd burned the place down myself."

"Why on earth?"

"Well, as you can imagine, there were a few galleries in Bodega Bay... Business had slowed down due to the economy." He shakes his head. "But anyone who knew me would know I would *never* burn my own paintings. What kind of a moron would do something like that?"

"Ah, so that's why your gallery is called the Phoenix?"

"Precisely." He nods. "We rose from the ashes."

"Well, I can't speak for Silverton, but I think you have a fine gallery here. And as I mentioned, if I wasn't so overloaded with art myself, I would consider one of your—" Then I stop myself. "Wait a minute, Garth."

"What? Are you okay?"

"I've just had an idea—perhaps it's even a good idea."

"I'm always open to good ideas."

"I'm sure you know who Sean Scully is..."

"Are you kidding? I'm a huge fan of his work."

"Well, I just happen to have an original in my home."

"Seriously?"

"Yes. I also have some other valuable pieces."

"Wow, would I like to see those!"

"And I was thinking…" I study this young man for a moment, wondering how honest I can be with him. For some reason I feel I can trust him. "Is there a place we can sit down?"

"Yes, of course." He points over to a seating area where a couple of attractive chrome and black leather chairs are set up.

"Eames?" I nod to the chairs.

"I wish. But they are a good reproduction, don't you think?"

"Yes." I sit down. "Comfortable too."

"So what's your idea?"

"Well, may I be frank with you?"

"Sure, you know my story." He grins. "Or some of it."

So I tell him who my husband was, and I am not surprised that Garth knows of him.

"No kidding? You were married to Gavin Fioré? I would've thought his wife would be about a hundred by now."

I clear my throat. "Well, his first wife would've been. As it is, I feel that I'm getting awfully close."

He shakes his head. "You don't look like you're even seventy, Mrs. Fioré."

"Call me Claudette." I smile. "All right, here's my idea. First, I will be honest and tell you, in all confidence, that Gavin's estate has gone through some hard times, and most of my finances have been seized."

"Is that why you moved here?"

"Exactly. I do, however, still have a fairly nice collection of art, including the Scully. However, because I am short of funds, I am thinking of selling a few pieces."

He frowns. "As much as I would love to have a Scully in here, there is no way I can afford something like that."

"Oh…"

"However, I might be interested in taking something on consignment." He looks unsure now. "But you might not care to do that."

"Can you explain what that would entail?" I ask, hoping not to appear too ignorant.

"We would write up a contract for your art, and it would hang in my gallery. If any sold, I would take a small commission and pay you the remainder."

"Yes." I don't want to seem too eager. "That sounds like a sensible plan, and perhaps if you have some collectible pieces mixed in with your work, you might get some recognition, possibly a write-up in an art magazine."

His eyes light up. "Definitely. Some well-known names in here could bring me some good attention…maybe some good foot traffic."

"Perhaps you'd even have a special show. Maybe for the holidays."

"Oh, Mrs. Fioré! Would you really be interested?"

I nod. "You know, I think I would. It's not anything I would've considered before. But now, well, things are changing. I suppose I am changing too."

"When can I see your pieces?"

"Whenever you like."

"How about now?"

I shrug. "I don't see why not."

"My sister, also my partner, is in the back room working on a frame. If you'll excuse me, I'll go ask her to watch the shop for me."

As he goes back, I walk around his gallery. While the art really is nice, it's very sparse. There is room for more. I pause in front of his abstract, the one I think would go well in my house. Perhaps I wouldn't miss my Scully quite so much if this one were to hang in its place. I look at the price. In the old days, $3,900 would seem like a trifle. But now...I'm not so sure.

"Okay," he says as he rejoins me. He has a coat slung over one arm.

"I'm thinking, Garth...my walls could look empty if I get rid of too much. Perhaps we could work a way to make some swaps."

"I don't see why we can't discuss it." He peers curiously at me. "You really do have an original Scully?"

"Trust me, it's the real thing. Gavin bought it years ago."

"What're we waiting for?"

He follows me to my house, and when we get out of our cars and go up the walk, I feel slightly apologetic for my humble abode. "It's not much—my house, I mean. It's been quite a transition for me...moving from Beverly Hills to here."

"It's a cute house," he says as I unlock the door.

"My stepson helped me set it up. Naturally only a small portion of my things could fit in here."

"Wow." He stops to admire an Avakyan abstract that's next to the window.

"Gavin got that for me just a few years before he passed away. It used to hang in our bedroom."

"It's beautiful."

I study it more closely. "It is, isn't it? And over here"—I point to the large painting above my sofa—"is the Scully."

Garth turns around and his eyes get so big that I'm worried he is going to faint dead away. He just shakes his head in silence. Finally he mutters, "Awesome...that is just awesome."

"Would you like some coffee or something?"

"That sounds great."

"You go ahead and look around," I say as I go to the kitchen.

Garth slowly works his way around my house making *ooh* and *ahh* sounds at the appropriate times. Finally he steps into the kitchen and lets out a big sigh. "Man, Claudette, your gallery is way hotter than mine."

I have to laugh as I hand him his coffee cup. "Well, let's discuss this in the living room."

Once we are comfortably seated, I tell him that I know I would greatly miss my Scully painting. "It's so warm and alive. I find it rather comforting in this room. But in some ways, it reminds me of that large piece you painted."

"Thanks, I take that as high praise."

"If you knew me, you'd know I don't hand out praise lightly."

"I'd gladly swap my painting for this one," he says quickly. "Not straight across, of course." He chuckles. "Maybe someday my work will be as valuable as a Scully. But for now, maybe we could work something else out—something that would make us both happy."

So we sit here, drinking our coffee and discussing what we might do. And while I certainly don't want to part with *all* of my art, I get a sense of excitement thinking that I might actually be helping this young man with his gallery. I've never been involved in anything like this before, but I want to be part of it now.

Finally we settle on several pieces, including the Scully. The agreement is that no money will cross hands yet—my paintings will be on consignment at the Phoenix, and if they should sell for fair market price, I will use some of my profits to purchase his paintings, which will be hanging in my house on loan in the meantime.

"I can get this all written up legally. My sister is the one with the business head. Celia is really good at that sort of thing."

"If you do get an exhibition scheduled, with some good media coverage and such…well, perhaps I can loan you the rest of my art. You know, to sort of fill up the gallery during that time."

"You would do that?"

I smile. "Gavin and I always considered ourselves to be patrons of the arts, Garth. But in all honesty, it was Gavin who walked the walk. I mostly just went along for the ride. Perhaps it's my turn to get involved."

"You won't hear me complaining."

We shake hands and exchange phone numbers, and I send Garth happily on his way. He plans to get back to me as soon as his sister puts something together. A part of me is rather stunned to think of what I'm doing. I'm sure some would question my sanity to trade my valuable art to a man I only met today. But somehow I think it's the right thing to do. And somehow I feel that Gavin would approve.

And I cannot deny that it feels slightly amazing to be helping someone else for a change.

27

On Saturday I get up earlier than usual. Garth called last night, telling me his sister has written out a contract that he wanted to bring by in the morning. So I invited them both to join me for coffee at ten.

It's times like this when I really miss Sylvia's cooking abilities. How nice it would be to have her whip up some fresh scones and muffins for my guests. As it is, I make do with a package of shortcake and some chocolate mint wafers. But I do arrange these carefully on a china plate. Before Garth and his sister arrive, I have everything nicely set on a sterling Chippendale tray, which I plan to serve in the living room. My only regret is that I have no fresh flowers. Oh, the pity of being poor.

My guests are prompt, and I welcome them into my humble abode. "It's not much," I tell them as I take their coats. "But I'm getting used to it."

"This is my sister Celia," Garth tells me. "Celia, this is Mrs. Fioré."

I shake Celia's hand, noting that she seems quite a bit older than her brother. And she's not as colorful as he. Her brown wool sweater is somewhat worn at the elbows, and her no-nonsense loafers suggest she is more practical than fashionable.

"It's a pleasure to meet you," I say. "But, please, call me Claudette."

"Your home is charming," she says. "I adore Craftsman style."

"And her art," says Garth, "is even more charming."

Celia laughs. "Yes, Garth has been going on and on about your collection."

"Please, sit down. I'll get our coffee."

"Let me help," offers Garth, right on my heels. The next thing I know, he is carrying the tray, which is actually rather cumbersome and heavy. He sets it on the oversized ottoman, and soon we are all comfortably settled. I wish I'd thought to make a fire in the fireplace. Still, it's nice and warm in here since the heating oil was delivered yesterday and the furnace has been running ever since.

"Here are the papers I've written up," Celia says after a bit. "I did some research as to current market values for the pieces Garth told me about. But you may want to consult with someone yourself on the prices; perhaps you have insurance estimates." She hands me a folder. "I have a copy of our gallery's insurance policy in there, as well as a brochure about Garth's work and some background about the gallery and our history. I expect you'll need some time to go through these things before you get back to us. As you'll see, our consignment rate is usually twenty percent, but you are doing us such a favor with these valuable pieces that we're willing to reduce it to fifteen."

I open the folder and skim over the pages. I am mostly interested in the values she's attached to my paintings. But I'm also considering her mention of insurance. I have absolutely no idea as to whether my belongings in this house are actually insured. That was one of the items on Michael's list—something I haven't gotten around to yet. It's unsettling to think that if something catastrophic happened, I might be left with nothing. Perhaps I should consign all my art to the Phoenix.

"Goodness," I say when I get to the values. "I didn't realize the paintings were worth that much. Are you sure?"

"According to my research, that's in the ballpark," says Celia. "Your husband had a good eye for art, especially investment art. These painters have all appreciated a great deal in the past two decades."

"I see that." I continue to skim the paperwork, and everything really does seem to be in order. I am tempted to sign them here and now, but I don't wish to appear overly eager or foolish. On the other hand, I'm uneasy about my own insurance situation. What if my house burned down tonight? Wouldn't I appear even more foolish to have lost all my art's value for lack of insurance coverage?

Just as I'm about to tell them it's a deal, I hear someone walking on the porch. Goodness, I hope it's not Busybody Bea. She should be getting home soon. "Excuse me." I go to answer the door. To my surprise, it's Irene.

"Hello," she says warmly. "I'm sorry to intrude like this, but I don't know if you'd gotten your phone hooked up yet. And besides, I don't have a number, but I wanted to stop by and ask you—"

"Come in, come in," I say, knowing that I will appear rude if I keep her standing on the porch. "I have guests, but you are—"

"Hey, Irene," Garth says as she enters the room. "Good to see you again. We sure had a great time at your house the other day. Thanks again for including us."

"Garth and Celia?" Irene looks at them and then curiously at me. "I didn't know you all were acquainted."

"We just met yesterday," I explain.

"Come join us." Garth pats the sofa beside him. "We're discussing art."

"Would you like some coffee?" I offer.

"No, thank you." She sits next to Garth. "But I might take a piece of that shortcake. I have a weakness for it."

"Of course." I pass the plate to her. "So, you are all friends?"

"Yes," says Irene. "Garth and Celia were part of my Thanksgiving gathering. Celia made the most incredible yam dish. I didn't think I liked yams...but she's changed my mind about that."

I feel a twinge of regret for not going to Irene's for Thanksgiving. Why was I being so stubborn? Or perhaps I was just being too proud. "I'm thinking of consigning some of my art to the Phoenix."

"Yes," says Garth. "Isn't it exciting? If we had artists of this caliber in the gallery, we could probably get some good media coverage."

"What a wonderful idea." Irene looks at me. "But I'm surprised you want to part with your paintings. They look so wonderful in here."

"Well, she might be willing to work a trade," Garth says happily. "Not straight across, of course. But she likes my art."

"In fact," I tell them, "I was just about to sign these contracts."

"Don't you want to go over them carefully?" asks Celia.

"They seem to be in order." I don't mention my fear about my own lack of insurance. "I don't see any reason to delay this. Besides, with Christmas around the corner, you might want to get something going right away."

"You know, the Christmas parade is two weeks away," says Irene. "That Saturday could be the perfect time for an exhibition."

"Yes, and that would also give us enough time to get out a press release," says Celia.

"And, if you like, I could let you borrow all my paintings for that evening's exhibit," I offer. "Perhaps for the following week as well."

"We could promote it as a one-time-only event." Celia writes down notes.

"Perhaps you could talk Page's friend Audra into playing violin."

"That's a great idea, Irene," says Garth. "And we'll serve wine and cheese."

Soon they are all spouting ideas, and I take the contracts into the kitchen and skim them once again. Then I sign each one and return the folder to Celia.

"This is so exciting." Celia signs her portion of the contracts and hands me back my copies. "It will be our biggest event ever."

"And Claudette will be our guest of honor," proclaims Garth. "Our personal patron of the arts."

"Well, you should at least ask her," says Celia. "She might be busy or not want to be involved—"

"Of course, I want to be involved. I'll do whatever I can to make this a huge success. In fact, I could contact some of my art friends in the Los Angeles area. Come to think of it, there were a number of people who had coveted some of Gavin's finds over the years. Maybe they'll want to come up here."

"Well, we have a lot to do," says Celia. "I want to work on the press releases."

"And I'll get the van to come back and pick up the contracted paintings," says Garth. Within minutes Garth and Celia are gone.

"How exciting," says Irene. "Garth and Celia are such dears, but it's been an uphill battle operating an art gallery in Silverton."

"Maybe that's about to change."

"I came by to invite you to the Festival of Trees," says Irene. I try to think why that sounds familiar and remember that horrid morning, only days ago, when my sister and friends came to invite me to this very same event. Just the thought of it brings a sour taste to my mouth. "I think I'll pass."

"Are you sure? I've heard it's rather nice this year."

"Yes, but thank you for thinking of me."

Irene smiles. "You seem to be getting along well, Claudette."

"Thank you. I am doing my best. But I'm afraid that I'm still not caught up. I have some laundry to do as well as some other household chores."

"Well, perhaps we can do something together next week," she suggests. "Even if it's just coffee."

"Yes, that would be nice. Perhaps later in the week." Hopefully I will have some money by then. I give Irene my phone number, hoping she might take this as a hint and call first instead of just popping in unannounced. I am growing very weary of unexpected visitors. Perhaps I should put a sign on my door: Occupant Will Be Seen by Appointment Only.

"Oh, another thing," she says as she's about to leave. "I wanted to invite you to church tomorrow."

I take in a breath. "I don't think so, Irene. I've never been much of a churchgoing person."

She laughs. "Yes, I figured as much. But perhaps you'd like to come to our women's book group. It's a very casual gathering of some interesting women. Page Turner leads it. We're doing a Christmas novella for December."

I consider this. "Can I think about it?"

"Of course."

As Irene drives away in her funny minivan, I wonder why I am so hesitant to participate in new things. Am I truly such a snob? Do I really feel I am superior to these people? Or is it something else? I remember when I lived in this town before, so many, many years ago. How I tried to keep myself apart from people during my youth as well. I think, in all honesty, I did this as a self-preservation tactic. I didn't want anyone to get close enough to see what my home life was really like. I didn't want to be teased for the fact that my father was a lush...or that my mother washed other peoples' laundry to feed her children.

Certainly I was aware that people knew these things. After all, Silverton was a small town. Even smaller than it is now. But I think I convinced myself that if I could hold people at bay—keep them a good arm's distance away—I could avoid the sort of intimacy that would lead to humiliation. Because, even as a child, I detested humiliation.

Thinking of these old things reminds me of my old best friend Caroline. She was the only person I ever allowed myself to get close to as a youth. And even then I held back some. But we did have some good times together, and I would actually enjoy seeing her again. That is, if I could erase the gruesome image she must still have of me from that frightful morning. I'm just not quite sure how one eradicates something like that. Perhaps it's better to let this friendship go. Or maybe in time, say six months or so, I might make an effort to spend time with her again.

I wish I could say the same for my sister. I am still greatly peeved at Violet, and I'm not sure that I'll feel differently in six months or even six years. Oh, I doubt she was really involved in a conspiracy against me. I probably blew that out of proportion. And I cringe to think of the accusations I made against her. The police most likely came to their own conclusions. Thankfully I didn't attempt to press charges.

What irks me most about her is the way she has treated me over the years...as if I am to blame for everything. I always feel as if she holds things against me. And yet they seem to be invisible things, for I am never quite sure what it is I've done. I chalk it up to jealousy. But you'd think that one could set such pettiness aside at our age. Still, I'm afraid we'll take it to our graves. I suppose that makes me sad.

By Saturday evening I have something else to feel sad about. Garth arrives with his van and packing blankets and removes the paintings I contracted for consignment. He promises to bring his paintings to my home after Celia writes contracts to cover them as well, but in the meantime my walls look rather stark and bare. Particularly in the living room. I did not know I would miss the paintings so much.

I go to bed early, taking the bundle of Gavin's letters with me. I'm not sure if I expect these letters to bring comfort and relief or if I am just setting myself up for more torture. Nonetheless, I sit in my bed and read, picking up where I left off, shortly after Gavin told my mother about my jealousy of Gala.

Dear Mother,

I think you must be right about your daughter's
insecurities. Although I have to admit I questioned that
at first. I'm sure most people who know my wife consider
her to be anything but insecure. I've heard her described
as haughty, superior, snobby, shallow…but never insecure. Her identity is so wrapped up in material things
and superficial appearances. She needs to dress a certain
way, talk a certain way, live a certain way…or she's perfectly miserable—and she can make others miserable
too. Once again, I must assume some of the blame here
since I have in essence enabled her. Sometimes I actually
feel as if I have created a monster! And yet I do love her.
I don't know what I would do without her. Especially in
my old age. She really has some fine qualities. Her
humor. Her mind. Her social abilities. Her lively spirit.
She really can be good company for an old fart like me.
So, please, don't take my candid communication as complaining. You really do have a fine daughter.

Love always,

Gavin

Well, I'm not quite sure how to take that last letter. I suppose I could see it as a veiled compliment, although that's a bit
of a stretch. And I'm afraid that I must admit that Gavin was
only speaking the truth—as he saw it anyway. Naturally I would
have thrown a fit if I'd read his letter back then. I would accuse

him of being disloyal and mean. Yet, somehow, I feel I can handle it better now. In a way it's like taking your medicine—it's bitter, but you hope that it's good for you.

There are similar letters of contemplations and musings, and some that seem written simply to cheer up my mother. Once again, I am reminded that Gavin really was a good man, a kind man…a man I took for granted.

By eleven o'clock, I've worked my way up to 1998. Just a few years before Gavin's death. To my surprise, it seems my mother has experienced some sort of personal revival and, perhaps because they are both in their nineties and facing their own mortality, they both seem to be openly speaking of God. This doesn't surprise me in regard to Gavin, since I do recall a change in him in the year before his death. But for some reason it surprises me about my mother.

Dear Mother,

I'm interested to hear more about this spiritual revelation you've experienced. What made you suddenly take an interest in God and the Bible? From what Claudette has told me, you were never religious, never attended church…and now it sounds as if that has all changed. Most people don't know that I was actually raised in a religious home or that my father was a preacher. It's a piece of my past I've kept hidden from everyone. Even Claudette. I suppose it was partly because I was embarrassed by it but also because my family disowned me when I expressed my interest in motion pictures. Our church was very conservative—no smoking, drinking, dancing, movies…and the list went on and on. As a teenager, I broke all the rules. I sneaked off to the movie theater, smoked and drank occasionally, and danced with "worldly" girls who wore makeup, jewelry, and fancy clothes. My parents didn't know what to do with me. At one point, I thought maybe I could give it all up. Except for movies. I loved the art of telling stories in film. Finally my parents said I had to choose. So I did. I picked film. Oh, in later years when I was a success, my parents "forgave" me. Their church had changed its position on movie-going (not on smoking or drinking or dancing), and because the films I made were more family friendly than some movies, I was partially "accepted." But never completely. When my parents died, a wide gulf still spanned between us. Something I was never able to bridge. So now you see my interest in whatever it is you have experienced in regard to God. Please, enlighten me. I am curious.

Love always,
Gavin

My eyelids refuse to stay open, and I set the bundle of letters aside, turn out the light, and consider Gavin's family history. I never knew any of that. I suppose I never even asked. All I knew was that his family was a bit old-fashioned and lived in Connecticut. The one time we went out to visit, while on our way to New York, Gavin's father had long since retired. I had assumed from business. I didn't feel very welcome in their home, and we only stayed for a few hours. But now it makes a bit of sense.

I can hear Gavin's hurt in that letter. I can imagine the young man who wanted to please his family but couldn't. I suppose in some ways I can relate to him. I never felt as if my family gave me the recognition I deserved for escaping the humdrum existence in Silverton. They never seemed to fully appreciate that I had made it in the bigger world.

In fact, I often felt judged and condemned, especially by my sister. As if her choice to go to college, become a teacher, and raise a family was morally superior to my lifestyle. My mother never said as much, but I suspected that she didn't completely approve of my choices either. It wasn't until shortly before she passed away that I began to feel a sense of acceptance from her. Now I wonder if Gavin didn't have something to do with that as well.

It is all too overwhelming to think about tonight. My brain is tired and weary. Perhaps I will think about it some other time.

28

On Sunday I feel dismal and gray—a bit like the weather. I walk about my house looking sadly at the barren walls and wishing I hadn't consigned my paintings to the Phoenix. What was I thinking?

To distract myself, and because I have only three bath towels, all of which are dirty, I decide to do some laundry. However, after I load the linens and turn the washer on, I discover I am out of laundry soap. I shake the blue jug several times, but only a drop or two comes out.

I stand there perplexed, wondering what to do, when it occurs to me that I do have dishwashing soap. Like the laundry soap, it's liquid and soapy, so why shouldn't it work as well? I go to the sink, retrieve the bottle of Joy, and fill the laundry soap dispenser cup with the proper amount. Then, quite pleased with myself, I pour this into the washer.

After that, I go back to the bedroom to get dressed. I would just as soon remain in my pajamas, perhaps even stay in bed all day. But I feel that is like giving in…and after all of my hard work, I don't think that's wise. So despite the fact that I have no intention of seeing anyone or going anywhere, I force myself to dress. Not only that, I force myself to make my bed as well.

To my surprise, I feel a bit better after accomplishing these two rather basic tasks. Perhaps to feel well, one needs to do well. Whatever the case, this little exercise in discipline was probably beneficial. I'm just plumping the last pillow when I hear a loud knocking on my front door, and then the bell is ringing. Not just once but over and over.

I hurry to see who it is. It's Busybody Bea. I am tempted to ignore her, but it is difficult to ignore the racket she is making.

"You're home," I say in a slightly bored tone, and the next thing I know, this obnoxious woman bursts through the door and marches straight through my living room. "Where are you going?" I say as I follow her.

"Your laundry!" she exclaims hysterically, hustling right to the kitchen, where she stops and points at the laundry room door, as if that should explain everything.

I am standing behind her now, trying to decide whether or not to call the police to remove this crazy woman from my house. Has she taken complete leave of her senses? "What on earth are you doing?"

"Your laundry!" she shrieks, turning to look at me. "Do you have any idea what is going on in—?"

I push past her and open the door to the laundry room porch, ready to prove that this woman has completely lost her mind, but suddenly there is a wave of white foaming bubbles pouring into my kitchen. I slam the door shut and turn to look at Bea. "What did you do to my laundry?"

"I didn't do a thing to your laundry," she says indignantly. "I just came to tell you there's a problem. Don't shoot the messenger, Claudette."

"But what on earth?"

"What kind of soap are you using?" She plants her hands on her hips.

I explain about the dish soap, and she just laughs.

"What is so funny?"

"You never, *never* put dish soap into the washing machine. Didn't anyone tell you that?"

I grab a couple of dishtowels, trying to mop up the mess of bubbles on my wooden kitchen floor, but they just keep spreading, almost as if they're multiplying.

Then Bea looks under my sink, takes out the dishpan, and uses it as a shovel of sorts, scooping up bubbles and tossing them into the sink. After a while, other than a ribbon of foam that continues to creep beneath the bottom of the door, it's fairly well cleaned up. Bea snatches the damp dishtowels, rolls them into tubes, and wedges them as a dam of sorts to stop the escaping foam.

"What do I do about it?" I ask Bea.

"Well, I tried to go in the back way. I was going to turn off your washer myself, but the door was locked."

"How did you know there was a problem?" I ask, still slightly suspicious.

"I was out in my backyard shaking a rug. I happened to look over here and saw what I first thought was snow piled all over your back porch steps. I couldn't figure that out. So I came over to see better and realized it was soap, coming from your laundry room. It appears you have a broken window there. But like I said, the door was locked. So I ran around to the front."

"Should I go around the back then?"

"That's what I'd do. That way the soap won't flood your house when you open the door."

So I get my key and traipse around to the back porch with Bea dogging my heels, and sure enough, white, foamy bubbles are everywhere. I'm not sure what to do. My wool pantsuit is dry clean only, and I'm sure the soap bubbles will ruin it. Oh, why do I bother to dress nicely at all?

"See," Bea proudly proclaims, "looks just like snow, don't it?" Then she points at the heap of garbage next to my trash can. "At first I thought that was some sort of snowman there too. Really had me going for a minute or two." She peers at me now. "You throwing those towels and things out?"

"Yes."

She frowns, then looks back toward the back porch. "Aren't you gonna go in there and shut that thing down?"

I look down at my expensive Versace boots and wonder how Italian leather holds up to soap bubbles.

"Give me that key," she snaps. "I'll do it myself."

Before I can answer, she snatches the key from my hand, marches up the bubble-encased stairs, unlocks the door, and disappears into a white cloud of foam. I stand there just staring with wide eyes. What if she can't breathe in there? What if she falls down and gets hurt? Will she sue me? Do I even have insurance against such things? I am actually holding my breath, waiting for her to reemerge, and when she does, she looks a bit like a snowman herself.

"Careful on those steps," I call out. "I'll bet they're slick."

She wipes the bubbles from her face and hair, then comes slowly down the steps and stands before me, where she shakes the remaining foam from her arms and legs like an oversized dog. I step back to avoid the flying bubbles.

"Thank you." I try to sound truly grateful instead of slightly irritated. "But I really didn't expect you to do that, Bea. I was simply deciding whether or not to change my clothes first."

She rolls her eyes. "There's one good reason why people shouldn't go around trying to dress like movie stars all the time."

I frown at her. "I am not trying to dress like a movie star. I simply enjoy quality clothing. I do not believe that's a crime."

"Well, it's a crime to put dish soap in a washing machine. And it's stupid. Why'd you go and do that, anyway?"

"Because I was *out* of laundry soap."

"Why didn't you go and get some more?"

I consider this. "Because it's Sunday," I say, knowing that's a weak defense. "I thought the stores might be closed."

"Pish posh, there's stores open on Sundays—even Raleigh's is open today. But I don't see why you're doing laundry on a Sunday. Who does laundry on a Sunday anyway?"

"I was doing laundry because I needed clean towels."

Once again she points to my melted snowman of white towels piled by the trash. "What happened to those towels anyway?"

"They are soiled." I hold my head high, thinking I am just about done with this conversation. Why doesn't this woman mind her own business?

"Why weren't you washing them too?"

"Because…they are *beyond saving.*"

She laughs. "Beyond saving? Just because they got dirty? You really do need to take some classes in housekeeping, Claudette."

"Perhaps you need to take some classes in etiquette, Bea."

"And maybe you should take a class in being neighborly."

"Only if you take a class in fashion and style—even if it's simply a beginner's class."

"Well!"

I glare at her, hoping she'll take offense and leave now, for I feel certain we've both said more than enough. But she just stands there, hands planted on hips, staring back at me. "You know what your problem is, Claudette Fioré?"

"No, but I suppose you're going to tell me."

"That's right. You are *full of yourself,* Miss High and Mighty. You are snooty and pretentious and shallow and mean and—"

"And you are *fat!*"

Her eyes grow wide, and for a moment I expect her to lunge at me with fists swinging. But she doesn't. Instead her pale little eyes start to fill with tears, and then she begins to cry.

"Oh, I'm sorry. I don't know why I said that. You just made me so mad."

She shakes her head. "No, it's true. I *am* fat. My daughter was just telling me that very same thing on Thanksgiving... I pretended not to mind, but it really hurt my feelings."

"Your daughter said that?" I blink and think that's a bit harsh coming from one's own daughter.

"She did. Right in front of everyone too. She thought she was being funny. But I thought it was downright mean."

"Well, if it makes you feel any better, what you said about me is true—I am shallow." I reach for the handkerchief in my pocket and hand it to her.

She nods and wipes her eyes. "Yes, yes, you are."

"So we both have our faults. What else is new?"

She smiles and hands me back my handkerchief. "Want me to help you clean that laundry room out?"

"How?" I look up to where bubbles cascade down the steps like a foaming fountain.

"You got a mop? a broom?"

I point to the laundry room. "In there."

"That'll work." She looks at me. "You want to go change your clothes first?"

"Yes, that's a good idea."

"I have a better idea," she says suddenly. "You go and make us a nice pot of tea and something to have with it, and I'll see what I can do here since I'm already soapy. Deal?"

"Are you sure?"

"Sure, I'm sure. And I'm guessing I'll be done before you are anyway."

So I go inside and put on the teakettle, then locate my Minton teapot and matching teacups, saucers, and sandwich plates. I set out some Earl Grey tea and then set off to find something I can fix to go with it. My refrigerator is beginning to look rather sparse again. I really do need to go to the store. But I can't very well go to the store without money. Oh, the complications of everyday living!

"Excuse me." Bea pokes her head in the door from the laundry room. "The bubbles are gone now, and I put the towels through another cycle on the washer, just to rinse out the last of that soap. But I am soaked to the skin, so I'm gonna run home and change. I'll be back in two shakes of a lamb's tail."

Relieved that I have a bit more time, I finally take out a round of brie cheese that I got at Raleigh's last week. I haven't opened the package yet since I wasn't quite sure how to properly warm it, and I cannot imagine eating it cold. But when I read the packaging, I am pleased to discover that I can put it in the microwave for one minute. I do this, watching anxiously as sixty seconds tick by. Then the bell rings, I remove it, and the temperature feels just about right.

I peel off the packaging and place the brie in the center of a platter, and then I slice some apples, which I arrange nicely around it, along with some Wellington water crackers. I stand back and look at my culinary creation. Even Sylvia might be proud of me. The teakettle whistles, and before long the Earl Grey is smelling lovely.

I'm not sure how someone like Bea will react to my offering, but by the time I get it all arranged on the table, it looks rather elegantly tempting. The only thing missing, once again, is fresh flowers. Not that Bea would notice.

"Hello?" I hear her calling from the front door. "I'll just let myself in."

Seeing that there's no stopping her, I call out, "Yes, do come in."

"Look," she says when she gets to the kitchen, holding her arms out as if she's modeling. "I dressed up for you."

Her pantsuit is a bit on the snug side, and the color, eggplant, is not a shade that looks good with her complexion. "Very nice," I say. "Have a seat."

She looks at the table. "Is that some kind of cheese?"

"Brie."

"Is that French?"

"Yes. Would you like to try it?"

"What do you do with it?"

I cut off a generous piece for myself, put it on my plate, and then cut a smaller piece, which I put on a cracker. "Just like that."

"Is that white stuff *mold*?"

"Yes. It's the rind, but it's meant to be eaten, and it's delicious."

She makes a face, and I suppress the urge to growl.

"Why don't you just try it." I take a bite to show her that it won't hurt her.

"Okay, but I don't think I want to eat that moldy part."

"Fine."

She puts a chunk of brie on her plate. Then, as if performing surgery, she removes the rind and finally spreads some on a cracker. She holds it up and smells it, wrinkling her nose. "It smells weird, Claudette. Sort of like a wet diaper, I think. Are you sure it's not rotten or something?"

I take a whiff, realizing that I really am hungry. "I think it smells divine." I take another bite, then reach for an apple slice. Really, this woman seems determined to drive me absolutely stark raving mad.

"Hmm," she says after finally taking a tiny bite. "It's not as bad as I expected. I suppose I could get used to it."

"Perhaps it is an acquired taste. And to be fair, I normally serve brie with wine not tea."

"Why don't we have wine with it then?"

I stare at her. "I do not usually drink wine in the morning."

"Oh…"

"But if you'd like…"

"No, no. I'm just not a fancy person like you, Claudette. I guess I never figured out when is the right time or wrong time to drink wine because I don't normally drink it at all. But I wouldn't mind giving it a try sometime."

I nod, trying to be a better sport. She did, after all, clean my laundry room mess. "Well, perhaps you can come over here sometime, say, fiveish, and we can have some wine and cheese."

"Really?" She looks pitifully hopeful now, and part of me is actually sorry for her. But a much larger part is sorry I just said that. What on earth am I getting myself into by befriending this woman?

Even so, I nod. "Yes, really."

"Because I think we could be friends, Claudette. I know you were married to someone famous and you were rich and all that. But, really, we're not so different now, are we? And we're neighbors. Besides, I know some things...stories about your family...things you might want to know..."

I restrain myself from making the sort of comment that would confirm her earlier accusations that I am pretentious, shallow...*mean.* "What sort of stories?" I ask halfheartedly as I freshen up my tea.

"Well..." She lowers her voice as if someone might be listening. "The frying pan story is definitely worth hearing."

"Yes, you mentioned that before, Bea. Just what is the frying pan story, anyway?"

She takes another chunk of brie and cuts the rind off again. "Well, it was a long time ago... I was about nine or ten, as I recall. My dad was working late one night, and Mom asked me to take out the trash for her. It was a real cold night, kind of like the weather we've been having lately. I was grumbling to myself and carrying out the trash when I heard yelling. Well, it wasn't too unusual to hear your parents arguing over at your house. I mean, they argued a fair amount when you and Violet lived at home, but after you left...well, it got a whole lot worse. I was used to it. But I was surprised that they were arguing outside since it was so cold and all. So I sort of hunkered down by the laurel hedge there and just listened."

She pauses to take a sip of tea, and I try to imagine the nosy little red-headed girl next door, holding her garbage bag and eavesdropping on my parents' marital squabbles. Not a particularly charming scene, mind you.

"So they were going at it pretty good," she continues. "And as usual, your dad was drunk as a skunk, and he was saying some awful mean things to your mom, swearing at her and all that. And your mom sounded like she'd had it. She was telling him to go away and to never come back. He was just getting madder and madder, saying really nasty things, kind of threatening things, and I was about to go tell my mom. I thought maybe it was time to call the cops on him.

"Then I heard this loud twang sound, and your dad groaned, and then there was a *clunk-clunking* sound like something fell down. I stood up and looked over the hedge, and there was your dad, laid out with his feet sticking up on the back steps, and your mom, standing at the top of the steps, just holding this great big black frying pan and staring at her husband with this scared look on her face."

I gasp and blink and stare at Bea. Is she making this whole crazy story up, just to get my attention? But I remember, once again, how Michael said he'd found a cast-iron frying pan wrapped up so neatly and hidden under my mother's bed. "Is that really the truth?" I finally ask.

She nods with wide eyes. "Yep. Your mom killed your dad."

I just shake my head, trying to absorb this. "Why didn't anyone know about this? Why didn't you call the police? Why didn't my mother go to jail?"

"Well, I just stood there looking at her, Claudette, and she looked so scared and sad, and I thought about all the mean things he'd just said to her and about how he'd treated her...and to be honest, I didn't really know if he was dead or just knocked out—or maybe even passed out. I'd seen him like that plenty of times. Besides, I always liked your mom, even when I was little. She was always really nice to me. And I didn't want to get her in trouble.

"So I thought to myself, *Let sleeping dogs lie.* I swear those exact words went through my little ten-year-old head. And that was that. I went and dumped the trash, and I never told a single soul. Well, except for your mother. I told her years later, after I moved back in here to help with Pop. We only spoke of it once, and I could tell it made her really uncomfortable, so I promised her I wouldn't tell anyone else."

"But you're telling me now." And even as I say this, I realize that this is a story I would just as soon have never heard. What good can possibly come from knowing that my mother murdered my father at this stage of life?

"There's a reason I'm telling you."

"And that would be?" I can hear the irritation in my voice, and I'm sure I'm beginning to sound haughty, but, really, I do not care. I am feeling utterly betrayed. I cannot believe I trusted this woman with my friendship, invited her into my house, fixed her tea, shared my brie with her—and this is how she rewards me?

"It was those mean words your dad was saying to your mother, Claudette. I didn't understand them at the time... I was too young. So I sort of hid them away inside. But as I got older and wiser in the ways of men and woman and all that, well, I knew what he was saying to her. I knew what she was saying back at him...and I just felt so bad. You know, for all of you."

"What—do—you—mean?" My voice sounds like an automated computer recording.

"You know, how your dad took advantage of you two girls when you were growing up. That night he was sort of bragging to your mom, saying how his girls...well, you know...how they were lots better in bed than your mother ever was. I'm pretty sure that's why she whacked him over the head with the frying pan. You can't really blame her, can you?"

I stand up now, glaring at this horrible woman. How dare she sit at my table, in my mother's house, and make these kinds of statements? "That is enough."

"I'm not telling you this to hurt you, Claudette. But just so you'll know, okay? It seems like you need to know."

"And I'll tell you this, Bea, *just so you'll know.* My father never did *that*—what you are suggesting."

Yet even as I say this, I remember that time my father wanted a back massage…how he got carried away…but it did not lead to sex! Even so, I'm sure my cheeks are flushed with the embarrassment of this memory.

"I am not saying my father was a saint. Obviously, he was not. But just for the record, he never sexually abused or molested me. Is that *perfectly clear?*"

"Yes…" She nods and stands. "But I guess you can't speak for your sister, now can you? I mean, you don't know her side of the story, do you?"

My hands are shaking as I fold my arms tightly across my chest. "No, well, I suppose I cannot speak for her."

"See," she says victoriously. "That's probably what it was then. Your dad was talking about doing those things with Violet, not you. I just naturally assumed…"

It is all I can do not to throw this woman out. But I think she can tell by my expression, my body language, that she is no longer welcome. The tea party is over.

29

I am so angry after Bea leaves. I walk around the house like a cat on a hot tin roof. I can't stop moving...and yet I don't know what to do. I keep asking myself, what difference does it make? So what if my mother murdered my father?

In some ways, it was probably self-defense. Or perhaps she didn't mean to kill him... Perhaps she was simply so angry that she bopped him over the head in the heat of the moment. Not a lot was said at the time about the cause of my father's death. Violet was the one to call. She told me that Mother had discovered him dead in the morning, that he'd been out the previous night and probably came home late and that he'd either slipped on the icy back steps or passed out from over imbibing.

Whatever the case, he had fallen and struck his head and either died from the head wound or from exposure from being outside all night or, more likely, both. End of story. No one ever questioned any of this. Well, no one except little Bea.

As angry as I feel toward Bea, I now consider the bigger picture—what might've been. Suppose Bea had told her mother and Mrs. Jones had called the police...and what if Mother had been arrested, either for murder or attempted murder if my father had survived? I imagine the scandal…the humiliation…the trial…my mother spending time in jail…my father continuing to live as recklessly as he had done in the past… Would I have preferred that sort of scenario? Of course not. If what Bea is saying is true, I should be grateful to her, and I should probably apologize for treating her the way I did. In time, perhaps I will. But not today.

Thinking of Bea reminds me of the towels in the washing machine, so I decide to put them in the dryer. As I'm turning on the dryer, I notice the movement of something eggplant-colored across my backyard. I peer more closely and see that it's Bea heading across my yard toward her house with a laundry basket that appears to be heavy.

Curious as to what she's carrying, I move closer to the window, and that's when I notice that my trash pile, the one that resembled the melted snowman, is gone. I just shake my head. Why should I care if Bea wants those horrible towels and ruined rug? She is more than welcome to them. Good riddance!

I continue to pace around my house, replaying Bea's strange story. I try to imagine my mother, a woman with the patience of Job, being driven to such an extreme corner that she would whack my father over the head like that. For years she quietly put up with his shenanigans, she looked the other way when he indulged in affairs, she cleaned up his messes when he came home intoxicated.

My mother, the one who was raised in luxury and affluence,

worked her fingers to the bone, paid the bills, and took care of everything while my father acted like a spoiled prince and refused to get his hands dirty. She put up with so much for so long. So why did Mother break down? Why did she suddenly and completely lose her temper that night? What would drive a person like her to act that way? And the more I consider all this, the more likely it seems that she had a reason to be enraged. What Bea reported must be true.

And the real victim here must be Violet.

My legs feel like rubber bands, and I am so weak that all I can do is sit in the living room and think...and remember. The mind is a remarkable thing. It's able to repress as well as to recall. And I realize now that I have probably repressed much in the past seventy years. It's a wonder I can remember these things at all now. Yet they come rushing back at me—with a force that's overwhelming.

It started shortly after the back rub incident, about the same time I began distancing myself from my father. Somehow I instinctively knew that my father was dangerous—and that I wanted no part of it. So I spent more and more time with Caroline, including spending the night at her house whenever I got the chance.

During this time, I didn't only push Father away, but I pushed Violet away as well. Instead of doing things with her, I did things with Caroline. Naturally, Violet was jealous. And, I suppose, she was hurt.

I am sure I convinced myself that my choices had to do with survival—*my* survival. I never even considered the possibility that my fight to survive might have included sacrificing my little sister. Violet was such a plain girl, so quiet and mousy, so wrapped up in her silly books. I don't think I could even imagine my father being interested in someone like her, not the way he had been interested in me.

In some ways, I didn't even blame him for his interest in me—certainly it was twisted and wicked—but I was a pretty girl. And I kept myself up. My hair was always clean and shiny and blond. I imitated the movie stars and dressed as well as I could, and I carried myself with pride. Naturally that was attractive. But Violet did none of those things.

Still, if I dig deeply into my memory…there *were* signs. Signs I chose to ignore.

At first I was jealous when Father began inviting Violet to do things with him. Whether it was a nature walk in the woods or going out to look at the stars on a summer night, it was Violet who was invited, not me. And if she protested, as she began to do later on, he would make her feel guilty by playing the poor injured father that nobody loved. He would make such a scene that Violet would finally give in. *Poor Violet.*

Before I can stop myself, I go to the phone, dial Information, and ask for McLachlan Manor. And the next thing I know, my sister is on the other end.

"Violet," I say with a thick voice. "This is Claudette."

"What do you want?" Her tone is sharp and guarded.

"I want to talk to you."

"Then talk."

"No, I want to talk to you in person."

"Why?" She sounds very suspicious now.

"Because I think we need to."

"Are you going to accuse me of trying to drive you crazy?"

"What?" Then I remember what I said to the police. "Oh, Violet. I really felt I was going crazy that day. You have no idea."

"I think I have some idea."

"Yes, perhaps. But it was even worse than you knew. Look, I am terribly sorry I said those things. All I can say is that, at the time, it seemed reasonable."

"Can you imagine how embarrassing it was to be questioned by the police?"

"More embarrassing than being cornered in my bedroom that morning?"

"Maybe… Fortunately I had good alibis. My friends at McLachlan stood up for me. Of course, now everyone here thinks that Claudette Fioré has lost her mind."

"Yes, I figured as much."

"What do you want to talk about, Claudette?"

"I want to talk about us, our family, just things… I thought perhaps I could pick you up tomorrow, bring you over here… We could talk."

She lets out a long sigh. "I don't know. You were acting awfully strange last week. I don't think I'd be comfortable alone with you."

I consider this. "How about if Caroline comes along?"

"That might make it better."

"Are you comfortable talking about family things in front of Caroline?"

"I'm sure she knows as much about our family as anyone. Didn't you tell her everything when you were girls?"

"Maybe..."

So it's decided. We will meet at nine thirty Monday morning. I offer to pick the two of them up, but Violet suggests they hire Roberto to drive them to my house instead. She still doesn't trust me. Perhaps she thinks I plan to kidnap her or maybe that I'm going to drive us all off a cliff like in that strange movie *Thelma & Louise*.

Then Violet, in a slightly cynical tone, asks if she should dress warmly, and I assure her that the heat is back on. As soon as I hang up, someone knocks on my door. I just hope it's not Bea. I do want to straighten things out with her. Just not right now. I brace myself as I open the door.

"Special delivery," Garth says with a wide grin.

"What?"

"The art we're swapping. I was enjoying the vibrancy your paintings brought to the gallery, and I got to thinking about you here with your empty walls, and I felt guilty. Celia wrote up some on-loan contracts this morning. Not as involved as the consignment ones, but if you'll look them over and sign them, I'll bring in the art and put it up for you."

So just like that, I have art and life and color again. I thank Garth for thinking of me, and to my surprised relief, I discover that I like his paintings nearly as much as the ones I'm forced to let go. Perhaps in time I will like his art even more.

Knowing that I'm having visitors tomorrow inspires me to dust and straighten my house. I want everything to be vastly different from the last time Violet was here. I even get the fireplace ready for a cheerful fire—and I get my hands dirty and open the flue.

Finally it's nine o'clock and everything seems to be in its place. My reward for my effort, besides a tidy house, is to sit down with the last of Gavin's letters to my mother. There are only a few left. And the main topic seems to be God and what happens when we die.

Dear Mother,

I wish I had the sort of faith that you described in your last letter. I can't imagine getting up one morning and suddenly believing that not only is there a God but that he is smiling upon me, ready to welcome me with open arms. That's not the God I heard about when I was growing up. The God my father preached about was an angry God. He hated sin and sent sinners to hell, where they gnashed their teeth and cried for millions of years. Naturally, according to my father's theology, I would be among them. So I quit believing in things like heaven or hell. I suppose I never completely quit believing in God, since that was ingrained in me. But I began to believe that if I did enough good things, if I treated people fairly, did my best, lived honorably... that God might reconsider sending me to hell when the time came. I'm sure that must sound silly. It even does to me. But it was the best I could do. Now I'm not so sure. I think I need something more. I'm just not sure how to go about it. Enlighten me.

Love always,

Gavin

As I fold the letter and replace it in the envelope, I consider Gavin's theory about God and heaven. As far as I know, Gavin was always a good man, an honorable man. In an industry with more than its fair share of scoundrels, Gavin's reputation in Hollywood was sterling, the gold standard even. And if dear Gavin was worried about not making it to heaven, I hate to imagine where I might be sent when my time comes.

Of course, I've never been inclined to believe anything the least bit religious. I've always felt life is what you make it. That's all. But now as I read Gavin's letters, which appear to be written in all sincerity, I am not so sure. And as I consider how many things in my life have recently been turned upside down, I think there is the distinct possibility that even more surprises could be in store.

The next two letters include a number of questions about whether faith is a gift or something we must fabricate in ourselves, whether the Bible is really "the inspired word of God" or just a historical document, and whether or not a loving God could really send "innocent people to hell." All good questions, I suppose, but not the sort of thing I would have ever given much thought. Still, Gavin was always a deep thinker. He always looked at all sides of a story. Some say that's what made him such a brilliant director.

Finally I have the last letter in my hand. Its date is March of 2002, just one month before Gavin's death.

Dear Mother,

Something amazing happened to me yesterday. You know how I've been pestering you with so many questions and how hard it's been for me to grasp the concept of faith. Yet you keep telling me that faith is a gift from God. You even wrote down the Scripture reference. And yet I could not get that through my thick head. Yesterday I was out in the yard, just sitting in the sunshine having a glass of iced tea, enjoying the sounds of the birds in the trees, the flowers, the air...and suddenly something happened inside of me. It was as if something inside me just clicked, or as if the hand of God turned the key that unlocked the door. I'm not even sure how to describe it because it is nearly indescribable. But I knew—I absolutely knew that God was real, that he loved me, and that he has made the way for me to enter into heaven. Just like you've been telling me, just like the Bible says. I knew all I had to do was to believe and to receive. So very, very simple. Isn't it just like you'd been telling me? Faith really is a gift that only God can give. And now it is a done deal. My soul is at peace. Thank you for helping me on this journey, dear woman. If I do not see you again in this earthly life, I do look forward to giving you a great big hug in heaven. What do you know!

Love eternally,

Gavin

While this letter does not surprise me, I do find it deeply unsettling. Primarily because it seems that both Gavin and my mother discovered something that seems just outside my reach. Suddenly I feel like that young girl who wanted it all—the fancy dresses, the expensive jewelry, the luxury cars, the beautiful mansions—and always it remained just beyond my reach. But then I grew up and took my life into my own hands. I did what it took to get what I wanted, and I thought that it worked.

But now I am not so sure. Now, I find myself back in that same place again—still reaching, still grasping, still wanting… never enough. Sometimes I think my curse in this life is never to be satisfied. Perhaps it will be my curse in the afterlife as well.

Or maybe what Gavin said in that final letter was true. Maybe faith really is a gift from God. But if that's the case, what must I do to get God to give it to me?

30

I wake up earlier than usual on Monday—a good thing, for I have much to do. I quickly but carefully dress, and then I go next door and knock on Bea's door. It's just a little before nine, but because Bea made herself comfortable knocking on my door at odd hours, I think I should be safe.

She opens the door, then blinks in surprise. She is wearing a fuzzy pink bathrobe and her hair sticks out in all directions. "Claudette?"

"I am sorry to disturb you like this, but I just wanted to say some things."

"What?"

"First of all, I want to apologize for how I reacted yesterday... when you told me about my mother...and my father..."

She waves her hand. "Oh, pish posh, who could blame you? I'm sure it was a shocking thing to hear. I could've told it a bit more gently. I've never been accused of being very restrained. My husband used to say I had hoof-and-mouth disease."

"What?"

"Meaning I was always sticking my hoof in my mouth."

"Oh…well, I gave what you told me some thought, and I realized that, as hard as it was to hear, you must've been telling me the truth. Not only that, but I should have been more grateful, Bea. I most appreciate that, even though you were a child, you were very thoughtful of my mother and her situation… You cared enough to protect her. I thank you for that."

"Well, I—I just don't know what to say."

"Now I should get back to my house. I've invited Violet to come over for coffee this morning. I want to talk to her about, well, what you told me."

Bea nods with a serious expression. "I expect that'll be a good thing for both of you." Then she grins. "Maybe you'd like some pumpkin nut bread to go with your coffee. I just happen to have an extra loaf. Could you use it?"

"That sounds very nice, Bea."

"Come in out of the cold while I go get it."

Now I'm not so sure that I really want to go inside her house. Yet I am curious. And once inside, I'm not surprised that Bea's house, like her, is a mishmash of clashing colors and unrelated styles. She also appears to have a fondness for cheesy porcelain figurines and knickknacks. Shelves cover her walls, filled with all sorts of things. I hate to imagine what would happen if we ever experienced an earthquake up here.

"Here you go." She hands me a foil-wrapped loaf. "Tell your sister hello for me."

"I will. Thank you for this." I make my way to the door.

"And I'm holding you to your promise, Claudette."

"What's that?" I turn and peer at her.

"You know, for happy hour. You said we'd have wine and cheese some night around fiveish. I'm looking forward to it."

"Oh yes." I nod uneasily. "That's right."

As I walk back to my house, I consider my "happy hour" promise. What could I have been thinking? Still, I have more pressing matters to focus on now. I will think about Bea another day.

I do one last check of my house. I want everything to be as perfect as possible. I light a fire, making sure it's venting properly up the chimney, and then I go to the kitchen and make coffee. I get out my sterling tray and set out my Limoges cups and saucers, cream and sugar, spoons and napkins. I carefully slice the pumpkin bread and arrange it on a Limoges plate as well. Then I check the clock. It's nine forty. Only ten minutes late… I know I shouldn't be concerned. After all, I've been known to be two hours late to a party in the past, fashionably late. Yet for some reason it doesn't strike me as either fashionable or polite now.

Then I see a dark green van pulling up with the words *McLachlan Manor* on the side. Violet gets out, then Roberto helps Caroline out. He peers at the house as if he'd like to come in and see today's carnival sideshow, but he just gets back into the van. He doesn't drive away. They probably asked him to wait.

My palms feel sweaty as I slowly walk to the front door. I have entertained movie stars, producers, directors, dignitaries... all with less stress than I'm feeling right now. I take in a deep breath, then slowly release it. Then, pasting what I hope is a congenial smile onto my face, I open the door and greet them.

"Thank you for coming," I say in my most gracious voice.

They both look at me curiously as they say a cautious, "Hello," and step inside. It feels as if they expect my head to begin spinning or some other such nonsense.

"May I take your coats?" I ask, still smiling.

"Thanks." Caroline slips off her parka and hands it to me.

"I'll keep mine on," says Violet.

Caroline is examining the photo montage. "Is that Shelley Winters?"

"Yes. And that's Rita Hayworth, Joan Crawford, Lana Turner..." And I go through the list of celebrities.

"You were really friends with all those people?" Caroline just shakes her head. "I wish I'd had a better idea about this when I was younger. I might've come down to visit you."

I nod. "I wish I'd thought to invite you."

"Really..." Violet looks skeptical.

"Would you like to see the rest of the house?" I offer, thinking it might be a good distraction or icebreaker or something.

"Did you hire someone to clean things up?" asks Violet.

"Actually, a couple of friends helped out. But I am trying to do it myself."

"I like what you've done with the place," says Caroline. "This is much classier than it used to be. I mean, your mom always kept it nice and cozy and comfortable, but this is, well, very sophisticated."

"It's easy to be sophisticated when you have money," says Violet.

"And taste," adds Caroline. "I've seen rich people with the tackiest taste."

"Actually, I don't have money anymore," I admit while we're standing in the kitchen.

Violet looks unconvinced.

"It's true. Gavin had an accountant who was a bit of a swindler. Instead of paying the IRS, he paid himself. I lost my house and most of my things for back taxes."

"Really?" Caroline shakes her head.

"Yes. I didn't want to tell anyone... It's rather embarrassing to be broke. But then so many other things have embarrassed me... Well, I decided perhaps it shouldn't matter so much."

"You really lost all your money?" Violet's expression has softened, ever so slightly.

"Yes. I'm even going to sell some of my art and things...so I can get by."

"Well, it's not as if you're destitute," says Violet.

"No, things could be worse."

We finish the brief tour, which puts my mind at ease, since they can see that things are a bit tidier than when they last visited, and finally we settle down in the living room with my coffee tray.

"This is so nice," says Caroline. "I'm so glad you invited me to join you today, Violet."

"I wasn't sure what to expect," says Violet. "I felt I might need the moral support."

"I told Violet that I'm sorry about my accusation the other day," I tell Caroline. "I was very upset, and I suppose it seemed reasonable at the time."

Caroline just laughs. "Well, under the circumstances, it's understandable."

"So what is this big thing you feel the need to tell me?" demands Violet. "Can we please just get whatever it is over with?"

"It's a somewhat private family matter, Violet. But I'm comfortable having Caroline here if you are."

Violet waves her hand. "I'm sure Caroline knows all the dirt on our family. Most of the town did."

"Not *all* the dirt…" I brace myself, unsure as to whether or not I can even relay Bea's story. But my sister urges me on, so I tell her exactly what Bea told me, or as near as possible. All except for the part that directly concerned Violet.

"That's absurd," says Violet.

"Yes, that's how I felt too…but then I remembered that Michael found a cast-iron frying pan under Mother's bed. He said it was wrapped neatly in an old towel and then in a box.

Rather mysterious, I thought at the time. But after Bea told me her story, I realized it must've been Mother's way of hiding the murder weapon—although I do feel in some ways it was self-defense."

Violet just shakes her head, and I can tell she doesn't believe this. "If you'd like to question Bea, I'm sure she'd be more than happy to cooperate. She's kept the secret for decades. Well, except that she spoke of it once to Mother, and Mother swore her to secrecy."

"I think it's believable," says Caroline. "You know that your dad was a real skunk sometimes, Violet. If I'd been married to him, I'm sure I would've clobbered him over the head long before your mother did."

"I don't think so..." Violet presses her lips together. "Mother put up with him for so many years. Why would she suddenly murder him?"

I study my sister. "It has to do with us, Violet. Apparently Father said some things to Mother about us—disturbing things."

Violet's eyes flash now. "What kinds of things?"

I glance at Caroline.

"It's okay, Claudette," Violet says in a surprisingly calm voice. "I want to know what kinds of things."

"I guess Father told Mother that he'd behaved improperly toward us, not in those words, of course, but it was an admission of sorts—even if it was a drunken one."

Violet's face pales, and I'm worried that I've said too much. "We don't have to talk about it anymore. I just thought you should know why Mother blew up like that. It was as if she suffered a form of temporary insanity because she loved her daughters so much, Violet. In a way, her reaction was in our defense."

"It wasn't *we* or *us* or *ours*, Claudette."

"What do you mean?"

"I mean it was *me*. I was the one who was abused. Not you. You escaped. You knew what was going on, but you got out. You left the monster to prey upon me." Violet begins to cry.

Caroline and I are sitting in the leather club chairs, and Violet is sitting alone on the couch. I get up and go over and do something completely out of character for me. I put my arm around her and pull her close to me.

"I don't know if I really did fully know at the time," I confess. "I've been thinking hard about this whole thing ever since Bea told me that story. And I do think a part of me knew, but another part couldn't admit that it was real. Or perhaps I suppressed it because it was too painful. Father hurt me too, Violet. Oh, not as badly as I'm sure he hurt you, but I suppose I wasn't as strong as you either. And you're right, I did run away."

Violet is sobbing onto my shoulder now, and Caroline comes over and joins us, putting her arms around Violet as well.

"I am so sorry," I say again. "If I could do it over...do it differently...I would."

Finally Violet is done crying. I hand her my handkerchief, and we all just sit there in silence.

Violet takes a deep breath and then looks at me with watery eyes. "You know, I've been through lots of counseling for all this, Claudette. I suppose I thought I was far beyond it by now. But the one thing I could never get past, the one thing that always got under my skin…was you. I felt like you abandoned me."

"You're right. I did. But I don't think I consciously abandoned you. I was just running for my life."

"That's not how it seemed."

"I know. And I'm sorry, Violet. I really am."

She slowly nods. "I know…"

"I was selfish and foolish and shallow… I think I spent my whole life just trying to escape my childhood. And look where it got me."

"You can run, but you can't hide," Caroline says with a wry smile.

"Maybe not."

Violet reaches over and embraces me. "I've missed you, Claudette."

"I've missed you too, Violet."

"Maybe we can start over."

"Yes," I tell her. "I'd like that."

"Now, doesn't it feel much better to have all of this out in the open?" Caroline pours herself a cup of coffee. "Now we can get back to the business of being old friends."

"With an emphasis on *old*?" I fill a coffee cup. "We have a lot of lost time to make up for." I hand the cup to Violet.

She shakes her head. "I'm still trying to imagine our mother hitting our father over the head with a frying pan. It's so unlike her."

"That was my reaction too."

"And yet...I remember something she said once, shortly before she passed away."

I lean forward. "What?"

"She'd been going to church for a few years by then." Violet glanced at me. "Did you know that our mother became quite religious in her final years?"

I nod. "I've recently become aware of this."

"It struck me as strange at first. You know how we'd rarely stepped inside a church growing up. But in those last years, Mother began reading from the Bible and attending church functions. And one day she told me that she could rest easy because she knew she was forgiven." Violet presses her lips together and shakes her head again. "I told her I couldn't imagine that she'd have done anything she needed to be forgiven for, and she just laughed."

"Laughed?" I set down my cup and wait.

"Yes, she laughed and then told me that for all I knew, she could be a murderess."

"She actually said that?"

Violet nodded. "Well, naturally, I just laughed too."

"Turns out it was true," said Caroline.

We all visit some more, and by the time Caroline and Violet

leave, I feel that we have truly initiated a new beginning. I even promise to come for lunch on Thursday.

As I'm clearing away the coffee things, my doorbell rings yet again. I suppress my agitation as I answer the door. No surprises here. It is Bea, and she has what appears to be a large black trash bag in her arms. I can only imagine what it contains. I hope she knows my trash can is full.

"Come in," I tell her, knowing it's useless to do anything else.

"I saw Violet and Caroline leaving," she says with bright eyes. "How did your conversation with her go?"

"It went quite well," I say as she follows me to the kitchen.

"I'm so glad." She drops her garbage bag onto a kitchen chair and grins. "I brought you something."

I set the coffee tray by the sink and turn around in time to see her retrieving a pile of neatly folded white towels, which she places on the kitchen table.

"What are those?"

"Your towels."

I frown. "The ruined ones I threw out?"

She lifts one now and then holds it up to my nose. "Smell?"

I take a cautious sniff and am surprised. Not only does it smell clean, it smells like fresh lavender. "Are these really my towels?" I touch the fabric to see that it feels like real Egyptian cotton. I brush it against my cheek and am amazed at the softness.

She grins as if she's terribly pleased with herself. "First I did a rinse cycle in really hot water, and after that I washed them in bleach and finally…" She produces a purple jug of what appears to be laundry soap from her black bag of tricks. "I washed them in this—lavender-scented laundry soap."

I now have tears running down my cheeks. "You did this for me?"

She simply nods.

"But I told you that you could keep them…"

"They're yours, Claudette. I just wanted to show you that even if something looks all useless and wasted and soiled and ruined…there's still hope. Sometimes things can be rescued."

"I believe you're right." Then to my utter surprise, I reach out and hug her. And I think to myself that not only things can be rescued but perhaps people as well.

Two weeks later and just two weeks before Christmas, Garth and Celia host their special art exhibit at the Phoenix. I've invited Violet, Caroline, and Eddie. I also invite Irene and Page and my new book group friends to come as well as many of the other friends and acquaintances I've made since moving back to Silverton. I fully expect it to be quite a well-attended show. At the last minute, I even invite Bea, and dressed in her eggplant suit, she happily rides with me to the gallery festivities.

Celia has somehow managed to get her press release about

the exhibit into many of the major papers along the West Coast, so expectations are high. And Garth has been dubbing the event as "a tribute to the late Gavin Fioré." To further liven things up, he has several reproduction movie posters from Gavin's films on display, and there is live music, wine, and appetizers. For Silverton, it is rather a big and impressive affair. I am a little disappointed that Michael and Richard can't make it, but they've promised to try to get out here before the exhibit ends on New Year's.

I am pleasantly surprised to see that a number of well-known and wealthy patrons of the arts make an appearance. Naturally, I know many of these people. I have socialized with them and attended benefits with them, and they know and recognize me. They politely pay their respects, inquiring as to my health and well-being and whatnot.

I smile and tell them that I'm finding life in Silverton to be rather charming and something of a delightful change from the hectic pace of Southern California—and this time I am not lying. Oh, I don't go into all the gory details, and I have no doubt they've heard of my financial ruin. But I don't really care. And I suppose that surprises me.

But what shocks me even more this evening is that I don't feel drawn to the old camaraderie. I feel no sense of comfort in their stuffy conversation, no real warmth in their slightly superior-looking smiles. Instead I feel strangely attracted to this new, and somewhat old, circle of friends. They are more genuine, more interesting, and yes, even more compelling than all my old friends—if they really were friends at all. And for the first time in my life, I feel entirely at home here in Silverton.

Not only that, but I feel I have more lessons to learn in this life, more things I must discover before I make my way into the next. And I'm starting to grasp what both Gavin and my mother believed in their final days: that God is real—and that he cares about me. Consequently, I now pick up Violet and Caroline on Sundays, and we all attend our mother's church together.

And I have begun to look at aging differently too... I'm beginning to understand that true beauty is not what you see in the limelight but what you experience once the lights have gone out.

Readers Guide

1. What was your first response to meeting Claudette? Did you dislike her? pity her? feel confused by her? Explain.

2. Do you know anyone like Claudette? If so, what is that relationship like? How would you like it to change?

3. Why do you think Claudette was so shallow?

4. Who was your favorite character in this book? Why?

5. What part of Claudette's personality, if any, can you relate to?

6. How many close friends do you think Claudette had before she moved back to Silverton? Describe what you think those relationships were like.

7. Do you have many elderly friends? Why or why not?

8. What's your personal attitude toward aging? Do you embrace it? hold it at arm's length? pretend it won't happen? take it in stride? Explain.

9. What part, if any, of your life do you think might be shallow? Why?

10. What incident(s) do you think brought about the most change in Claudette? Why?